# STARDUST NATION

First published 2016
by SelfMadeHero
139–141 Pancras Road
London NW1 1UN
www.selfmadehero.com

*Stardust Nation* is adapted from Deborah Levy's story of the
same title from her collection, *Black Vodka* (2013).

Page design and lettering by Kate McLauchlan
Cover design by Andrzej Klimowski and Kate McLauchlan

Publishing Assistant: Guillaume Rater
Sales & Marketing Manager: Sam Humphrey
Publishing Director: Emma Hayley
UK Publicist: Paul Smith
With thanks to: Natalia Klimowska-Nassar and Richard Doust

A CIP record for this book is available from the British Library

ISBN: 978-1-910593-13-4

10 9 8 7 6 5 4 3 2 1

Printed and bound in Slovenia

# STARDUST NATION

## DEBORAH LEVY   ANDRZEJ KLIMOWSKI

SELF MADE HERO

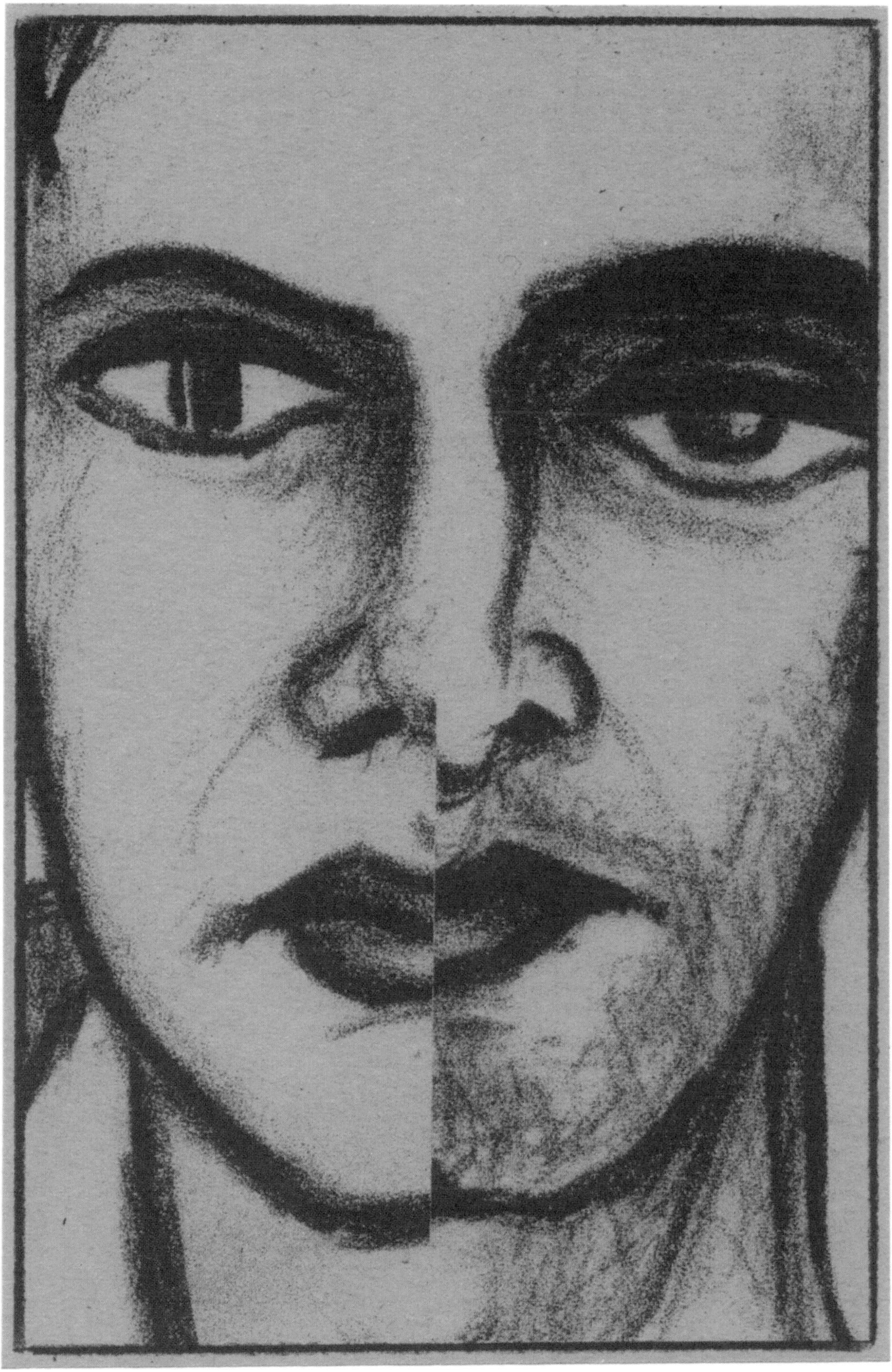

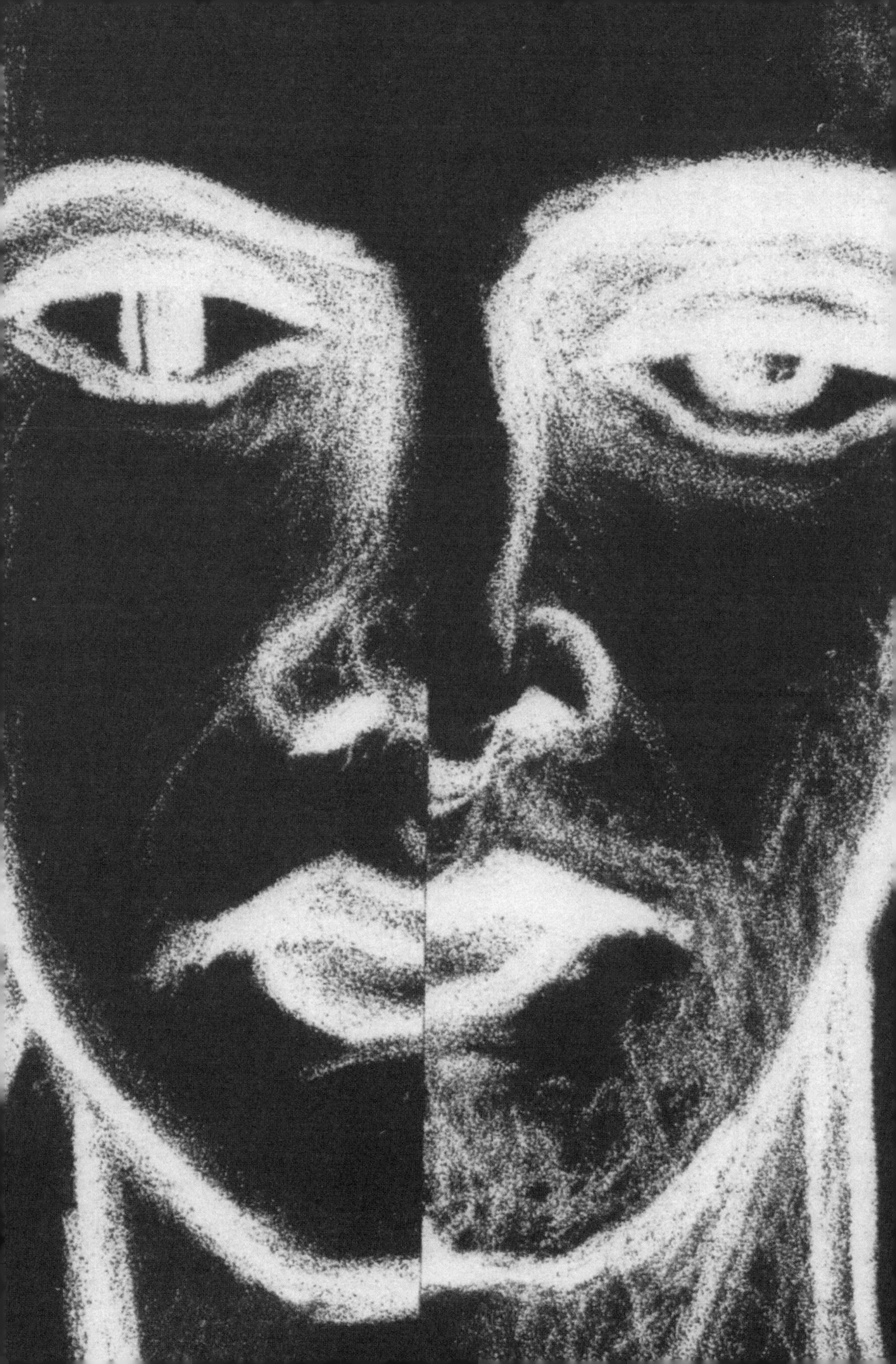

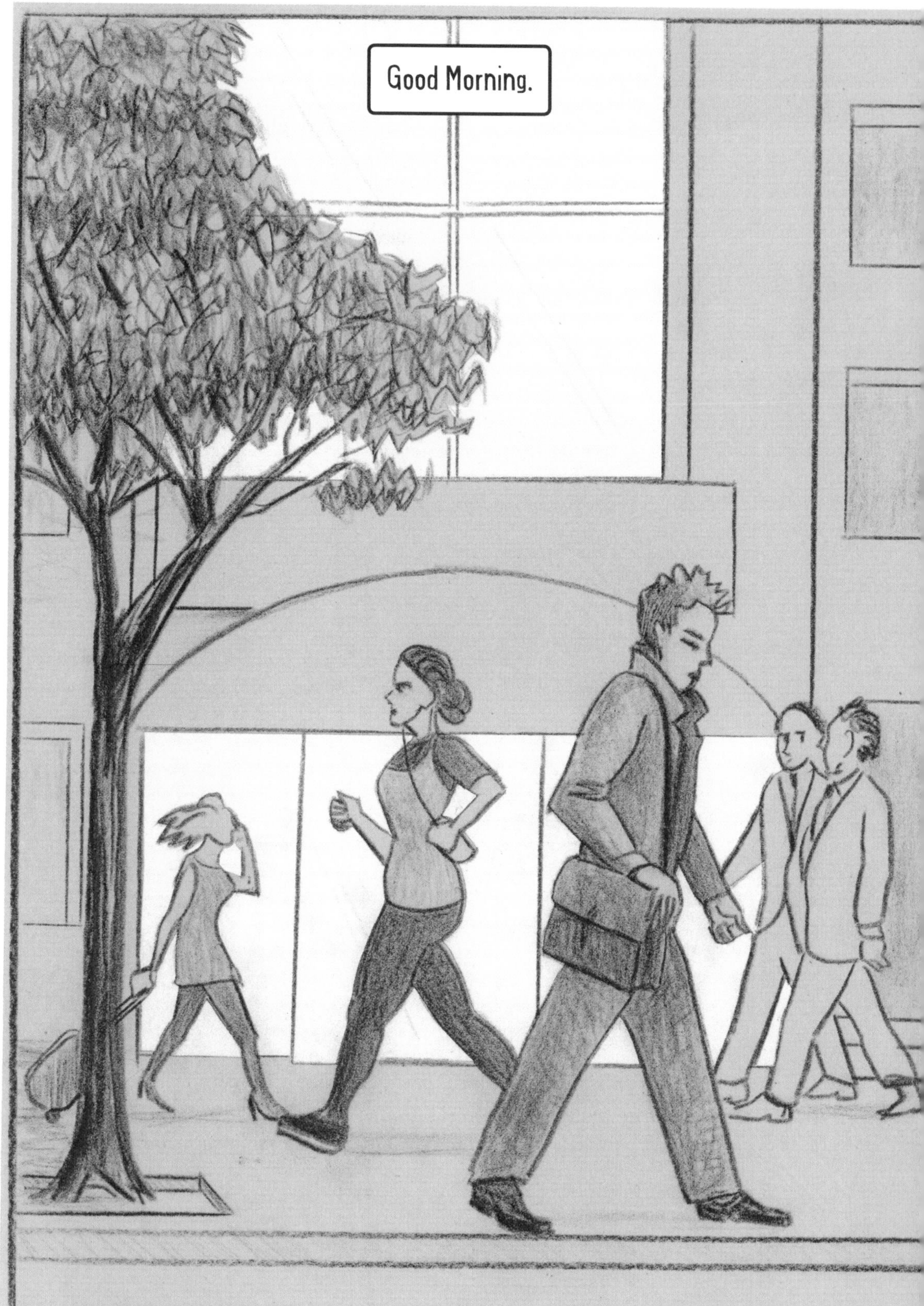
Good Morning.

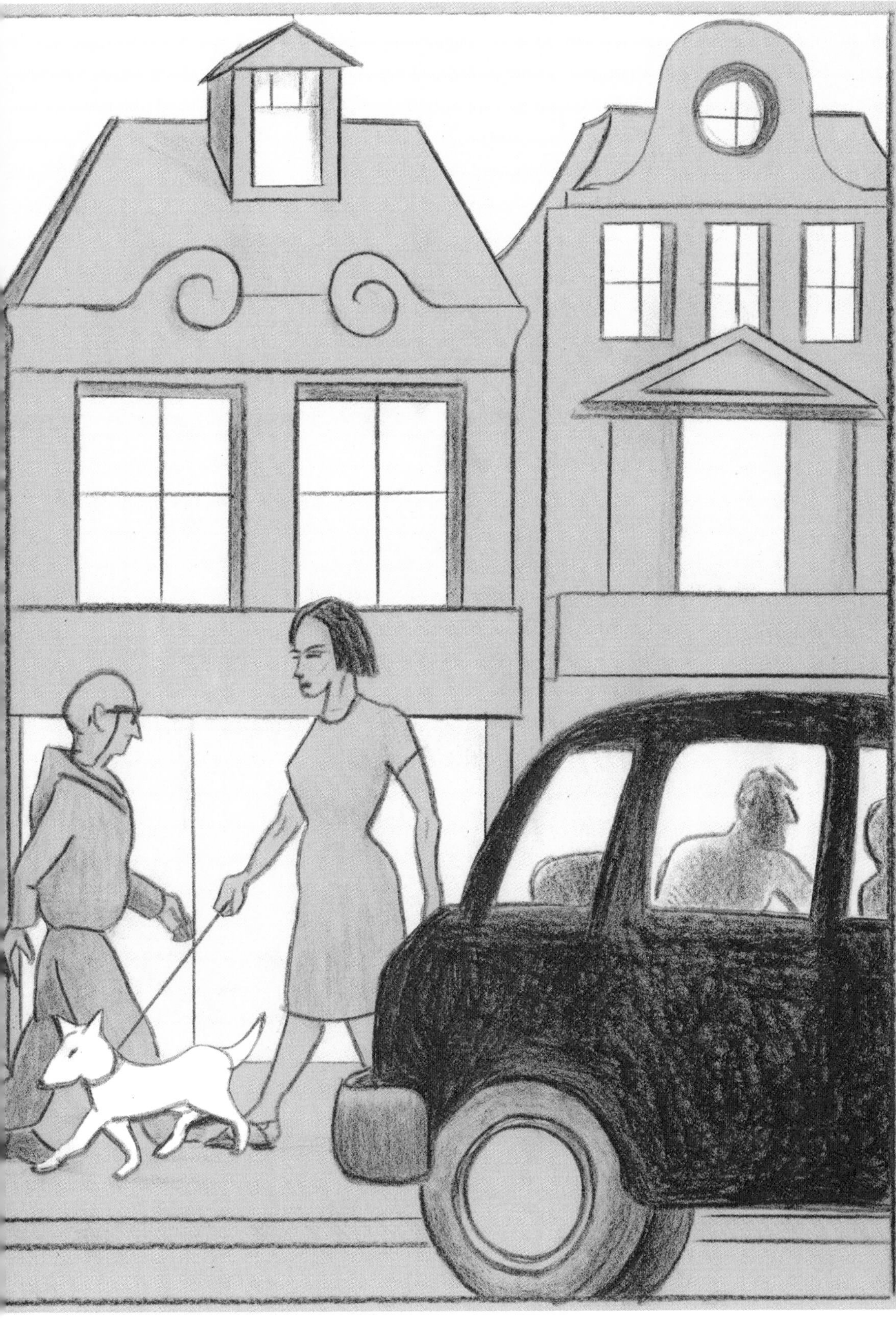

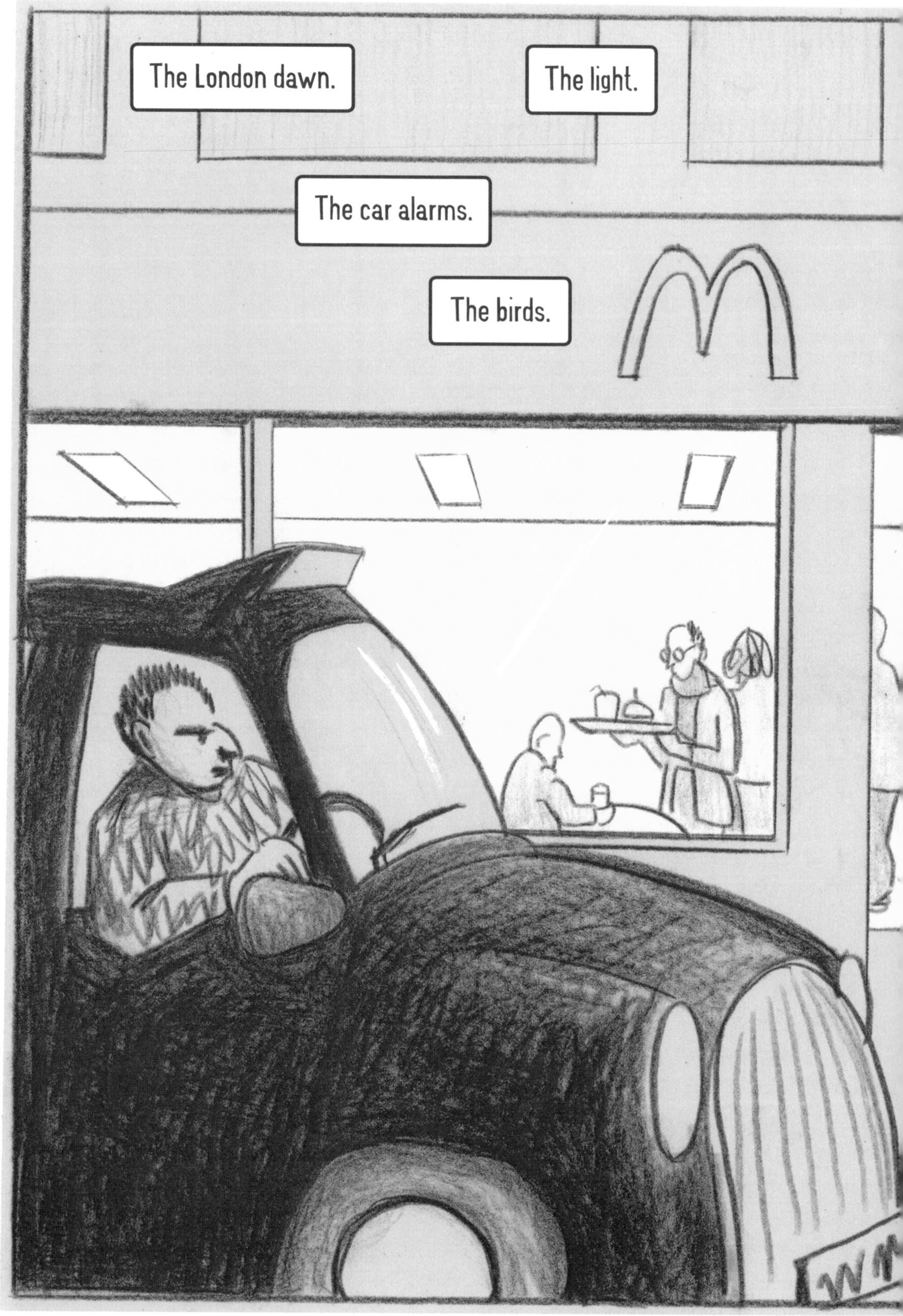

The London dawn.
The light.
The car alarms.
The birds.

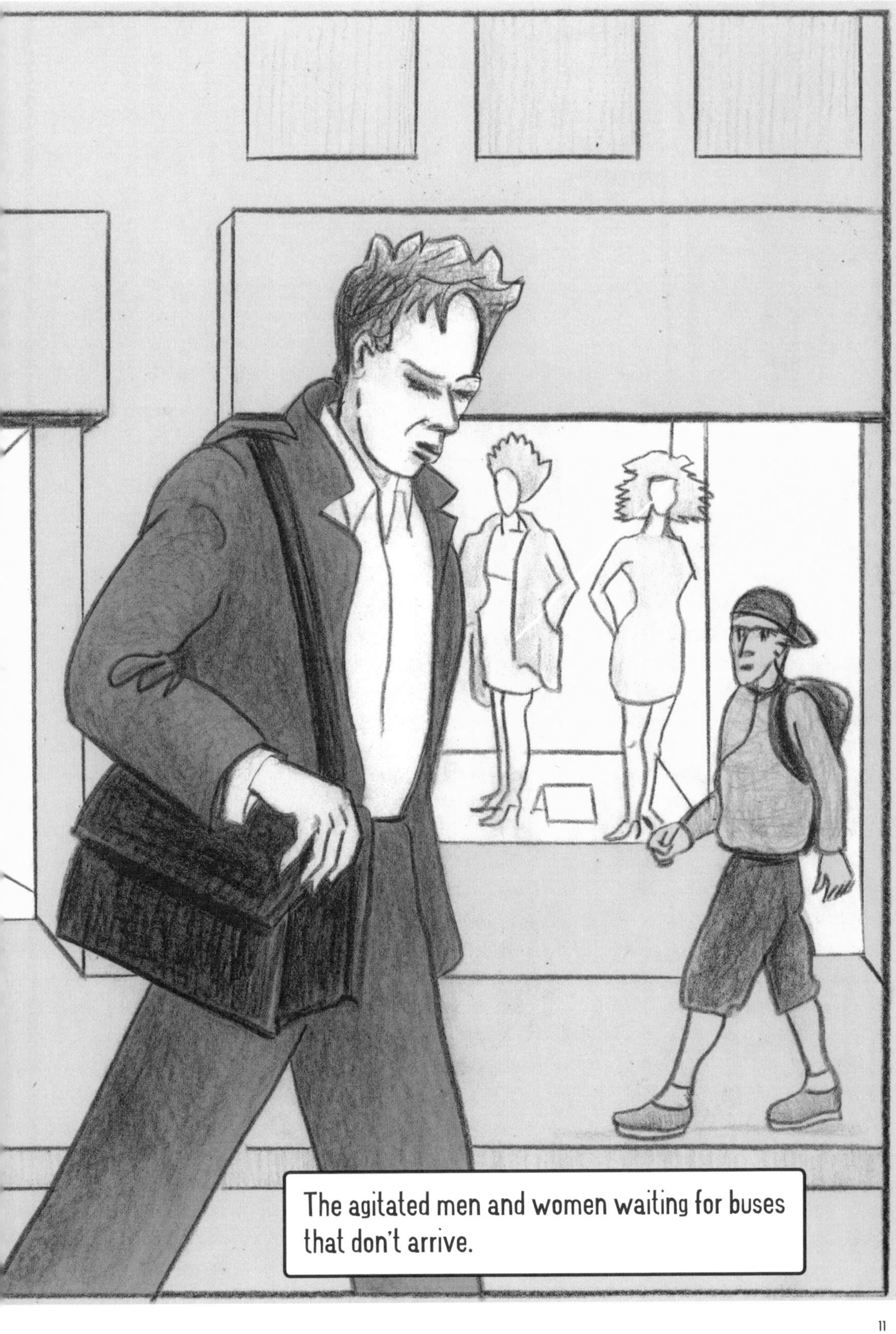
The agitated men and women waiting for buses that don't arrive.

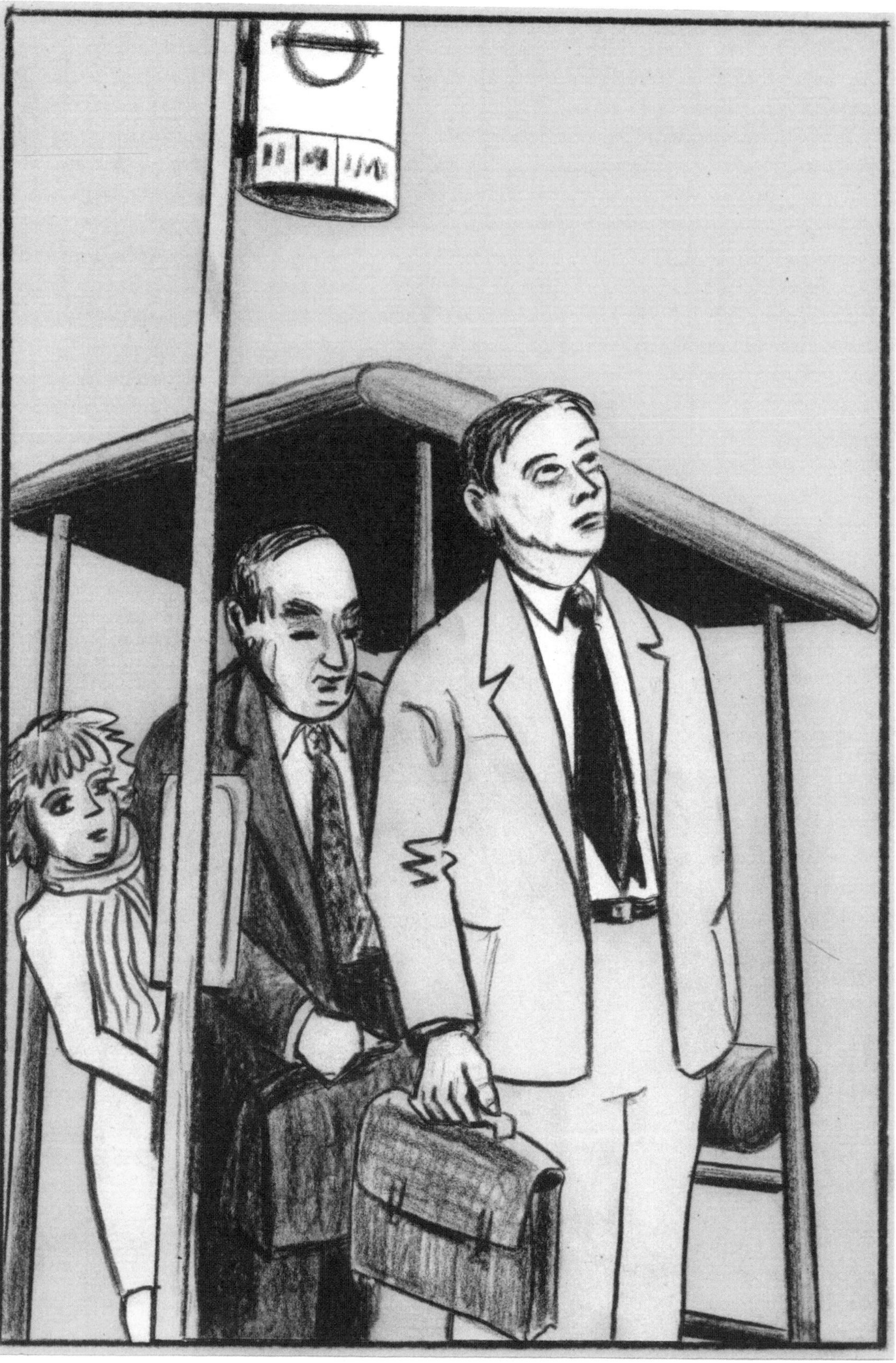

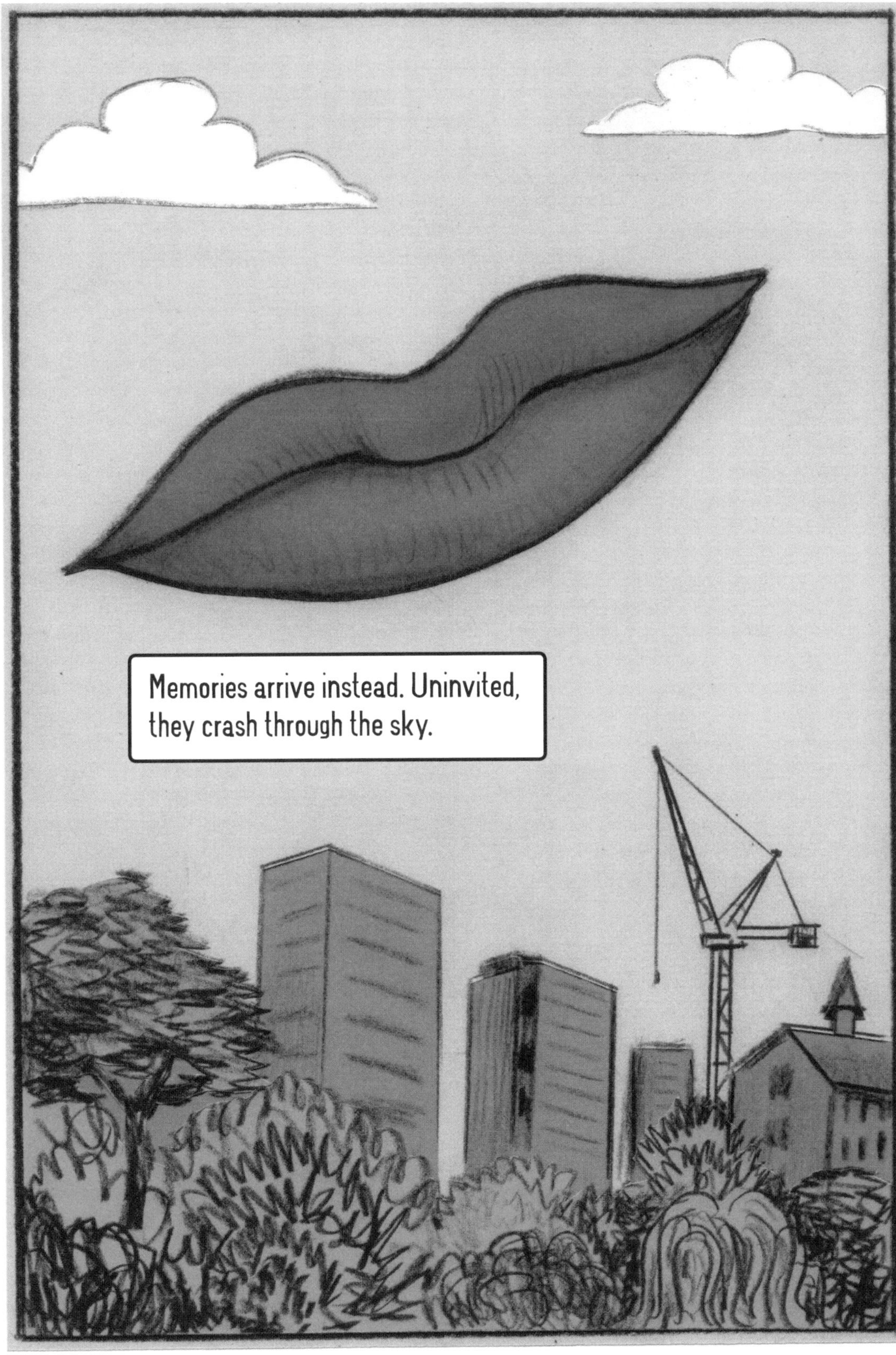
Memories arrive instead. Uninvited,
they crash through the sky.

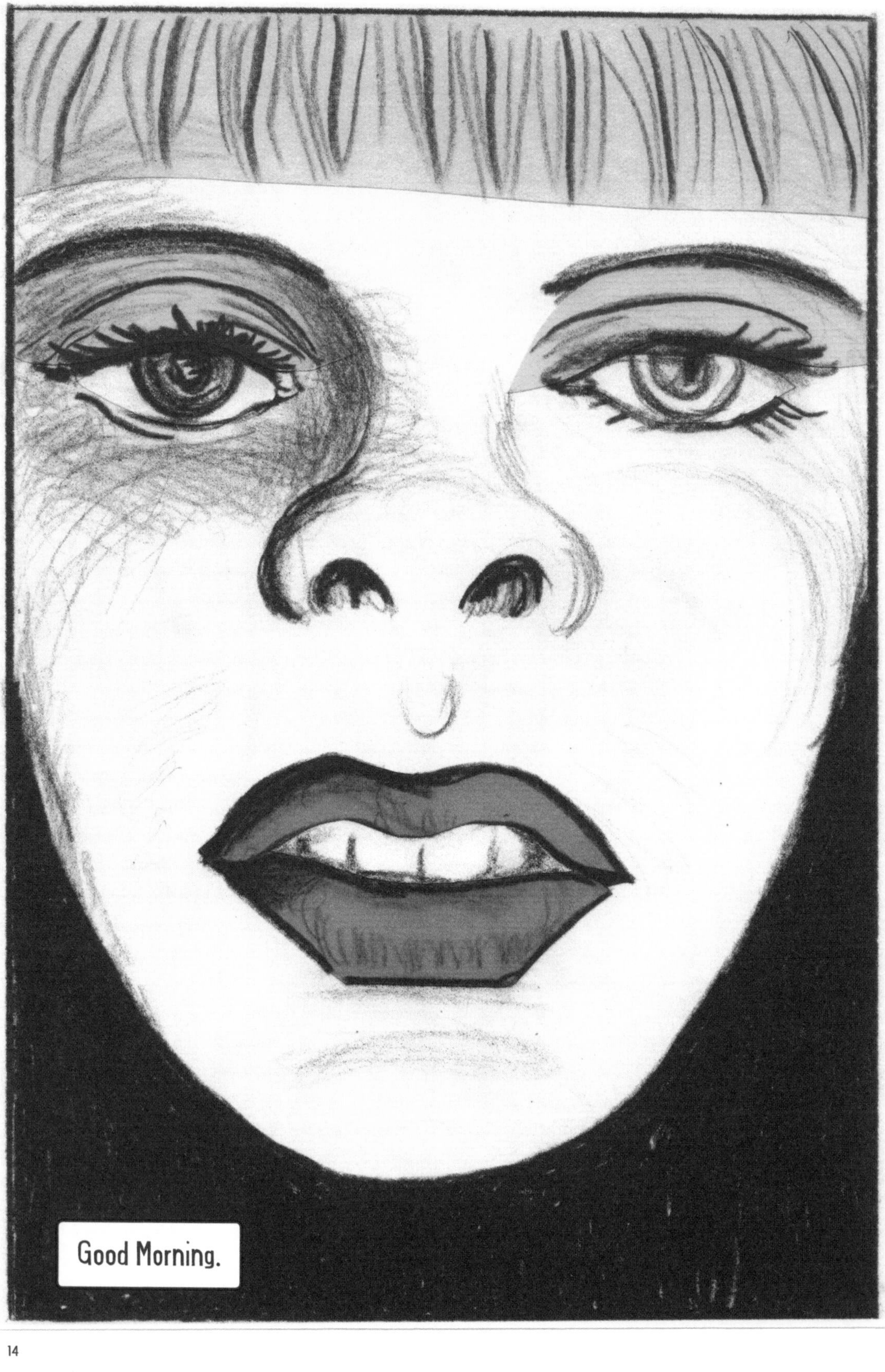
Good Morning.

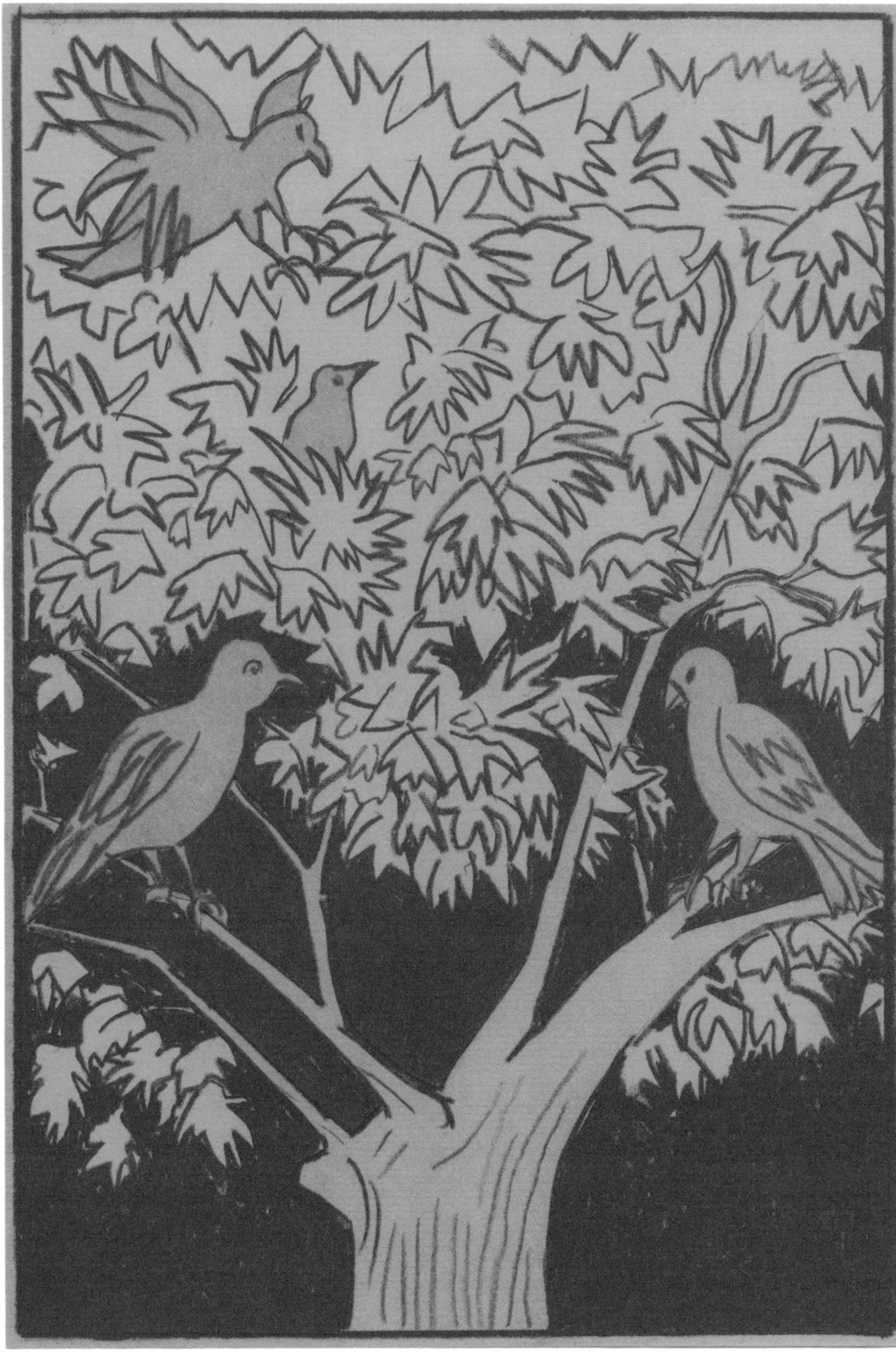

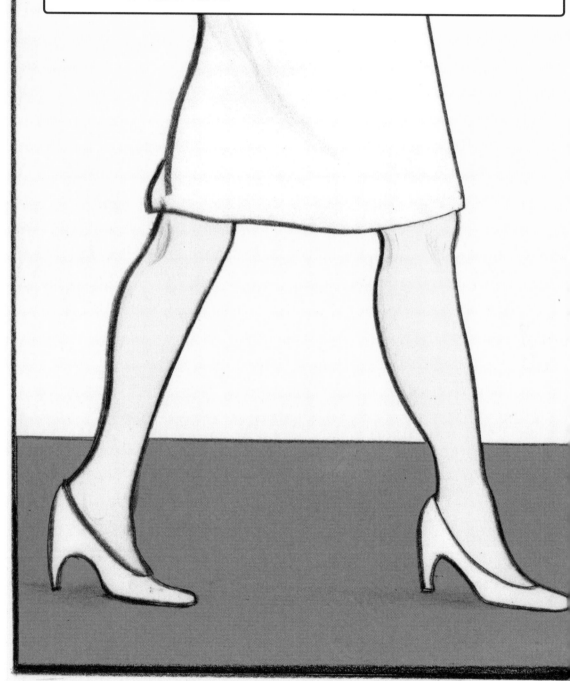

When I was five years old my mother employed a Dutch female tutor to teach me mathematics and biology. I have forgotten her name now but she always had a breezy morning manner when she walked into the nursery in her high-heeled white leather shoes.

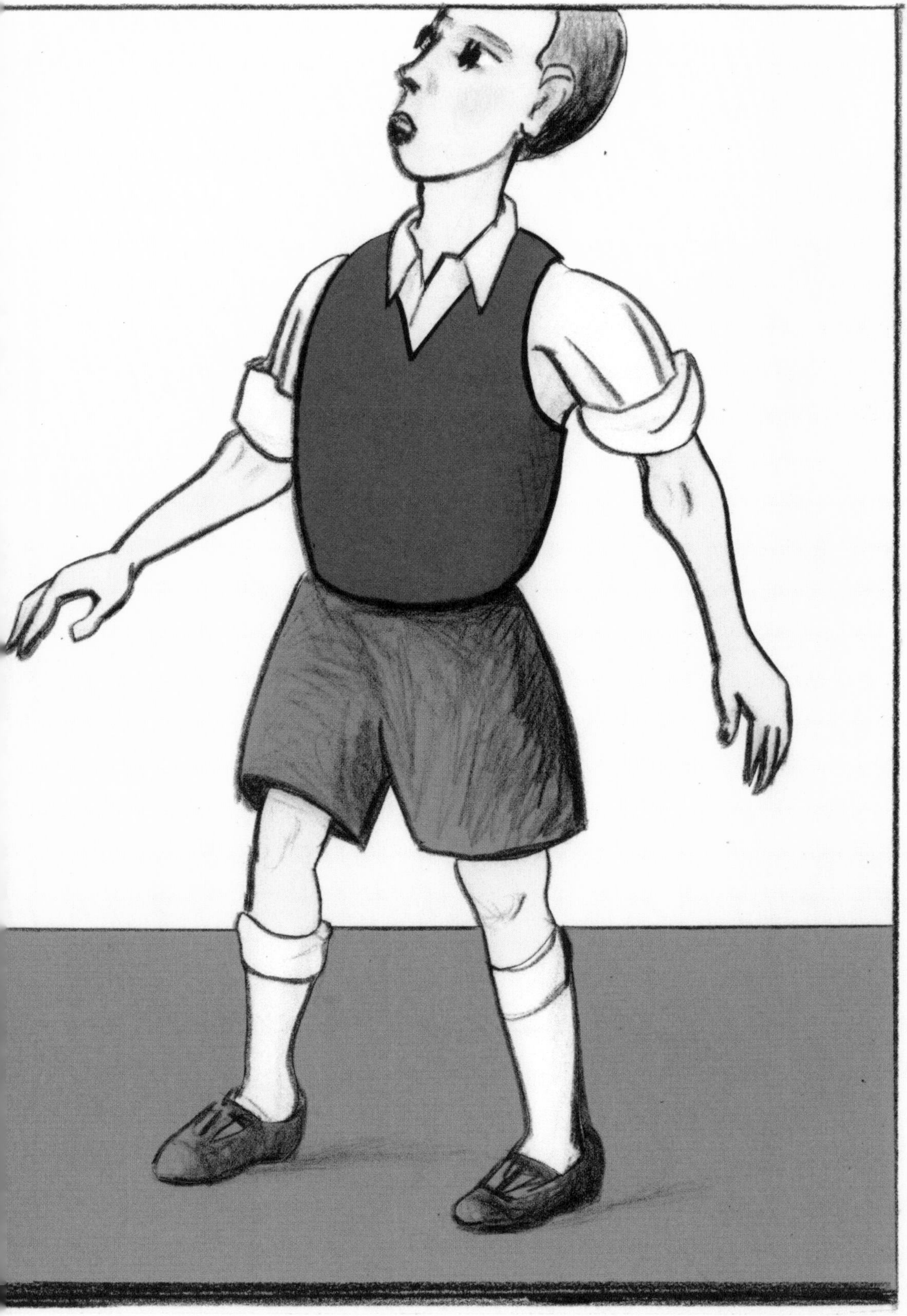

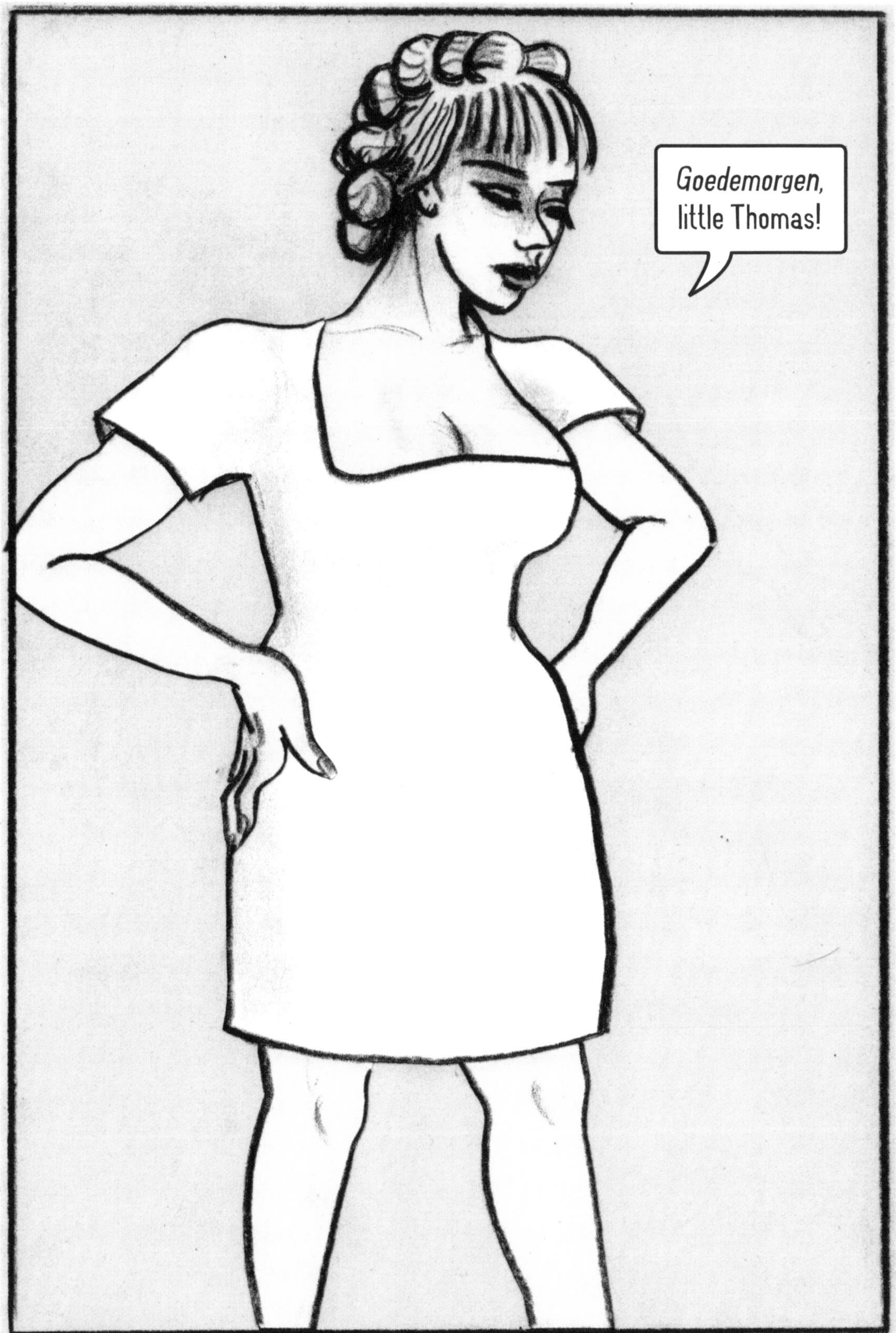
*Goedemorgen*, little Thomas!

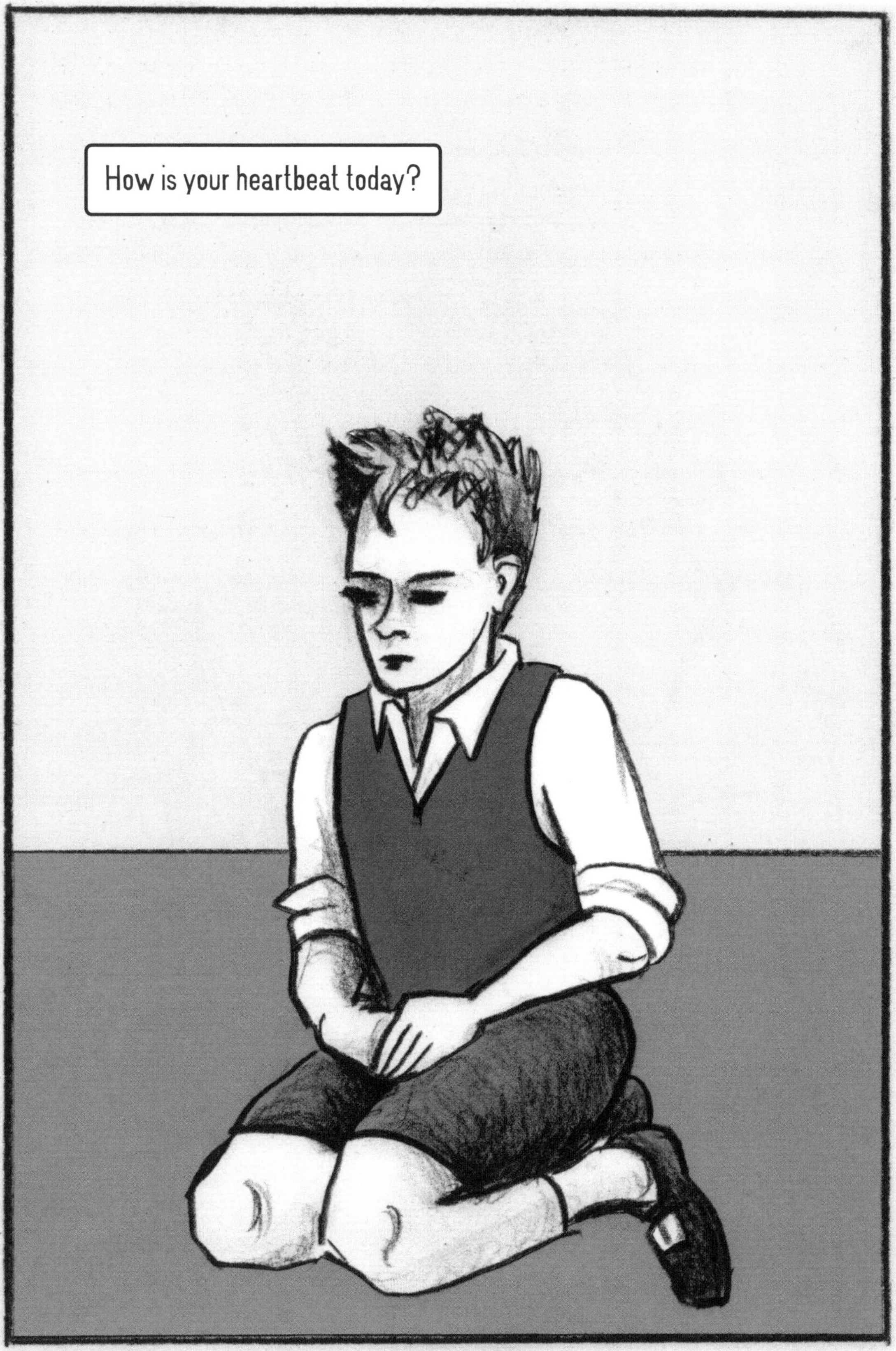
How is your heartbeat today?

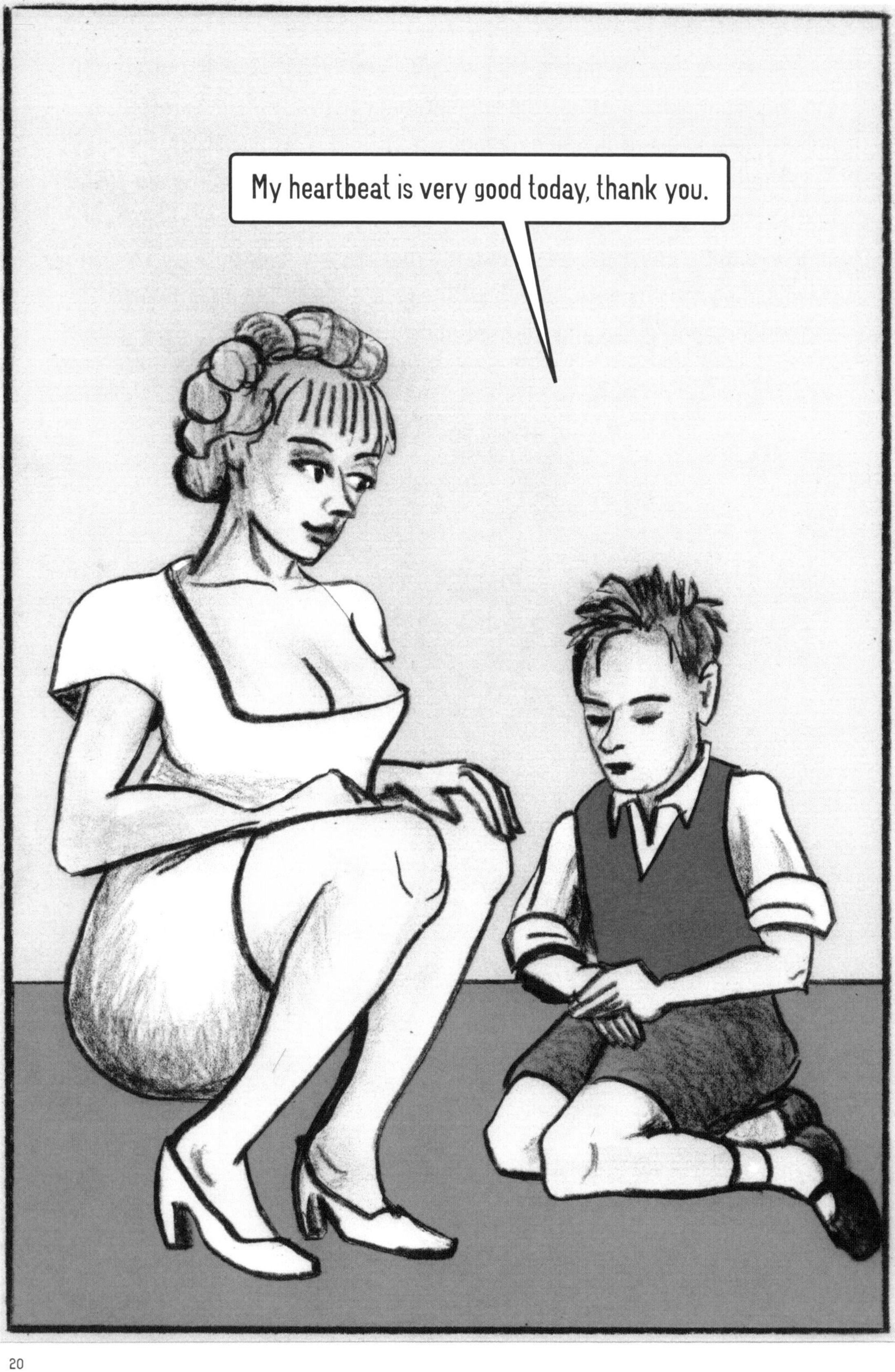
My heartbeat is very good today, thank you.

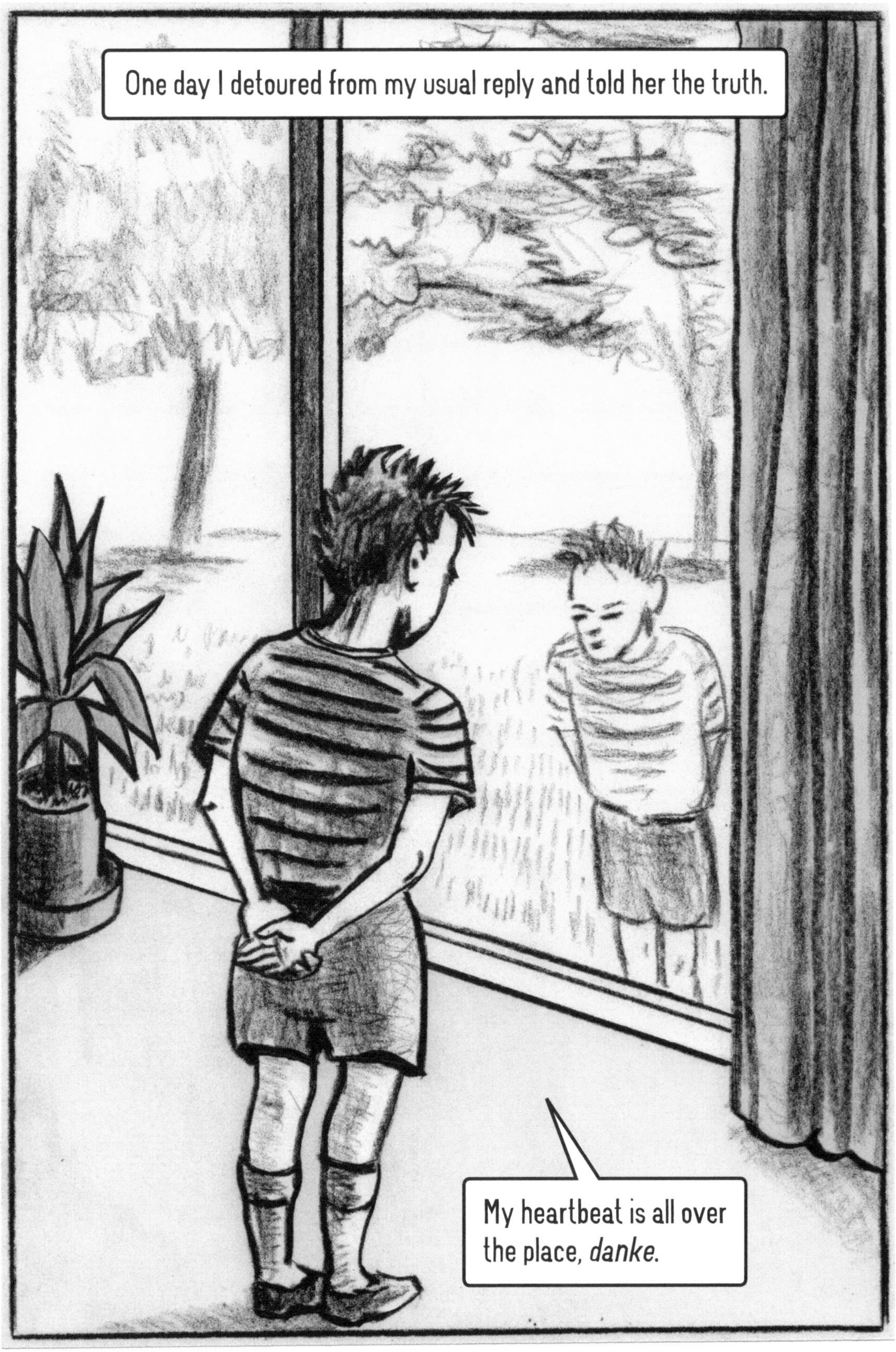
One day I detoured from my usual reply and told her the truth.
My heartbeat is all over the place, *danke*.

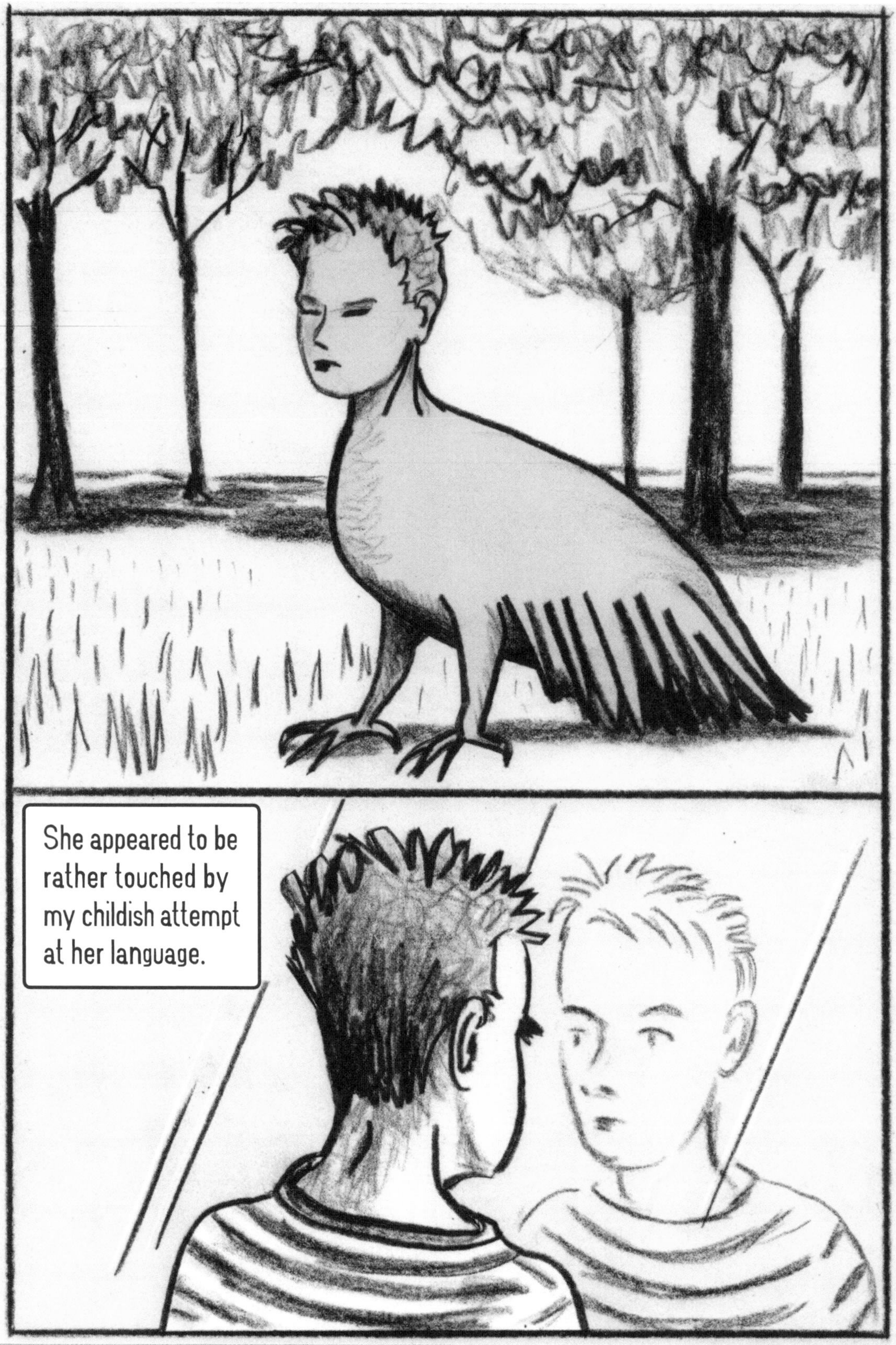
She appeared to be rather touched by my childish attempt at her language.

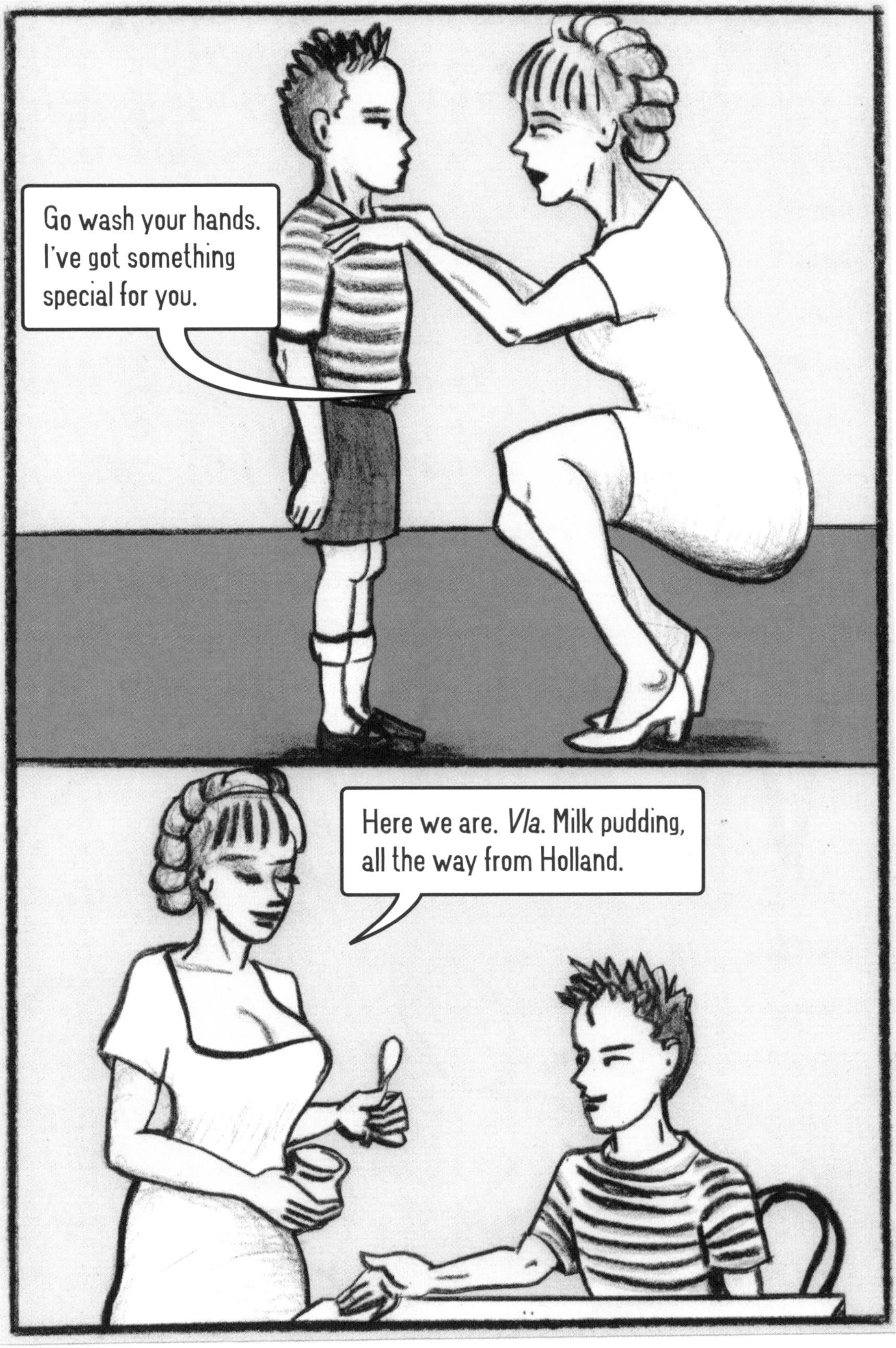
Go wash your hands. I've got something special for you.
Here we are. *Vla*. Milk pudding, all the way from Holland.

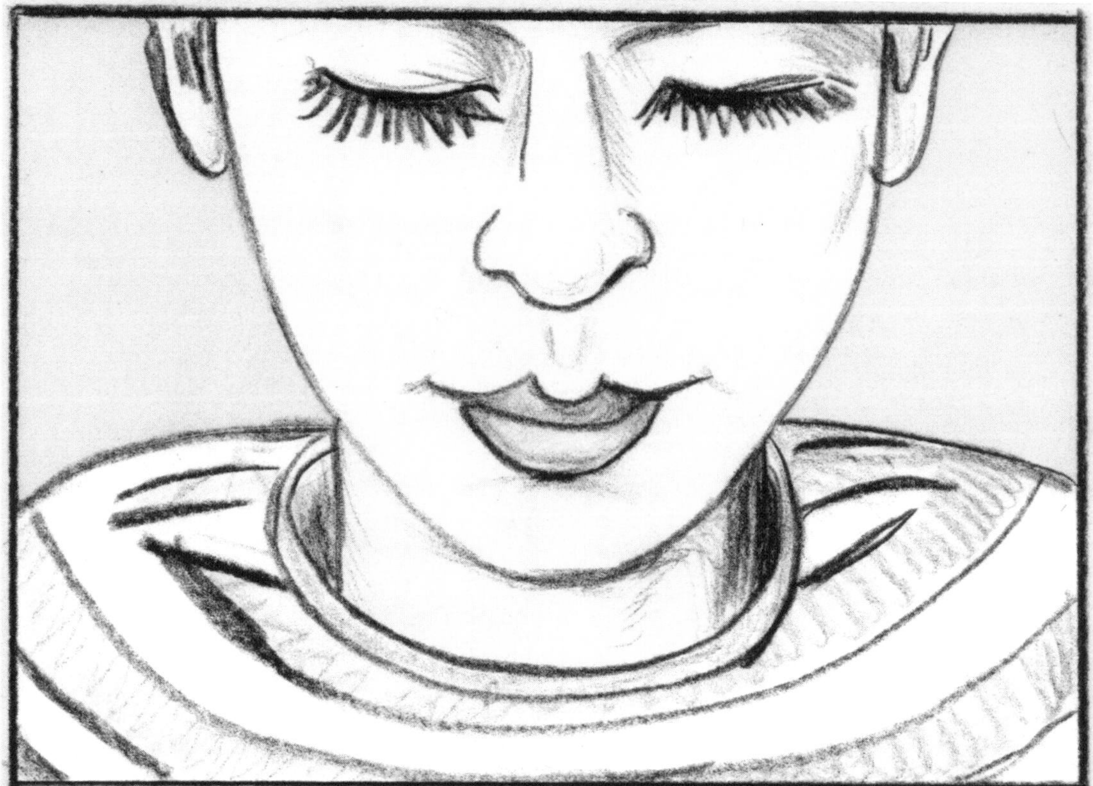

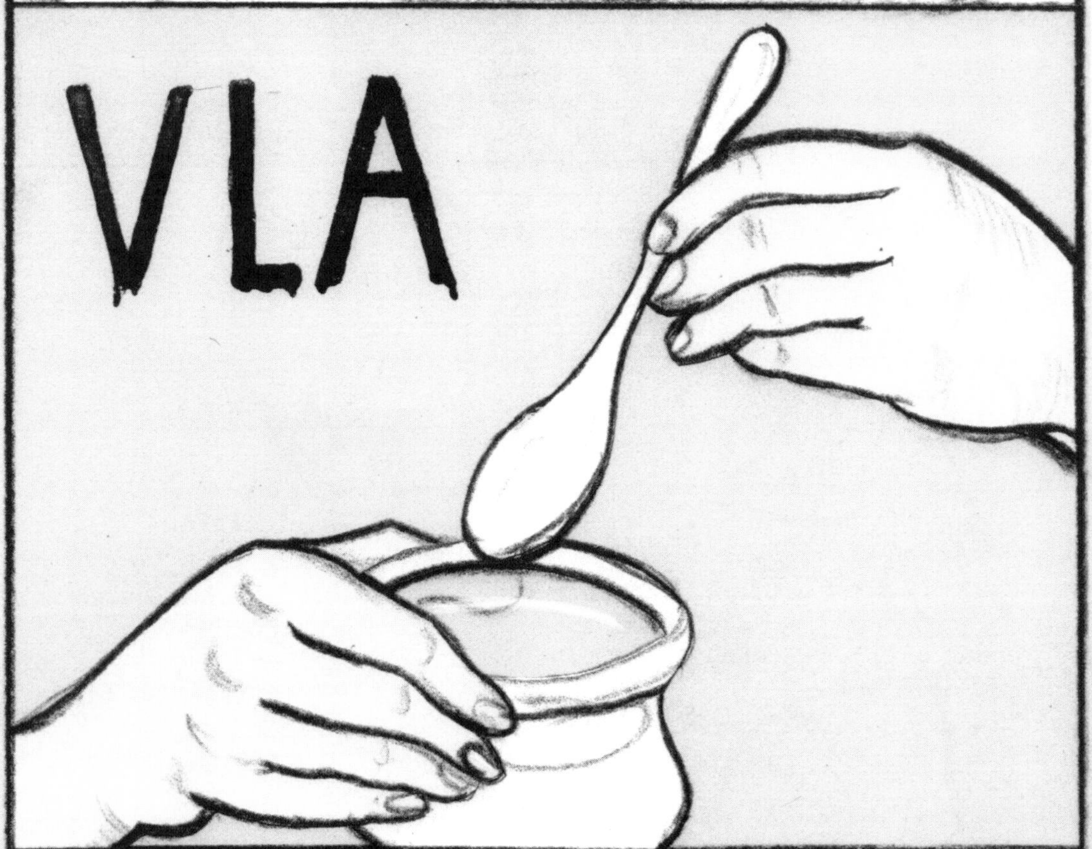
VLA

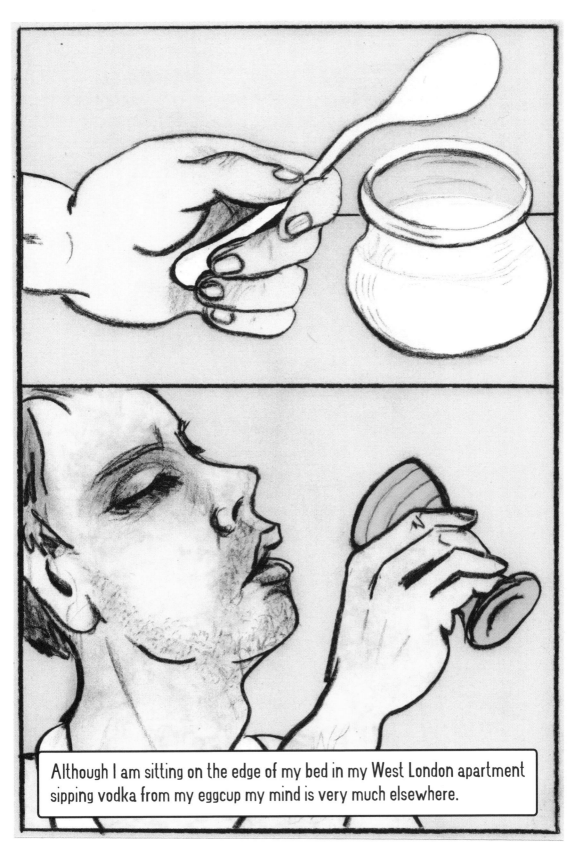

Although I am sitting on the edge of my bed in my West London apartment sipping vodka from my eggcup my mind is very much elsewhere.

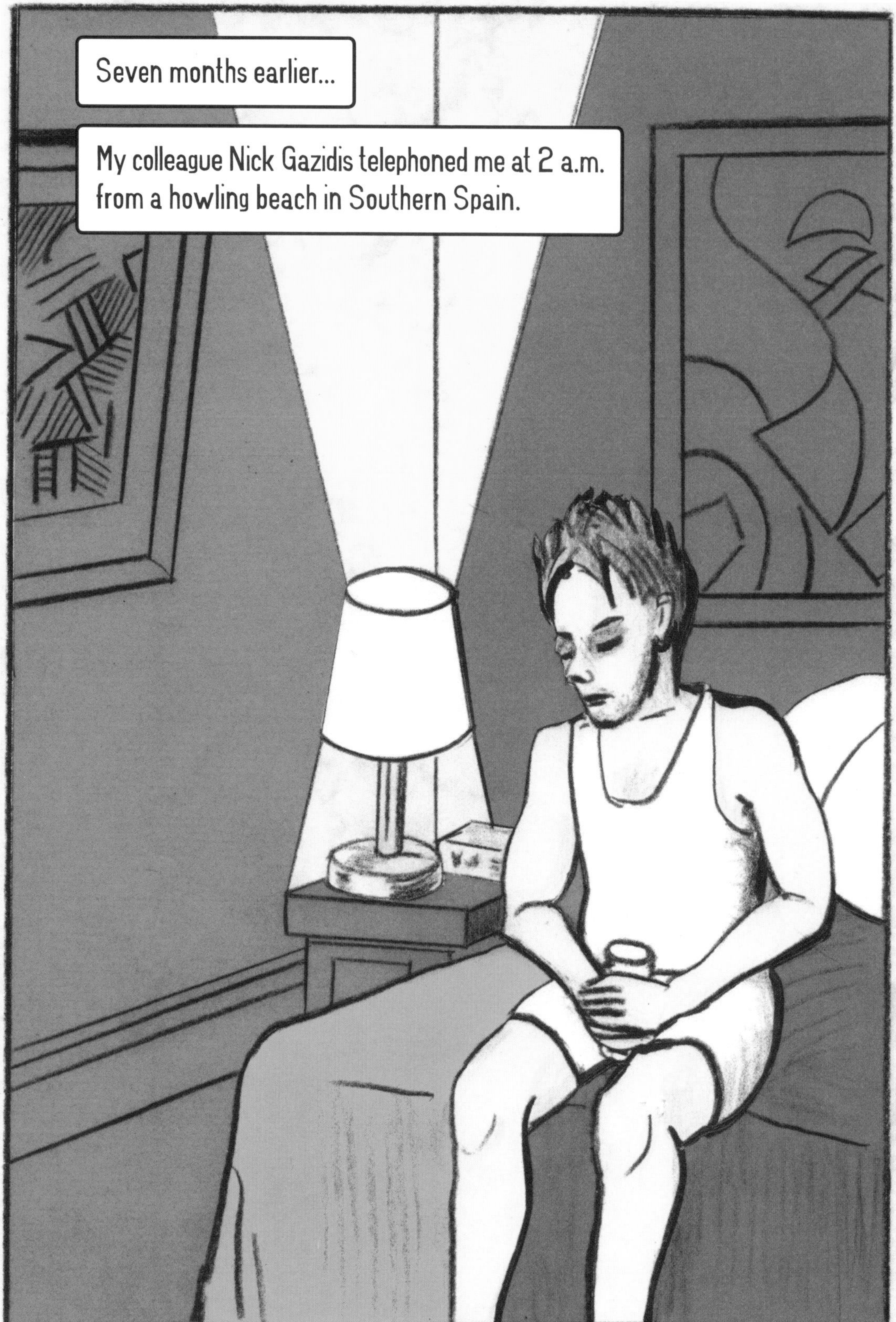
Seven months earlier...
My colleague Nick Gazidis telephoned me at 2 a.m. from a howling beach in Southern Spain.

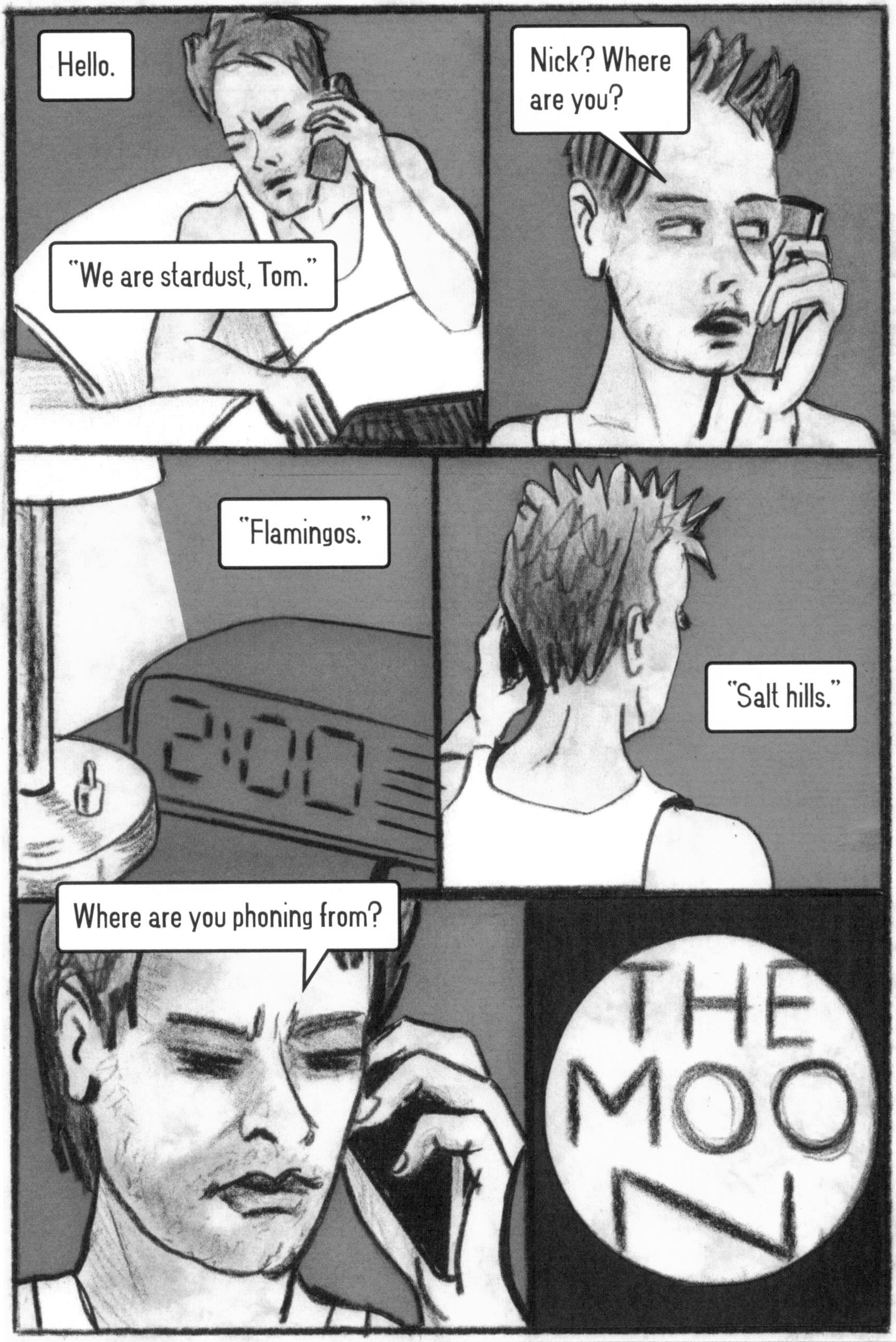
Hello.
"We are stardust, Tom."
Nick? Where are you?
"Flamingos."
2:00
"Salt hills."
Where are you phoning from?
THE MOON

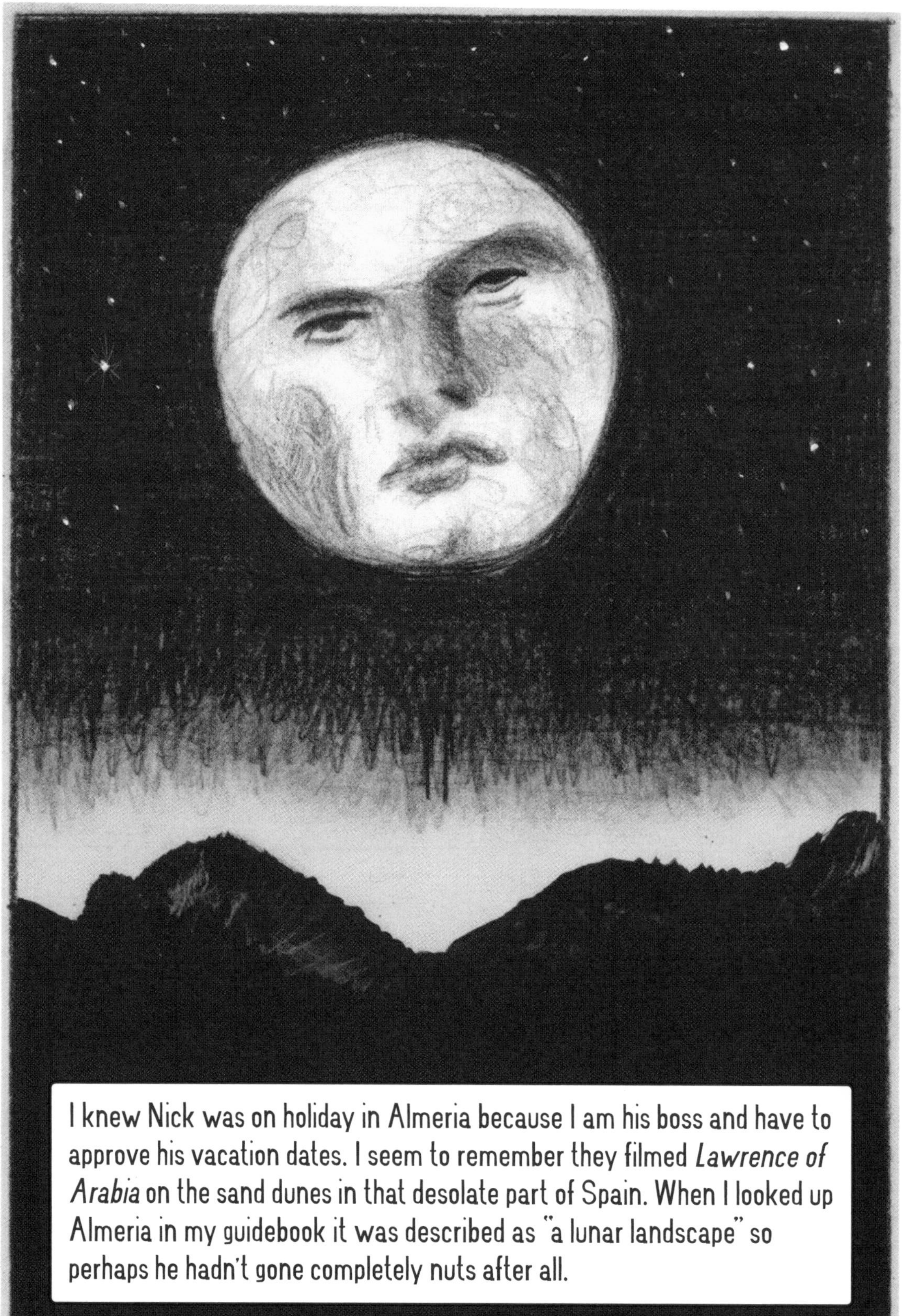
I knew Nick was on holiday in Almeria because I am his boss and have to approve his vacation dates. I seem to remember they filmed *Lawrence of Arabia* on the sand dunes in that desolate part of Spain. When I looked up Almeria in my guidebook it was described as "a lunar landscape" so perhaps he hadn't gone completely nuts after all.

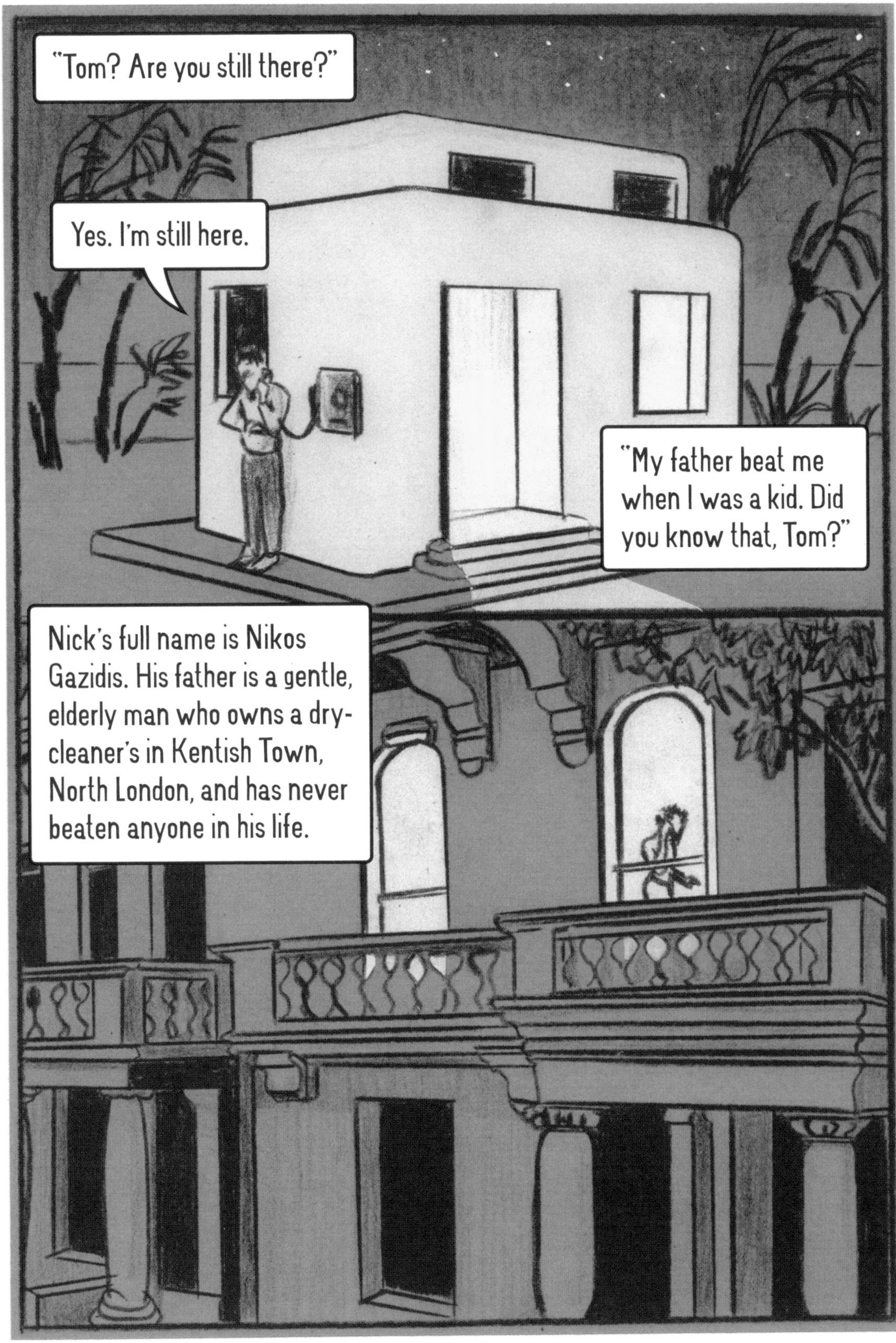
"Tom? Are you still there?"
Yes. I'm still here.
"My father beat me when I was a kid. Did you know that, Tom?"
Nick's full name is Nikos Gazidis. His father is a gentle, elderly man who owns a dry-cleaner's in Kentish Town, North London, and has never beaten anyone in his life.

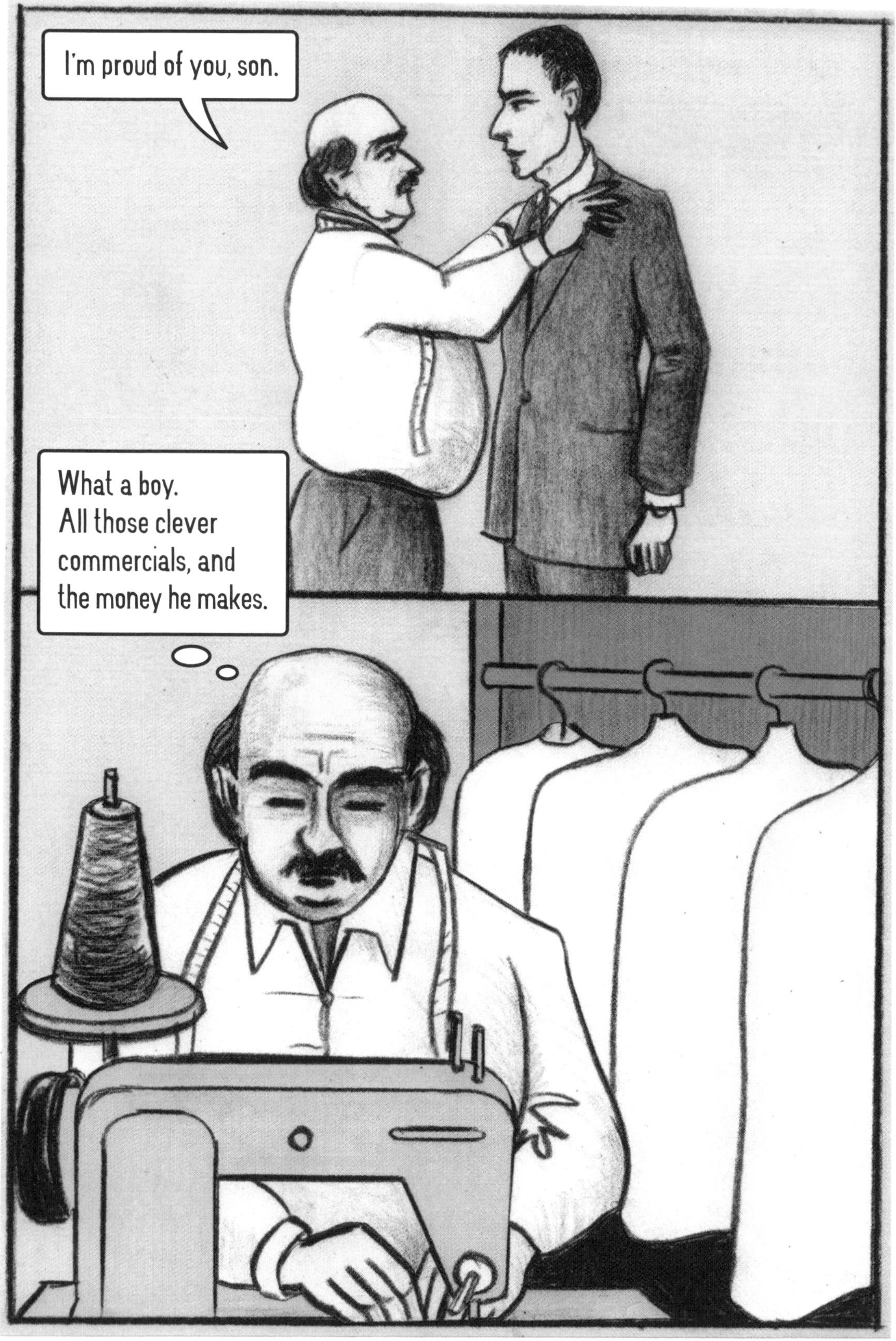
I'm proud of you, son.
What a boy. All those clever commercials, and the money he makes.

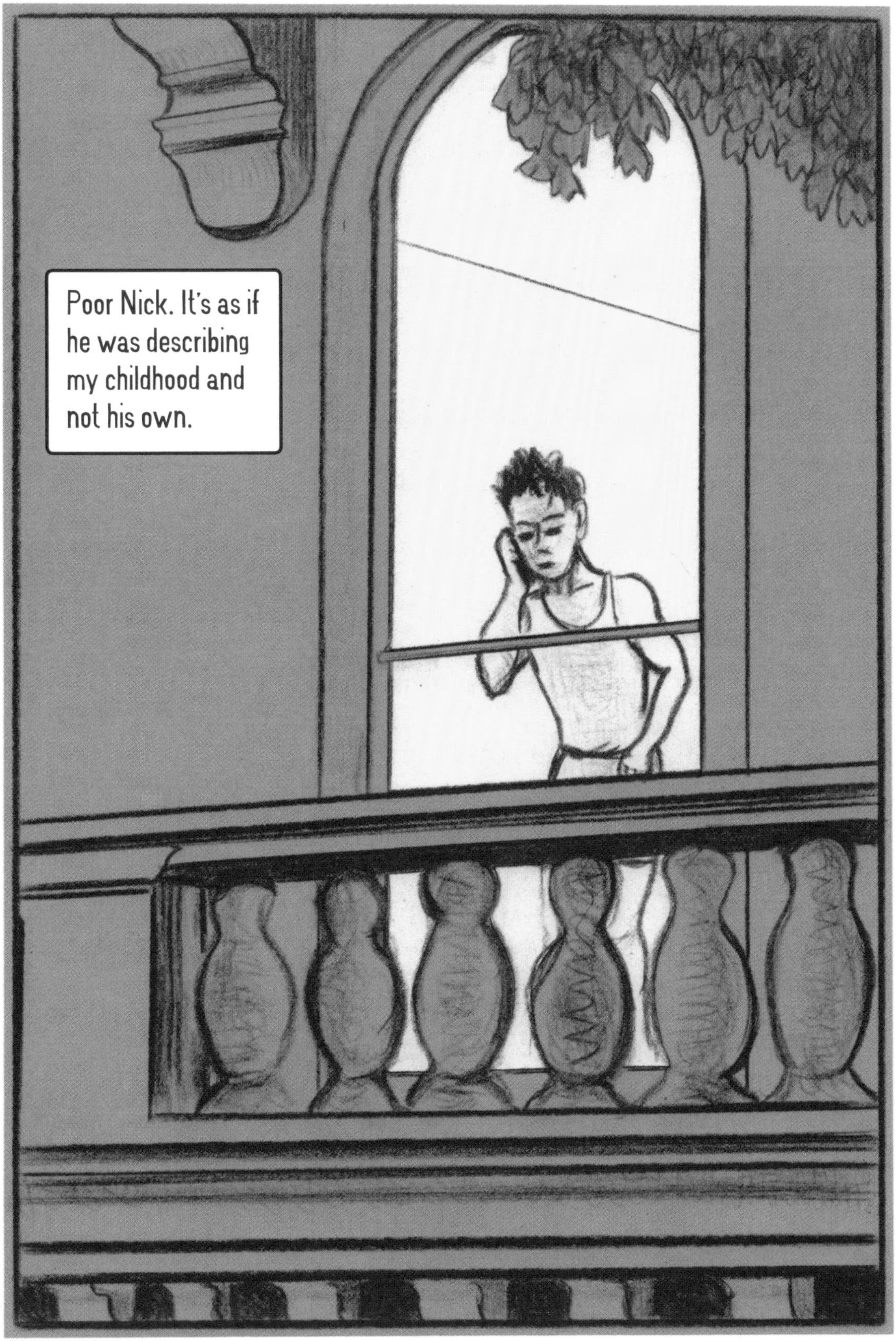
Poor Nick. It's as if he was describing my childhood and not his own.

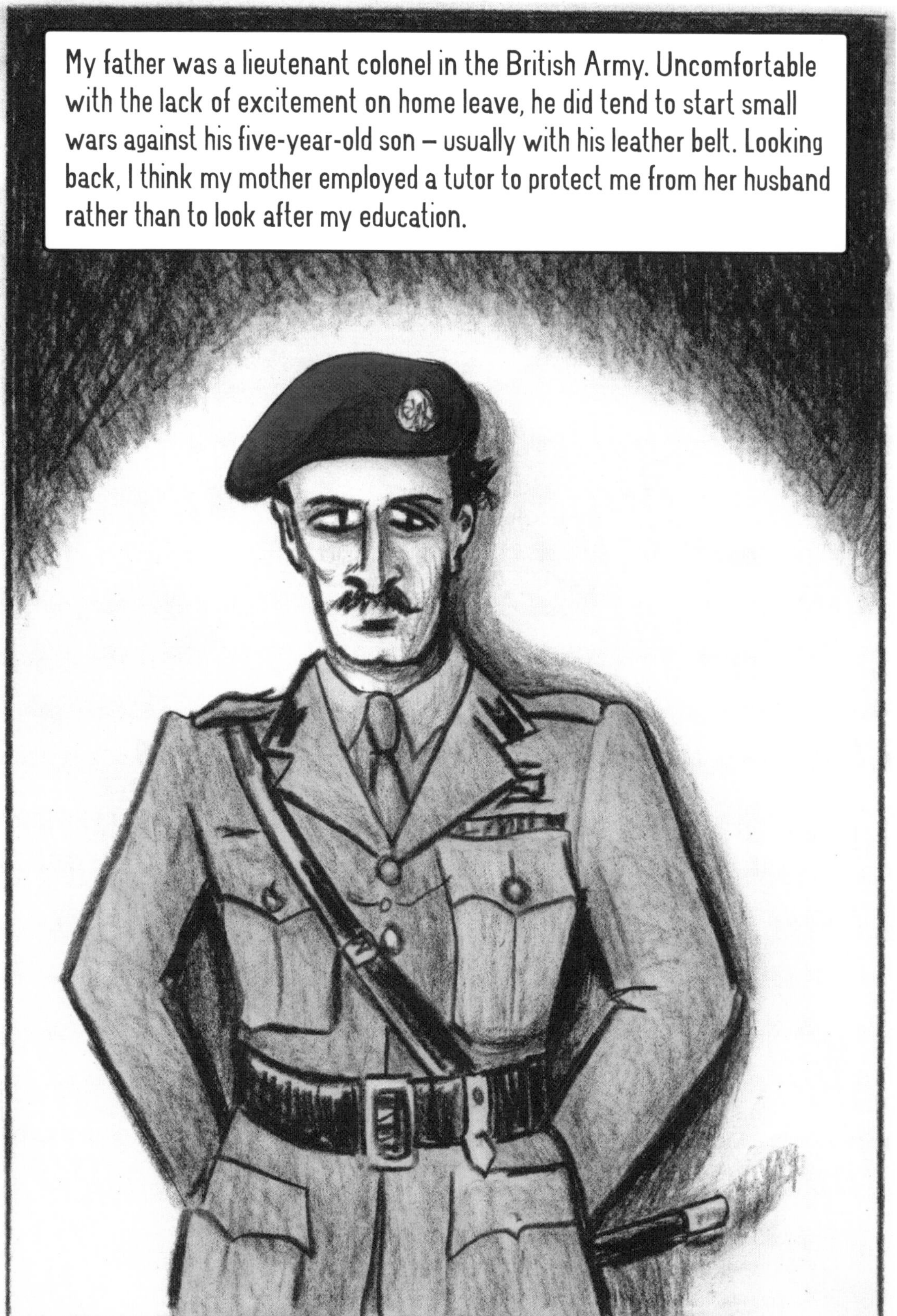
My father was a lieutenant colonel in the British Army. Uncomfortable with the lack of excitement on home leave, he did tend to start small wars against his five-year-old son – usually with his leather belt. Looking back, I think my mother employed a tutor to protect me from her husband rather than to look after my education.

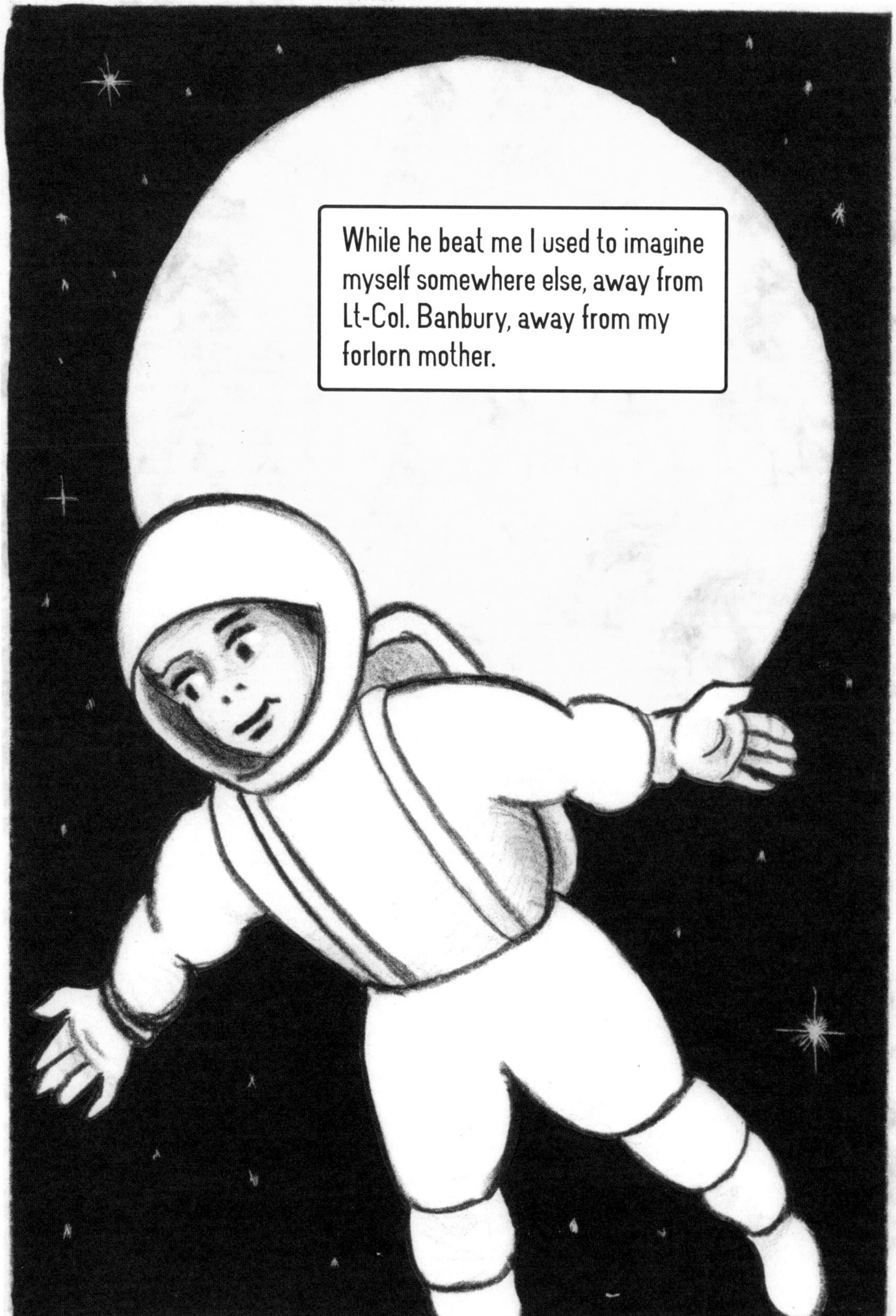
While he beat me I used to imagine myself somewhere else, away from Lt-Col. Banbury, away from my forlorn mother.

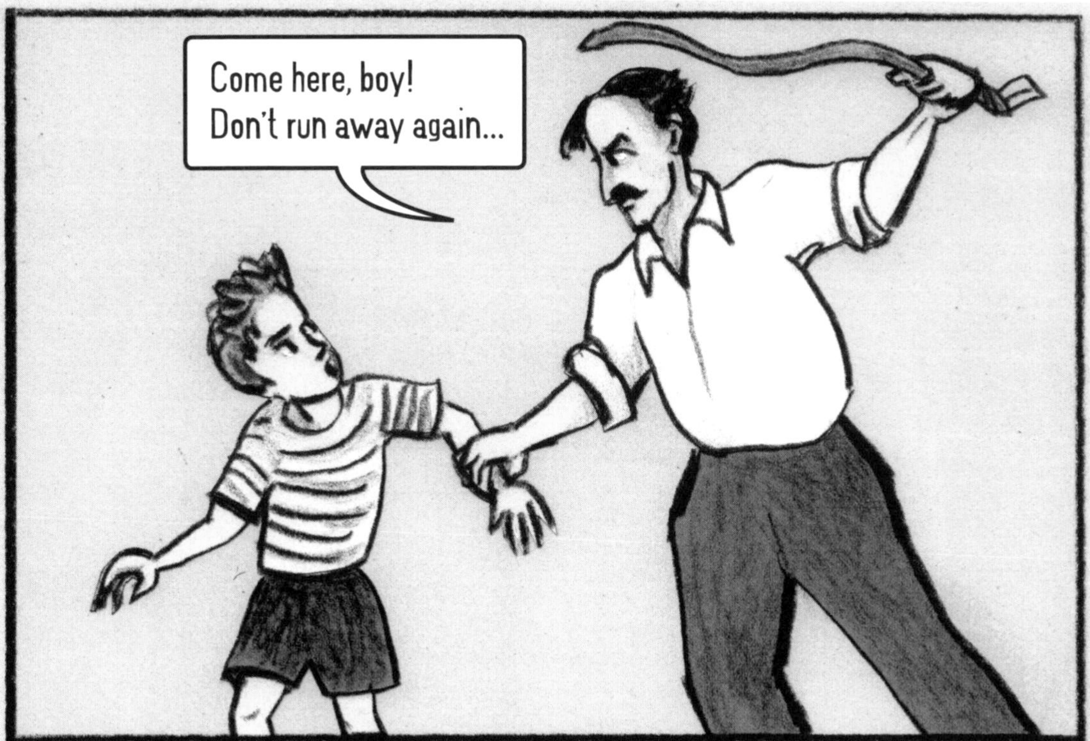
Come here, boy!
Don't run away again...

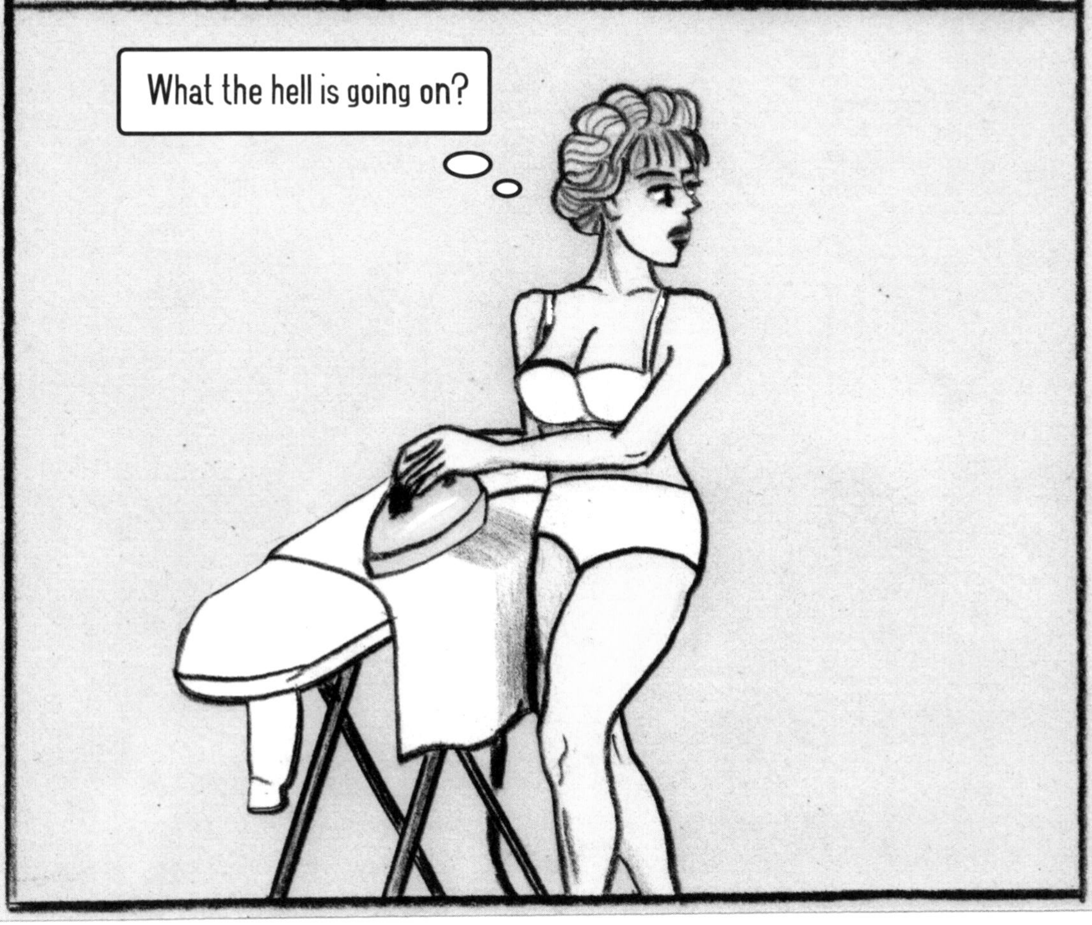
What the hell is going on?

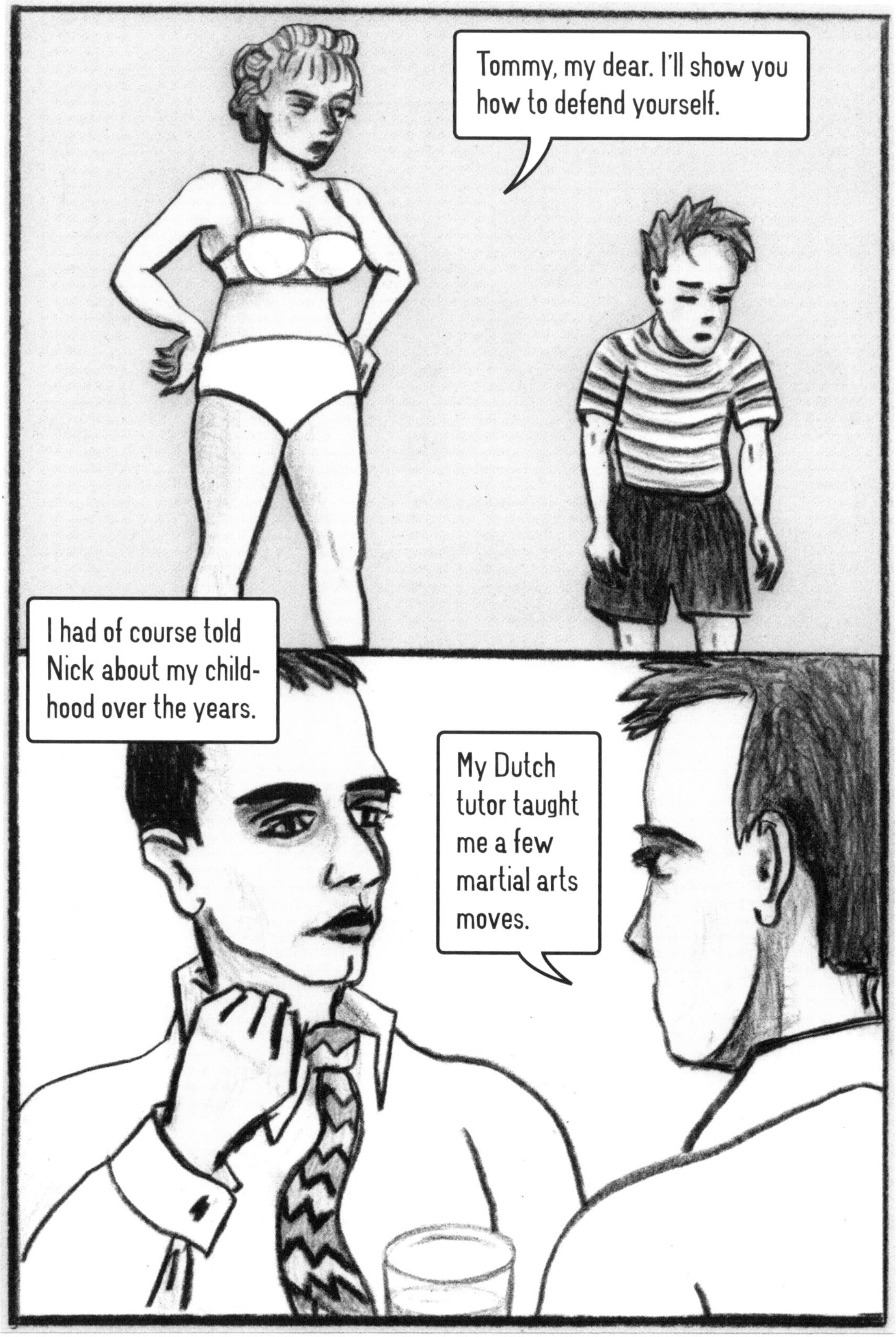
Tommy, my dear. I'll show you how to defend yourself.
I had of course told Nick about my child-hood over the years.
My Dutch tutor taught me a few martial arts moves.

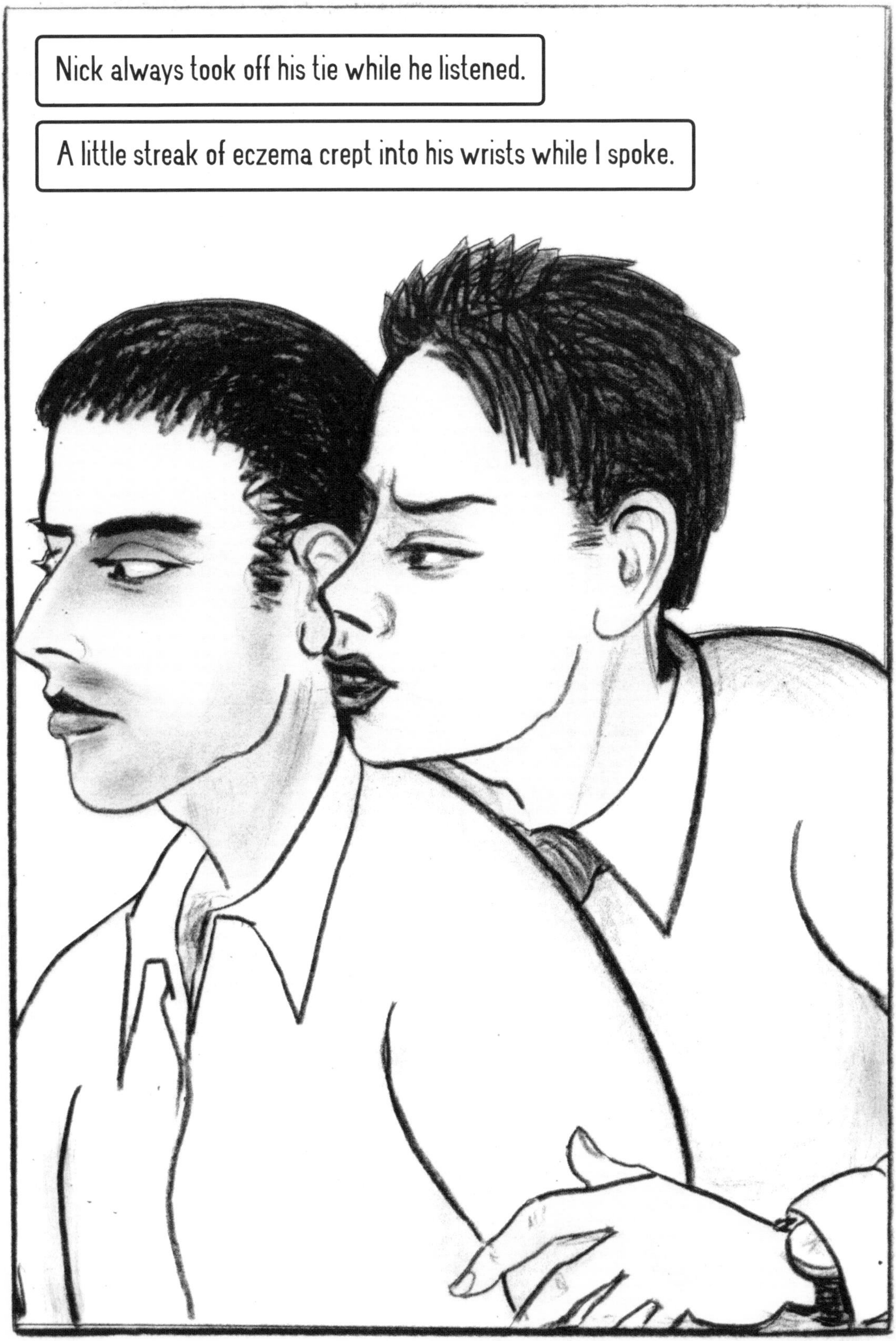
Nick always took off his tie while he listened.
A little streak of eczema crept into his wrists while I spoke.

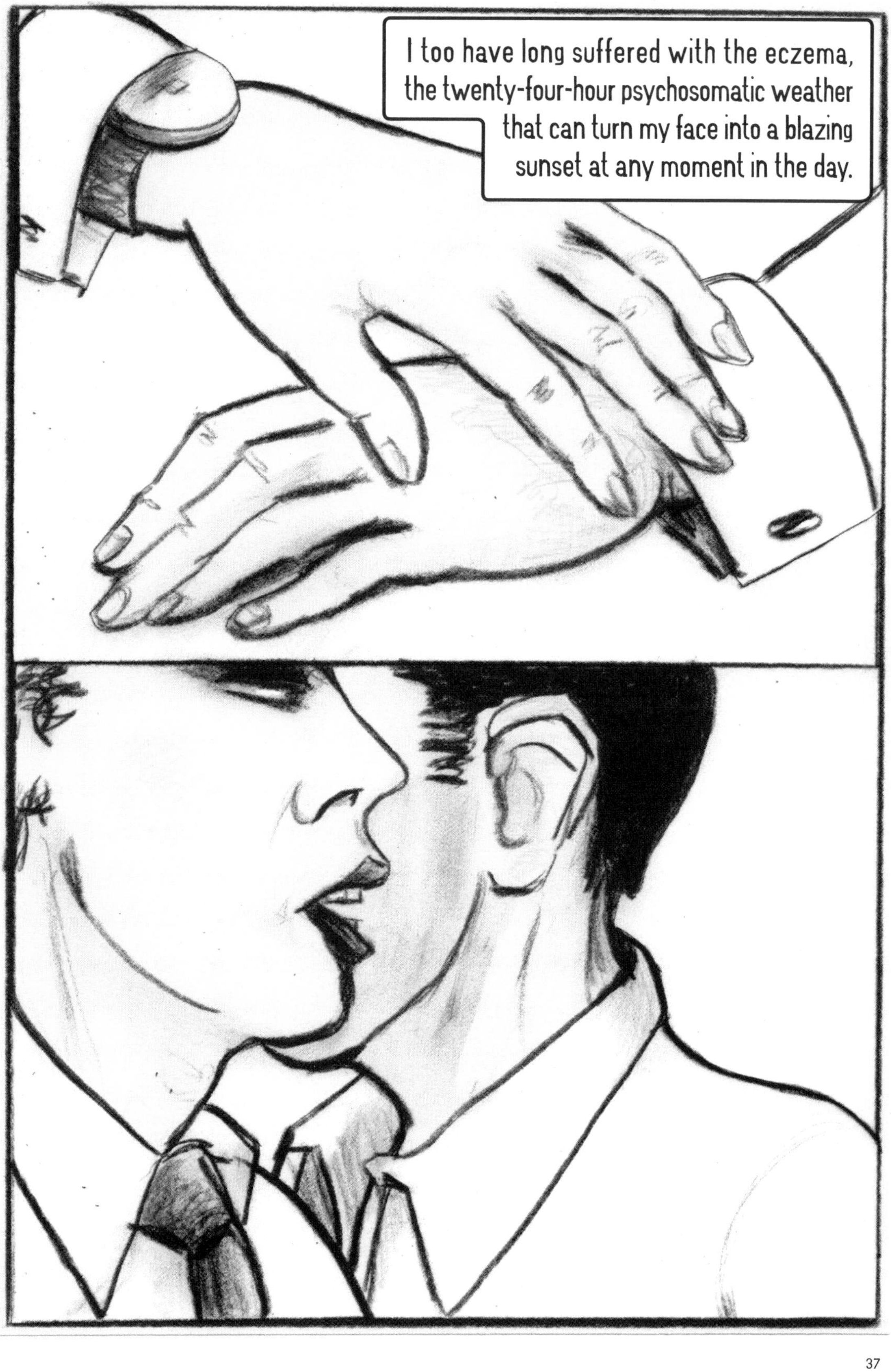
I too have long suffered with the eczema, the twenty-four-hour psychosomatic weather that can turn my face into a blazing sunset at any moment in the day.

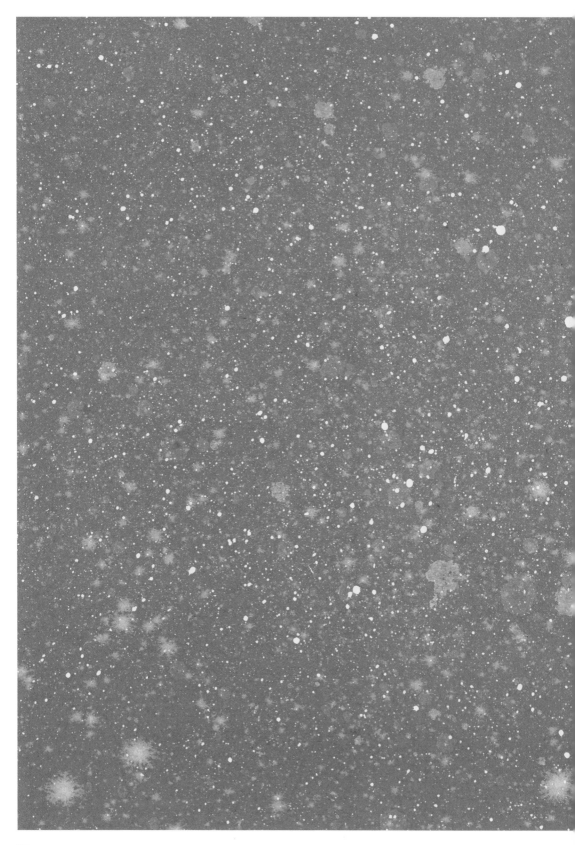

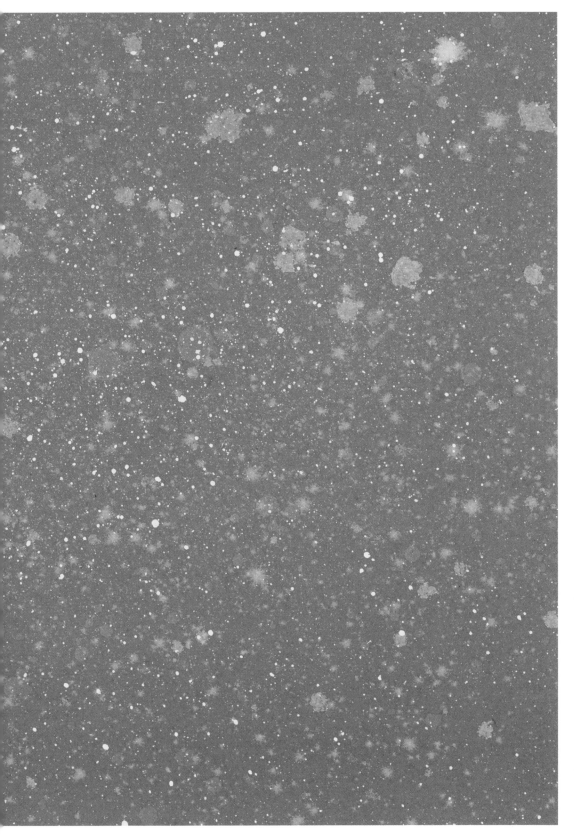

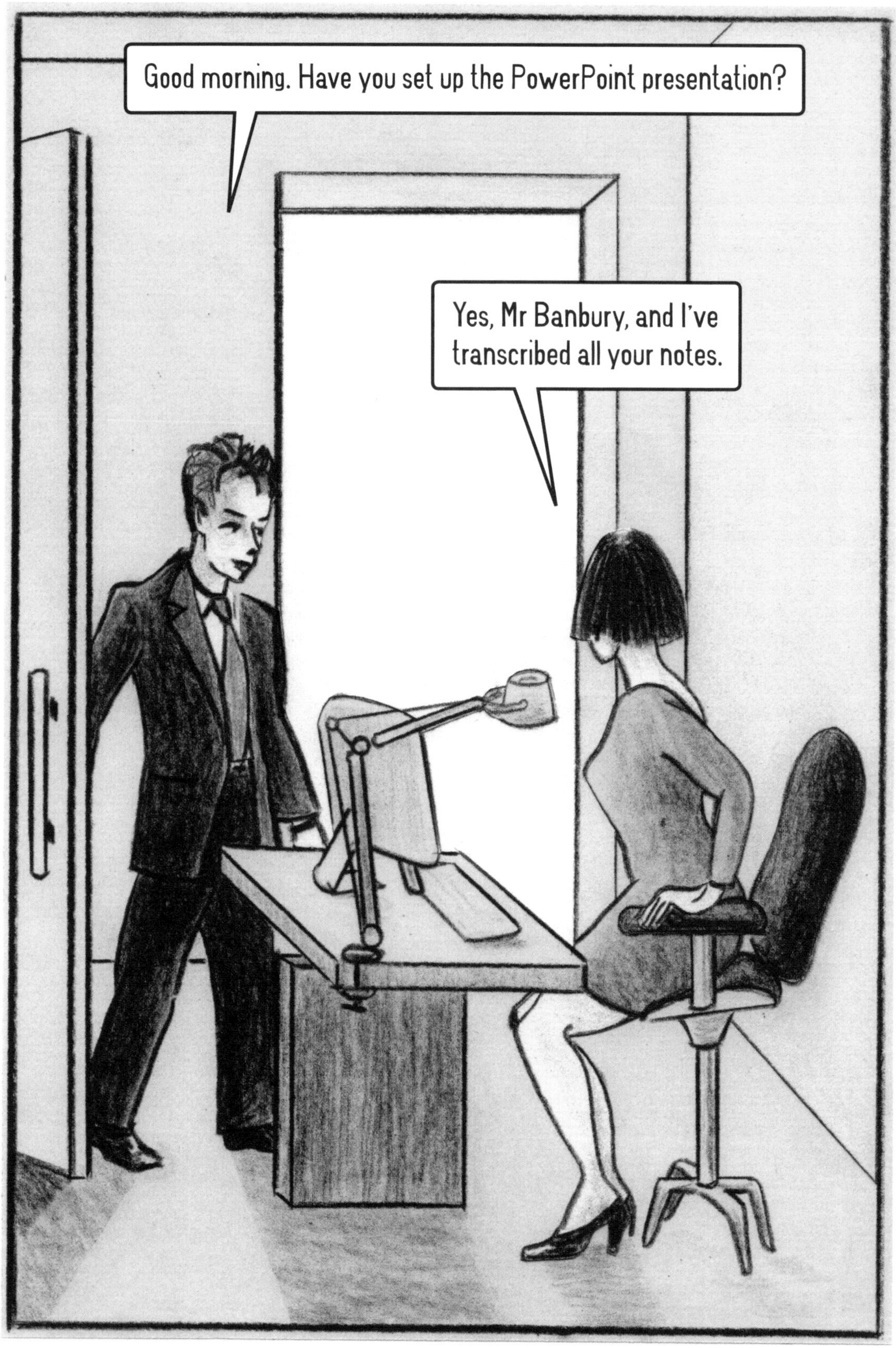
Good morning. Have you set up the PowerPoint presentation?
Yes, Mr Banbury, and I've transcribed all your notes.

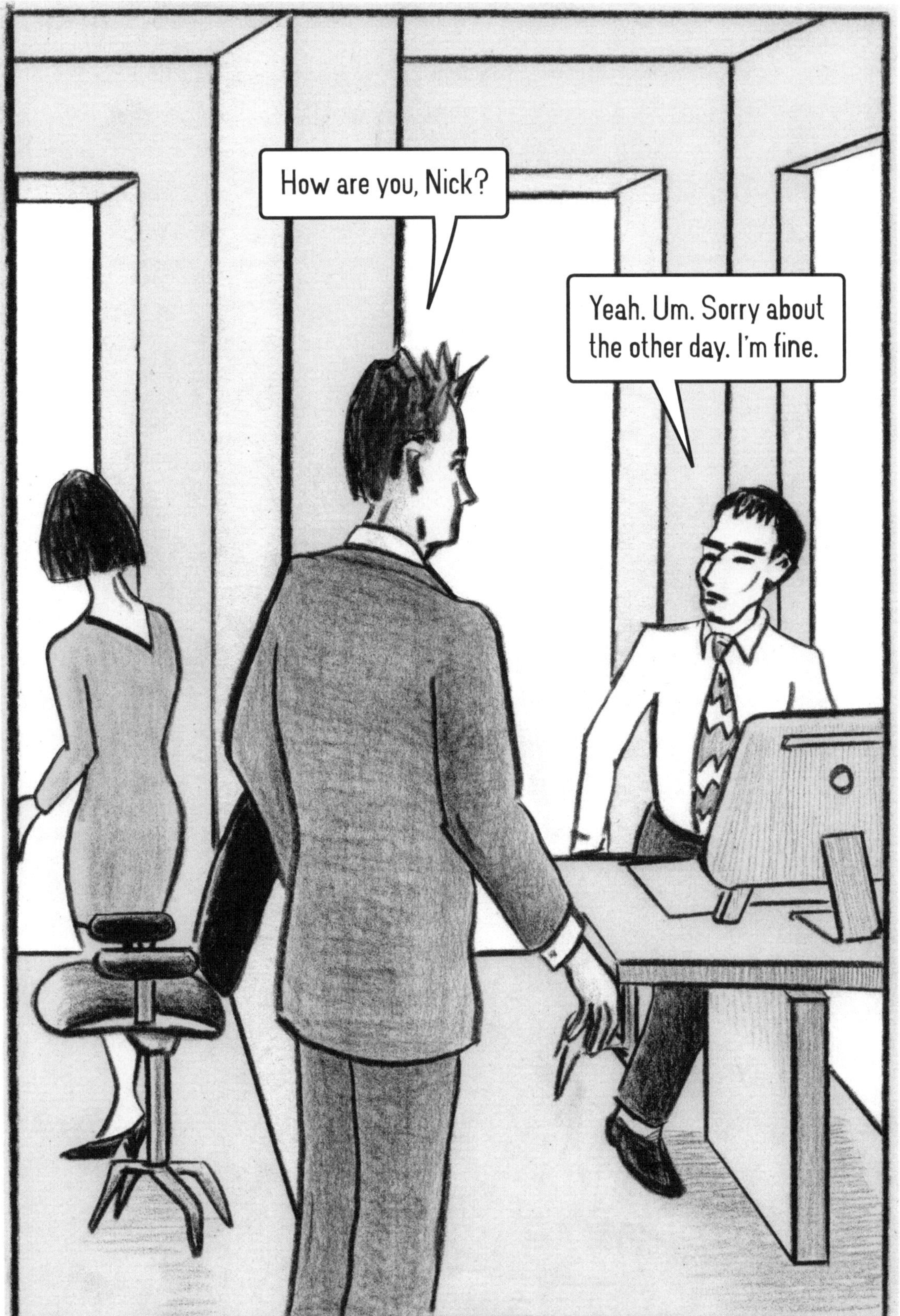
How are you, Nick?
Yeah. Um. Sorry about the other day. I'm fine.

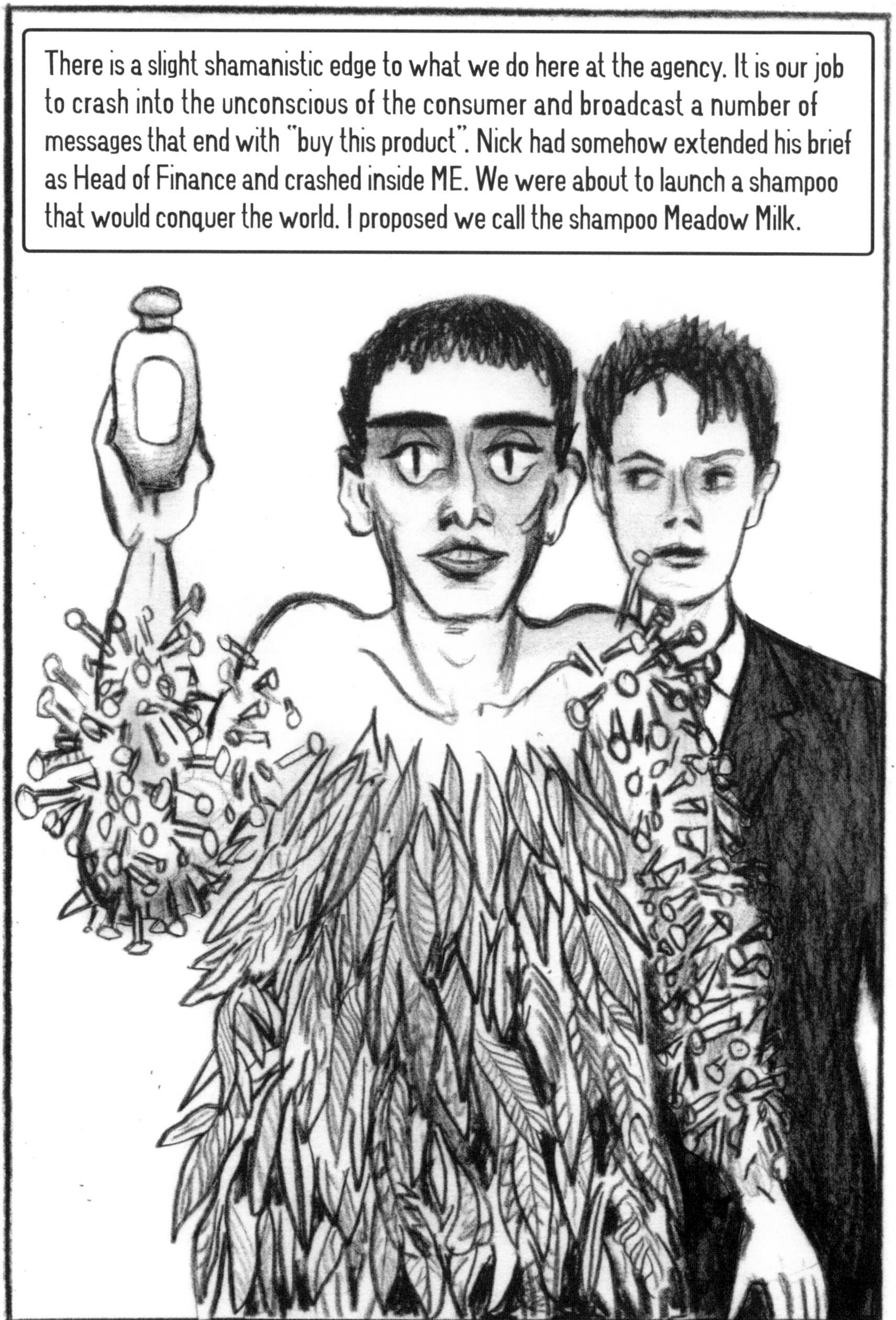
There is a slight shamanistic edge to what we do here at the agency. It is our job to crash into the unconscious of the consumer and broadcast a number of messages that end with "buy this product". Nick had somehow extended his brief as Head of Finance and crashed inside ME. We were about to launch a shampoo that would conquer the world. I proposed we call the shampoo Meadow Milk.

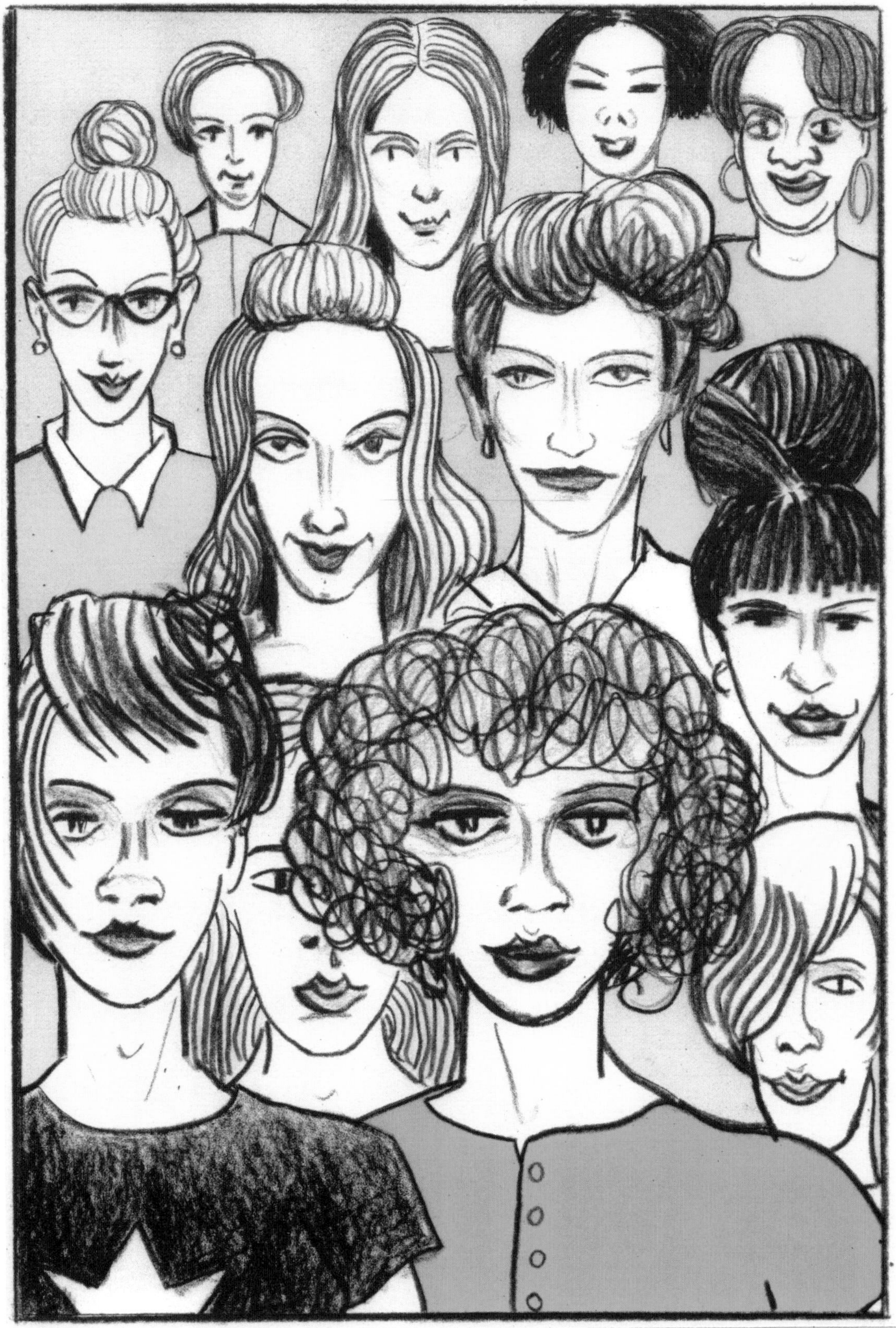

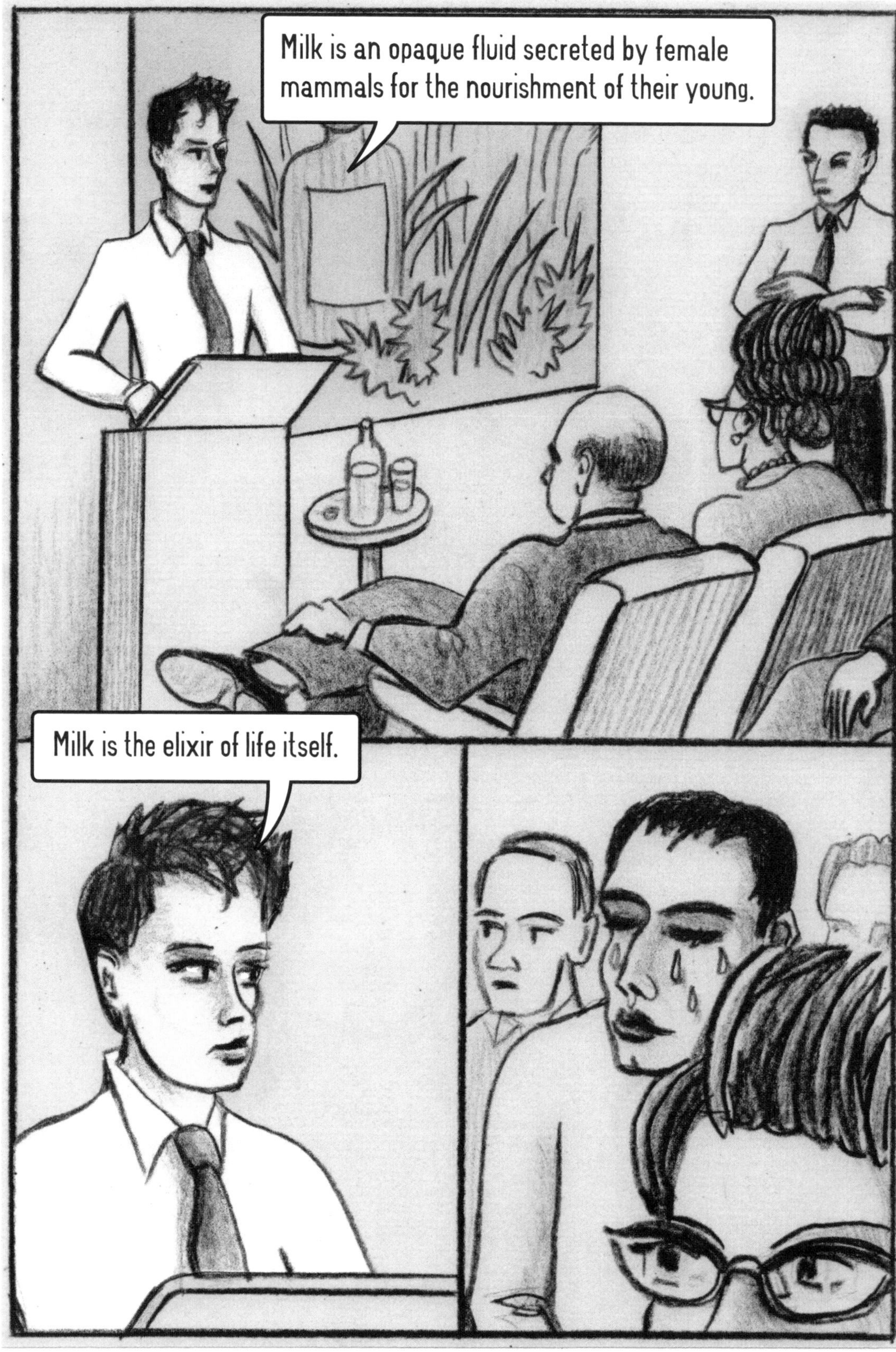
Milk is an opaque fluid secreted by female mammals for the nourishment of their young.
Milk is the elixir of life itself.

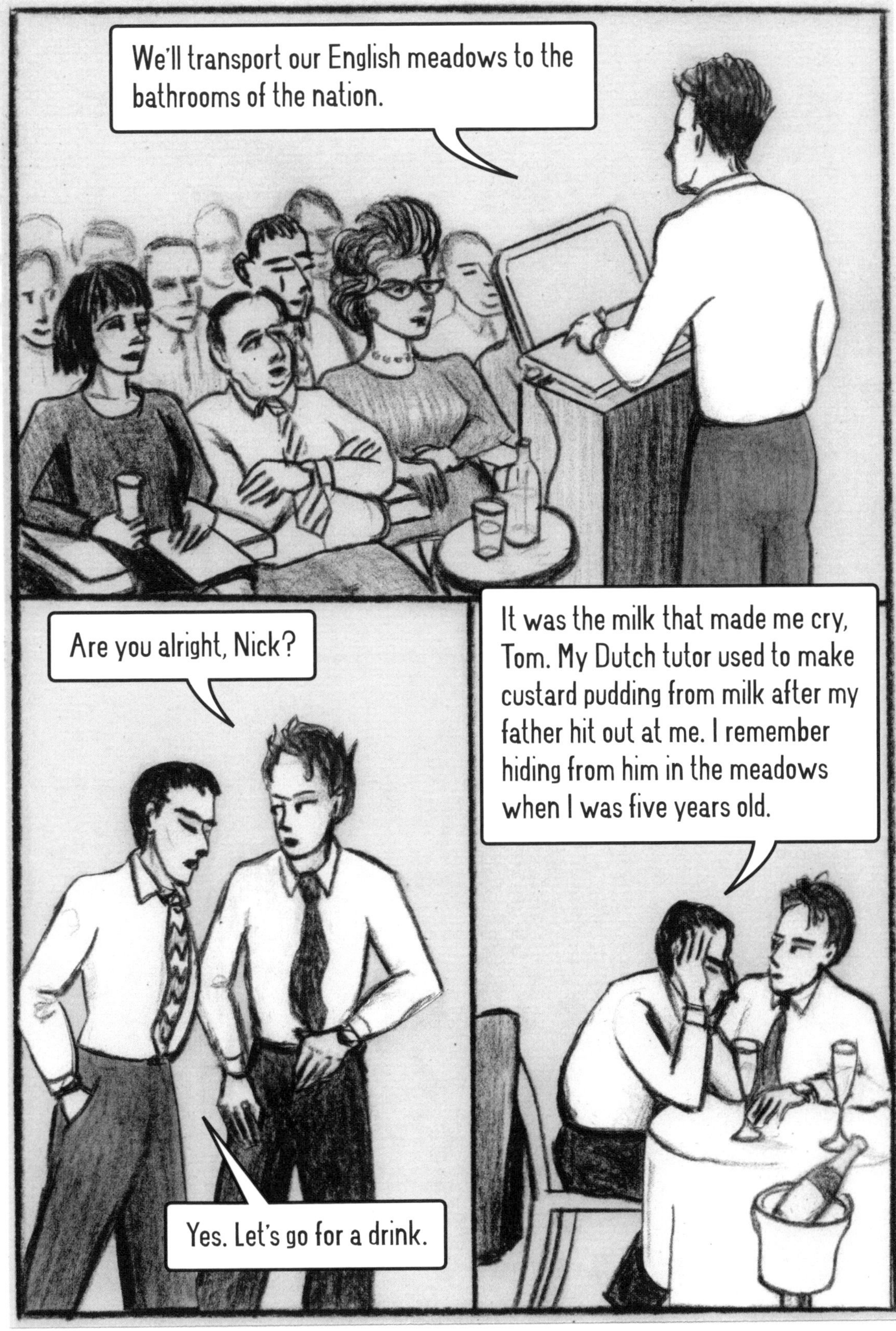
We'll transport our English meadows to the bathrooms of the nation.
Are you alright, Nick?
Yes. Let's go for a drink.
It was the milk that made me cry, Tom. My Dutch tutor used to make custard pudding from milk after my father hit out at me. I remember hiding from him in the meadows when I was five years old.

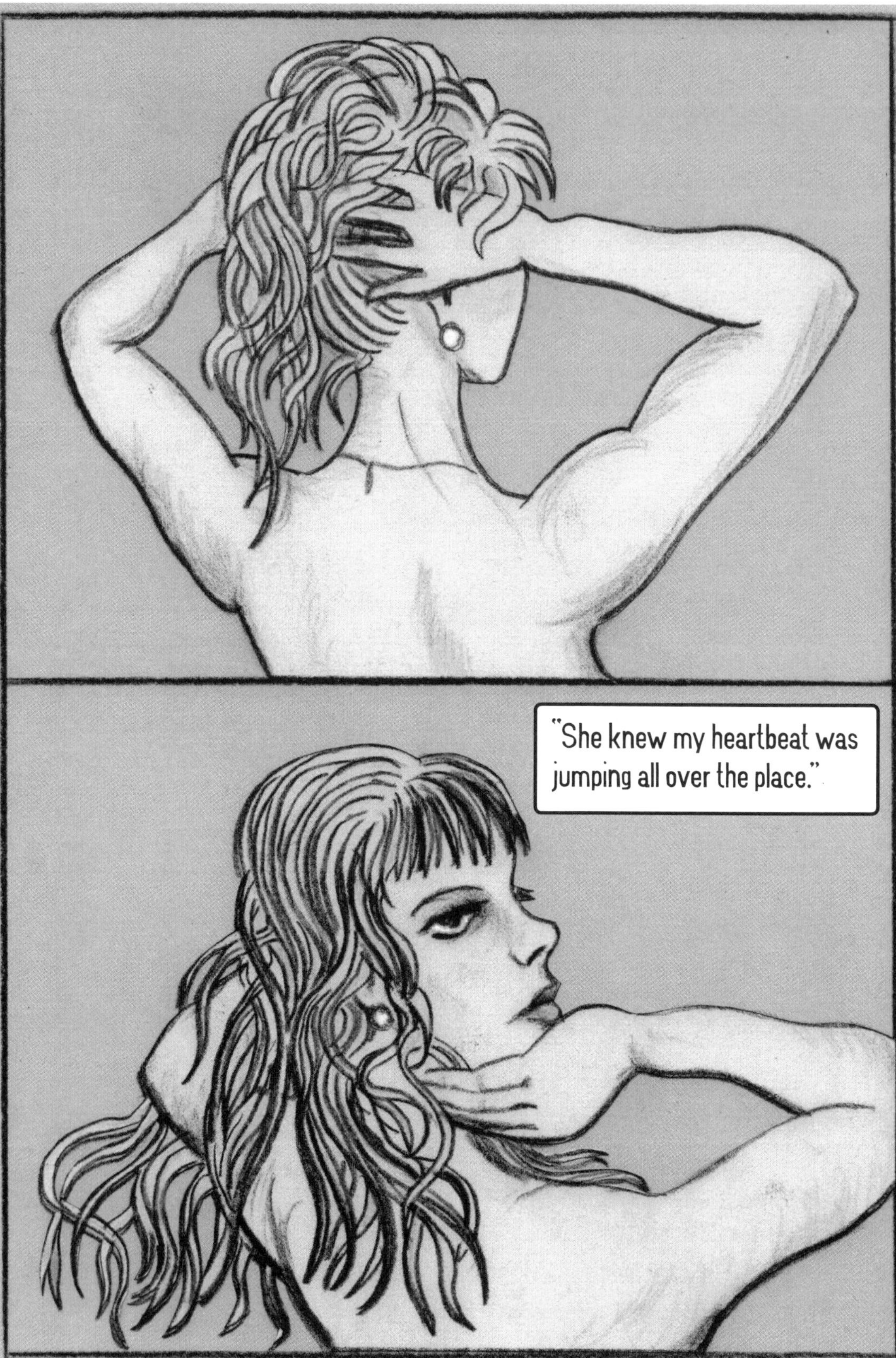
"She knew my heartbeat was jumping all over the place."

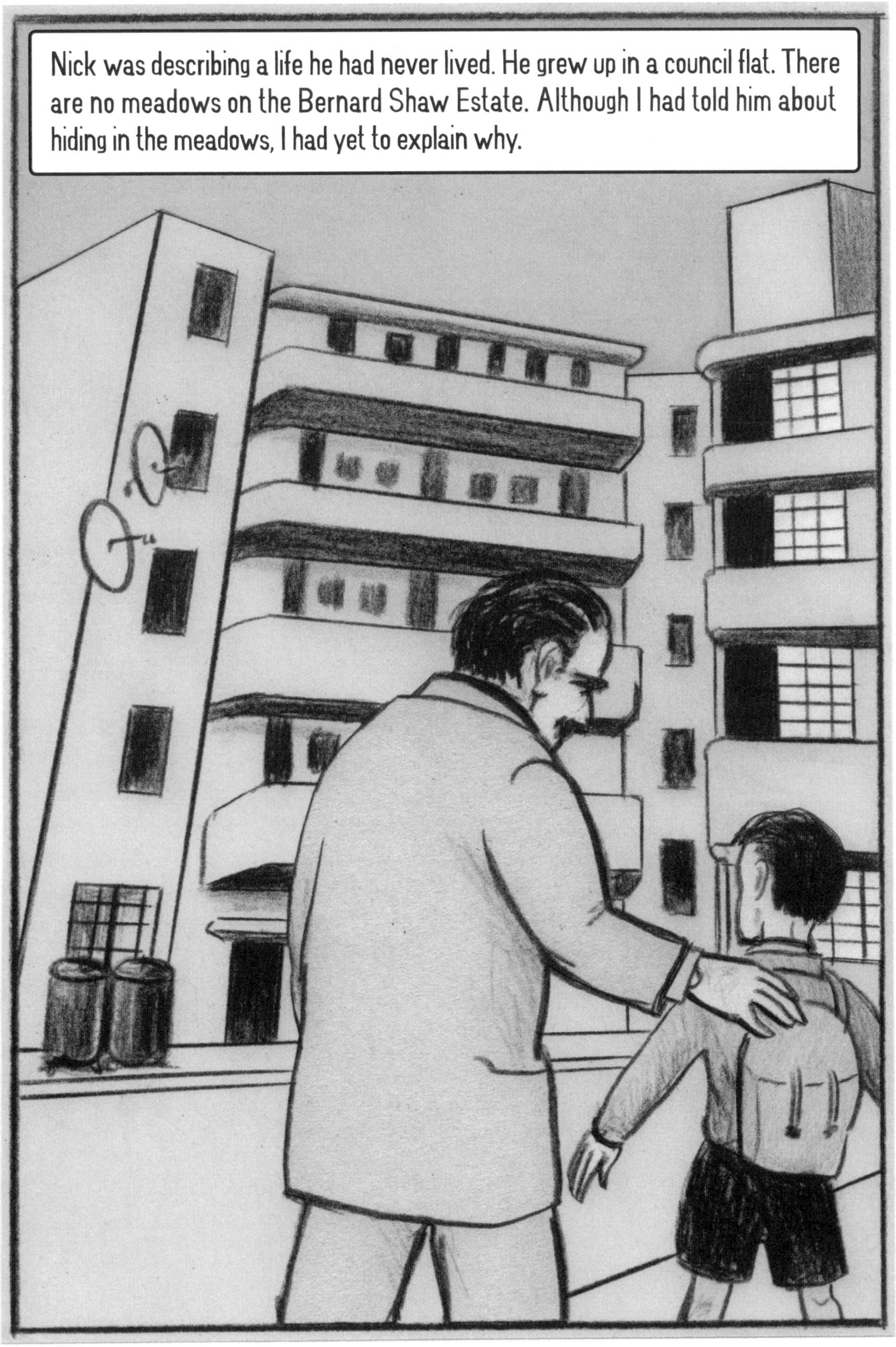
Nick was describing a life he had never lived. He grew up in a council flat. There are no meadows on the Bernard Shaw Estate. Although I had told him about hiding in the meadows, I had yet to explain why.

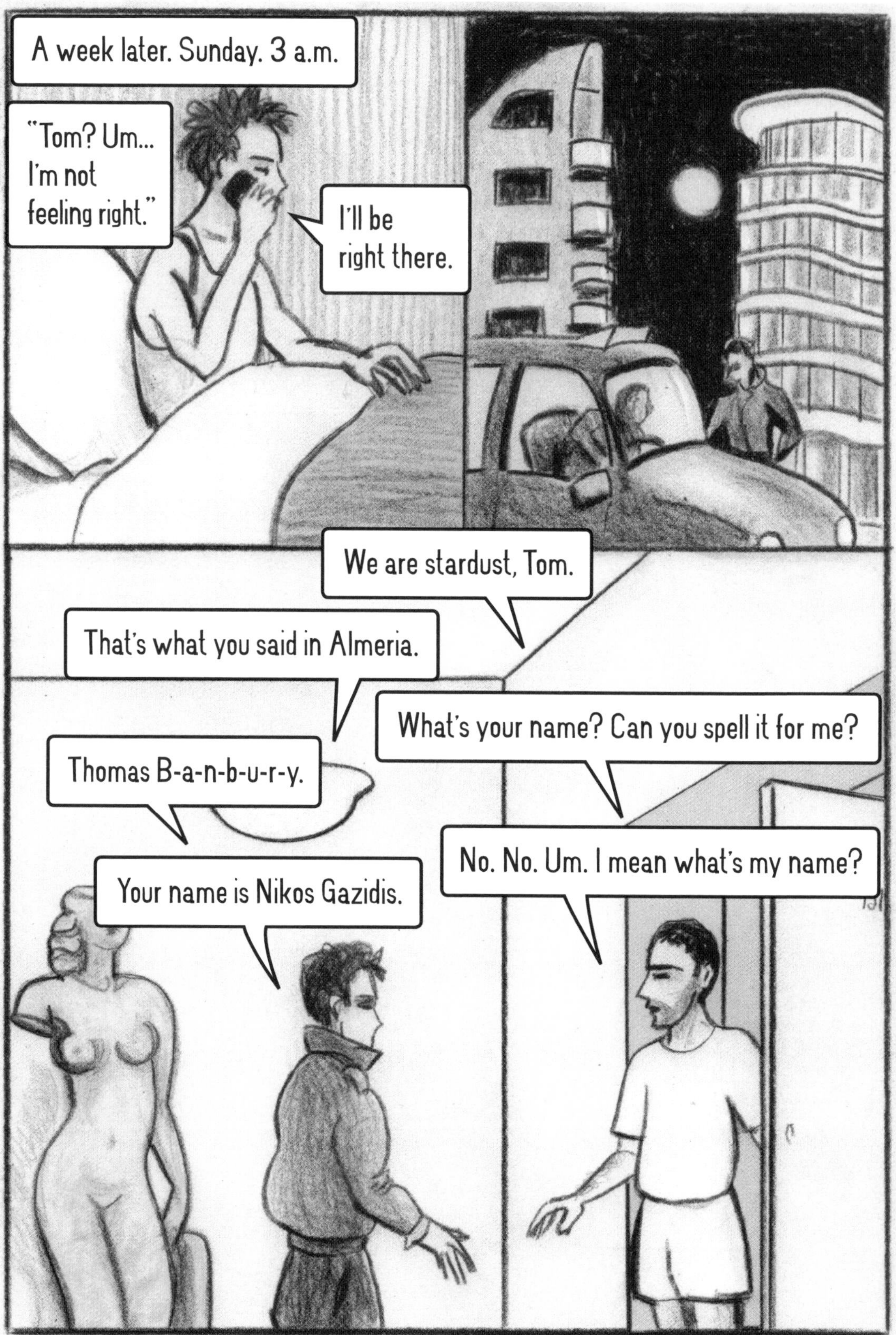
A week later. Sunday. 3 a.m.
"Tom? Um... I'm not feeling right."
I'll be right there.
We are stardust, Tom.
That's what you said in Almeria.
What's your name? Can you spell it for me?
Thomas B-a-n-b-u-r-y.
No. No. Um. I mean what's my name?
Your name is Nikos Gazidis.

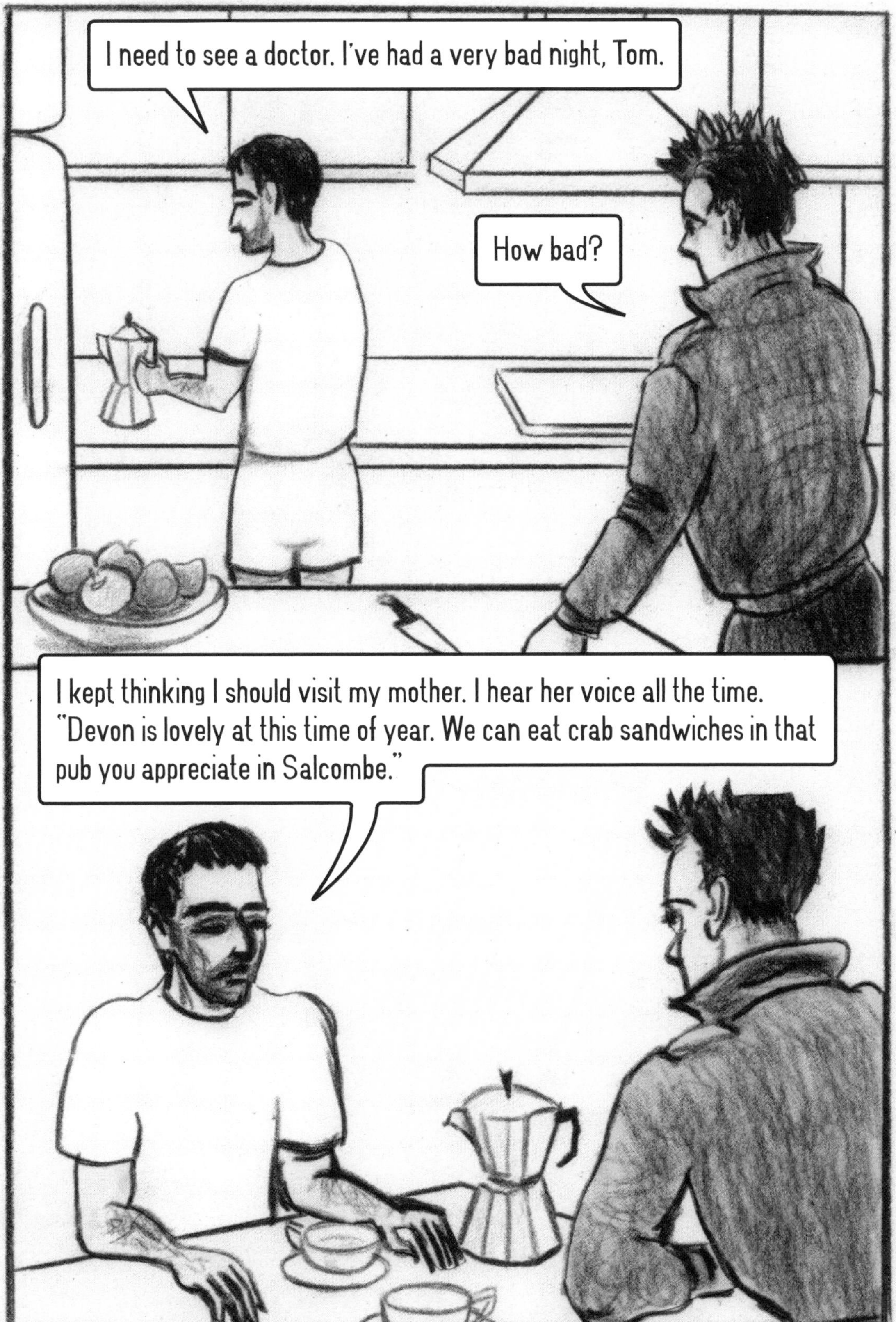
I need to see a doctor. I've had a very bad night, Tom.
How bad?
I kept thinking I should visit my mother. I hear her voice all the time. "Devon is lovely at this time of year. We can eat crab sandwiches in that pub you appreciate in Salcombe."

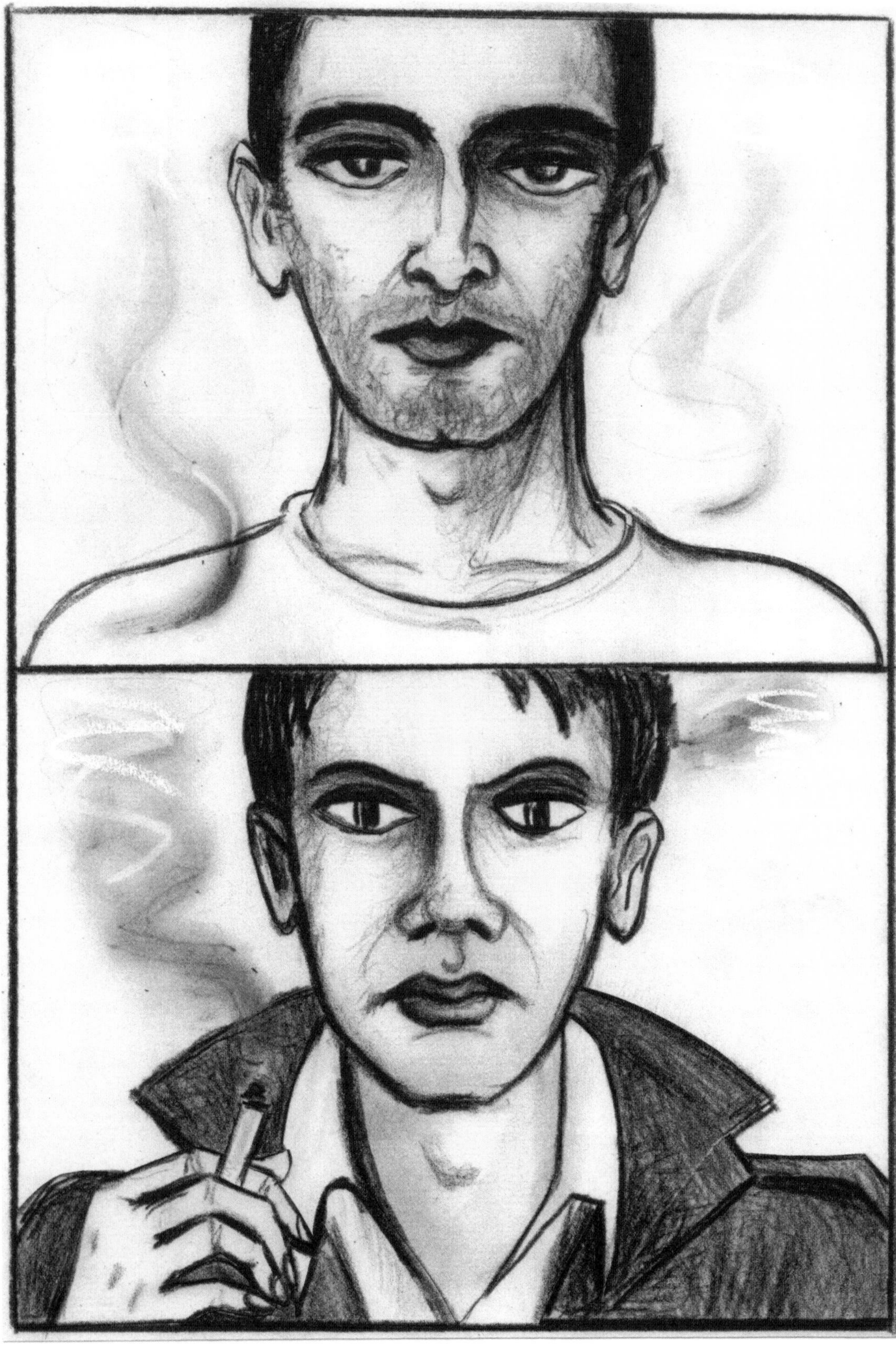

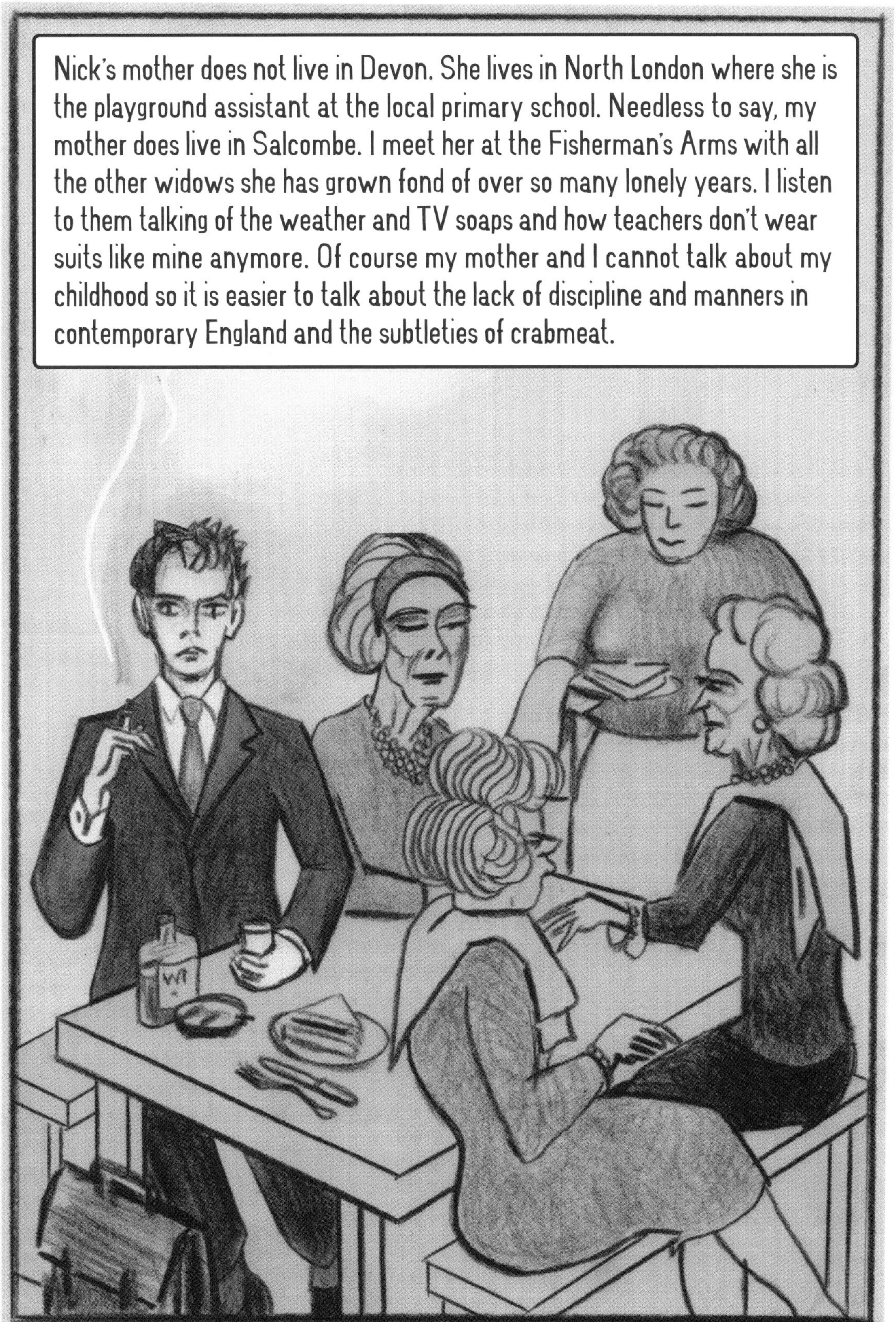
Nick's mother does not live in Devon. She lives in North London where she is the playground assistant at the local primary school. Needless to say, my mother does live in Salcombe. I meet her at the Fisherman's Arms with all the other widows she has grown fond of over so many lonely years. I listen to them talking of the weather and TV soaps and how teachers don't wear suits like mine anymore. Of course my mother and I cannot talk about my childhood so it is easier to talk about the lack of discipline and manners in contemporary England and the subtleties of crabmeat.

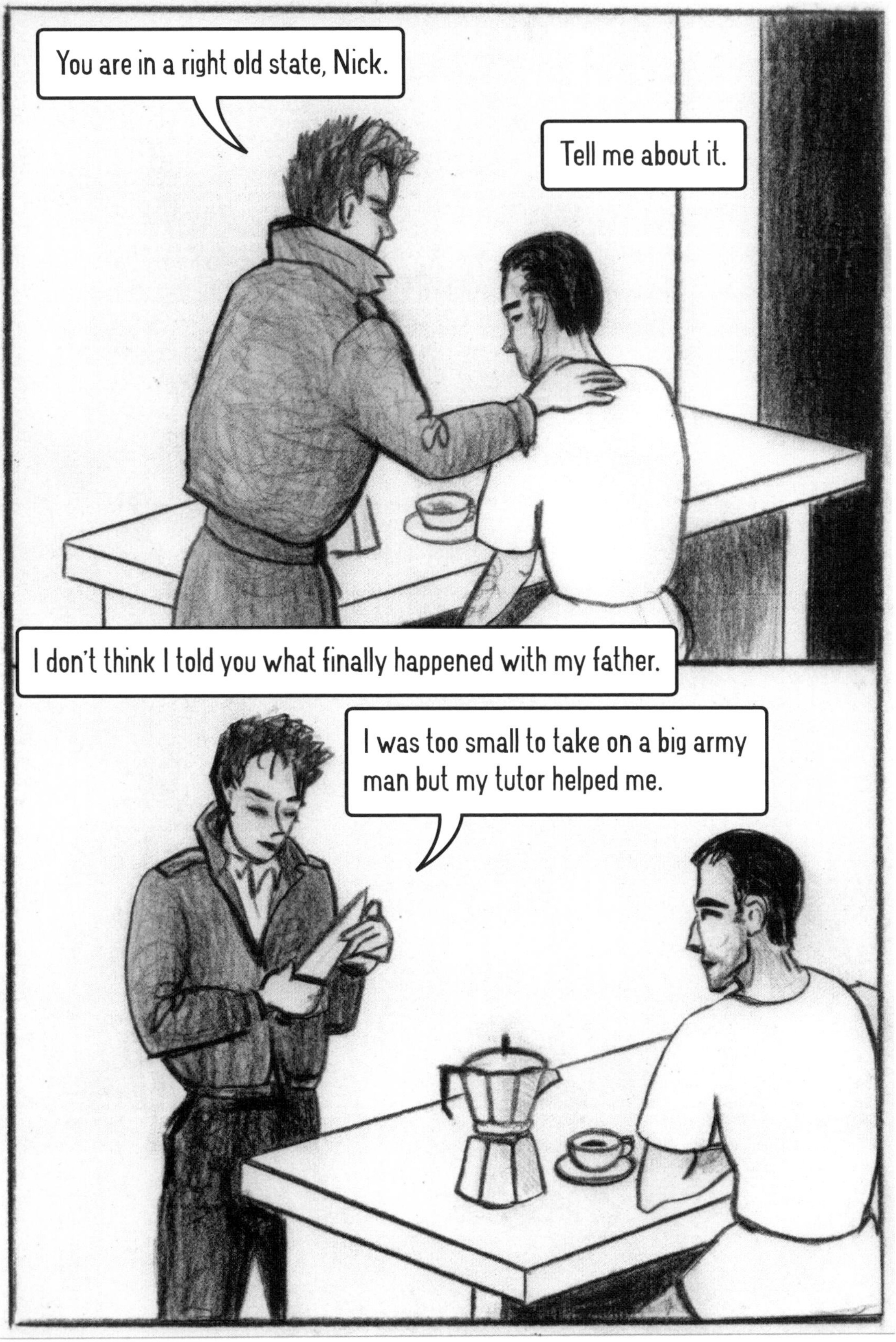
You are in a right old state, Nick.
Tell me about it.
I don't think I told you what finally happened with my father.
I was too small to take on a big army man but my tutor helped me.

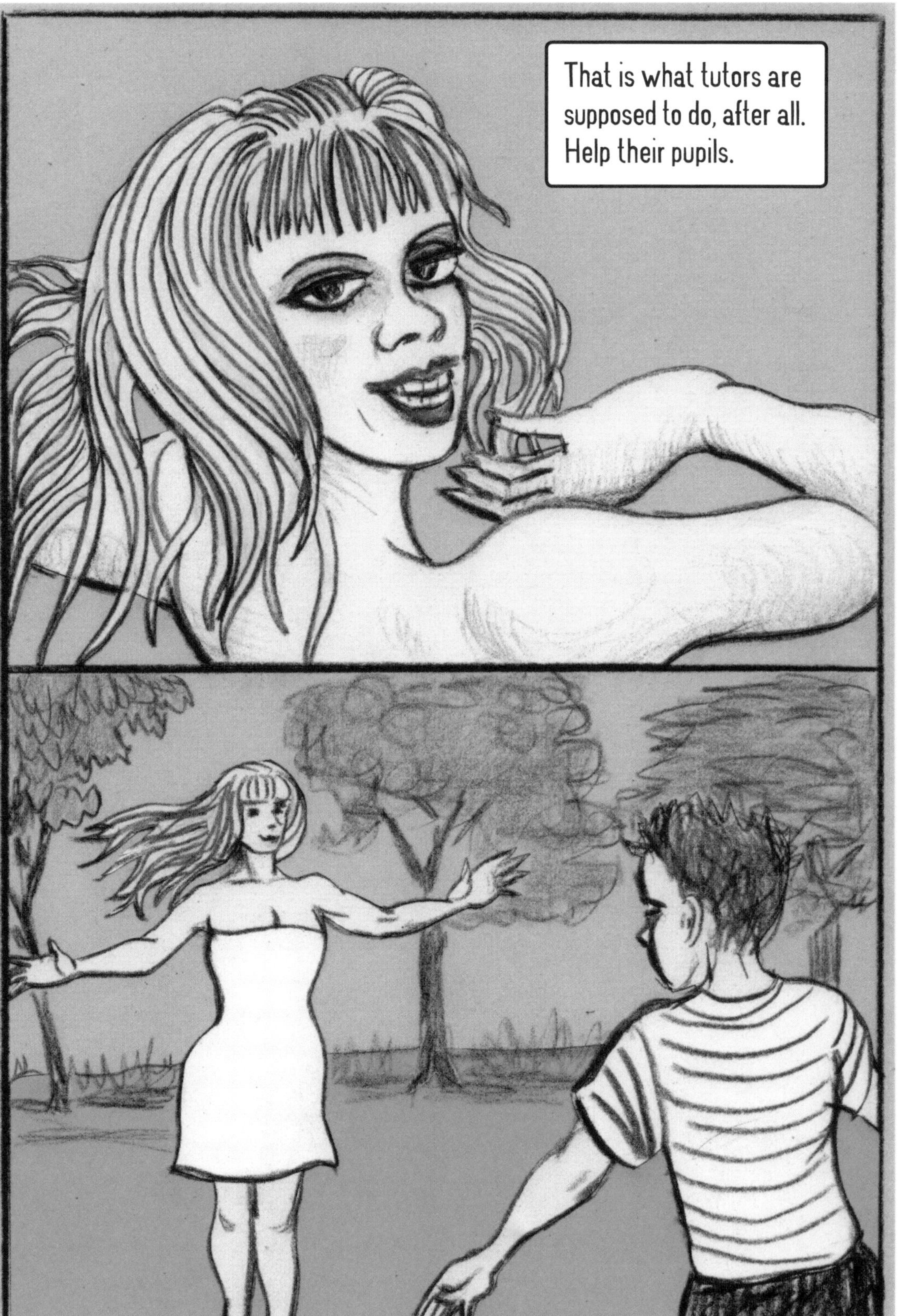
That is what tutors are supposed to do, after all. Help their pupils.

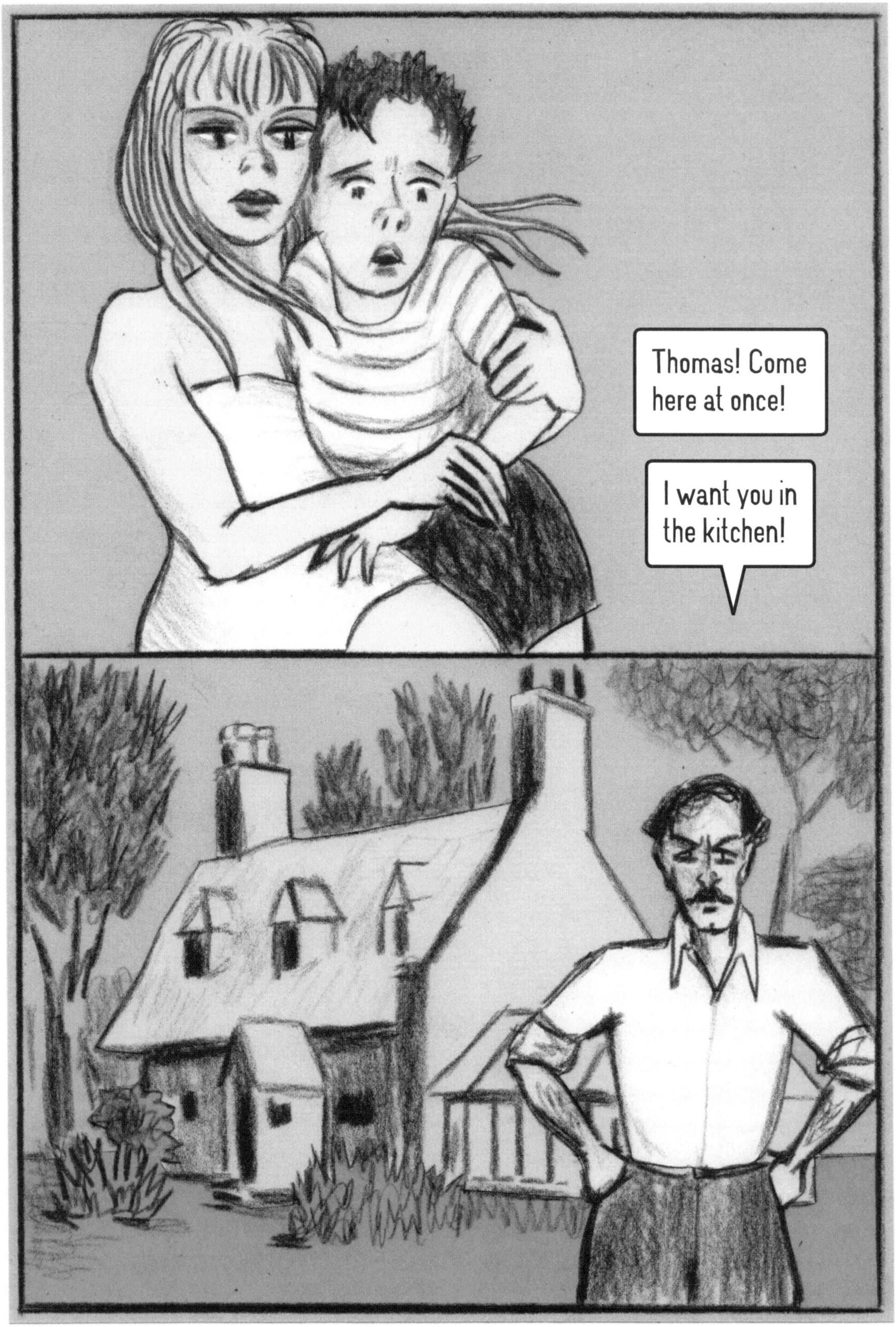
Thomas! Come here at once!
I want you in the kitchen!

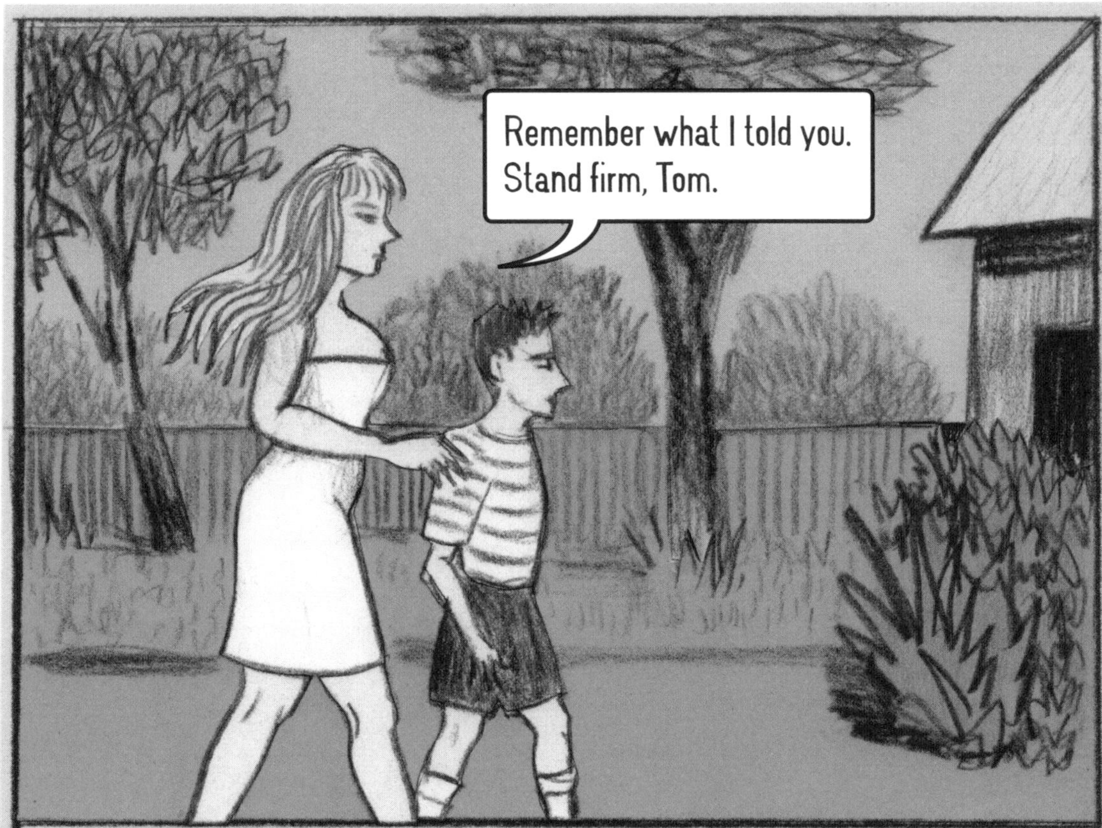
Remember what I told you.
Stand firm, Tom.

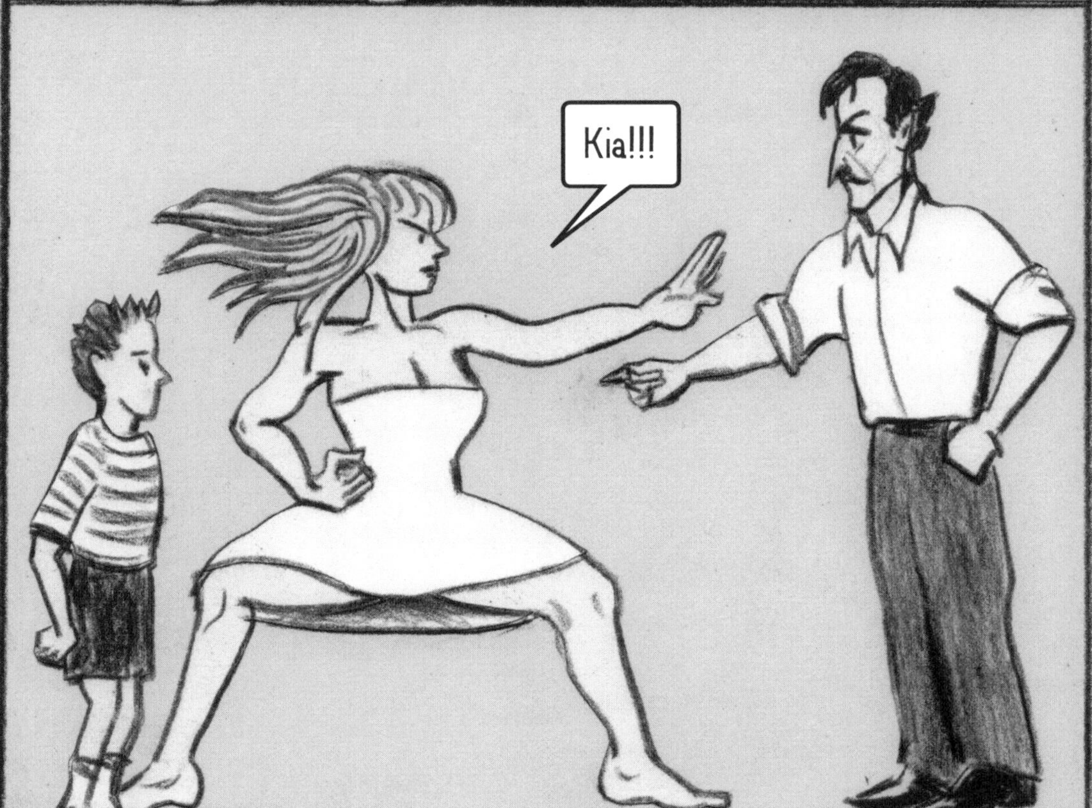
Kia!!!

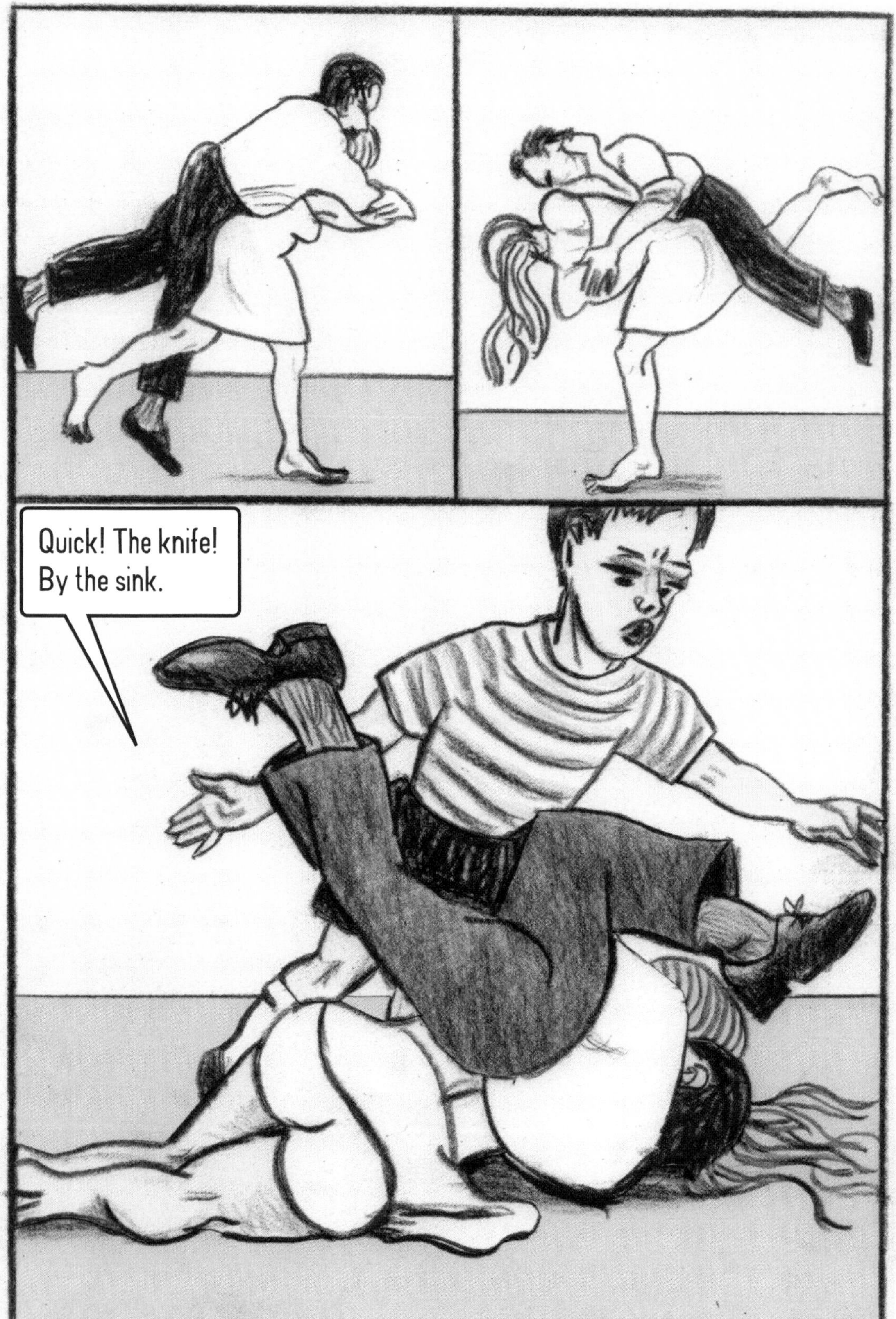
Quick! The knife!
By the sink.

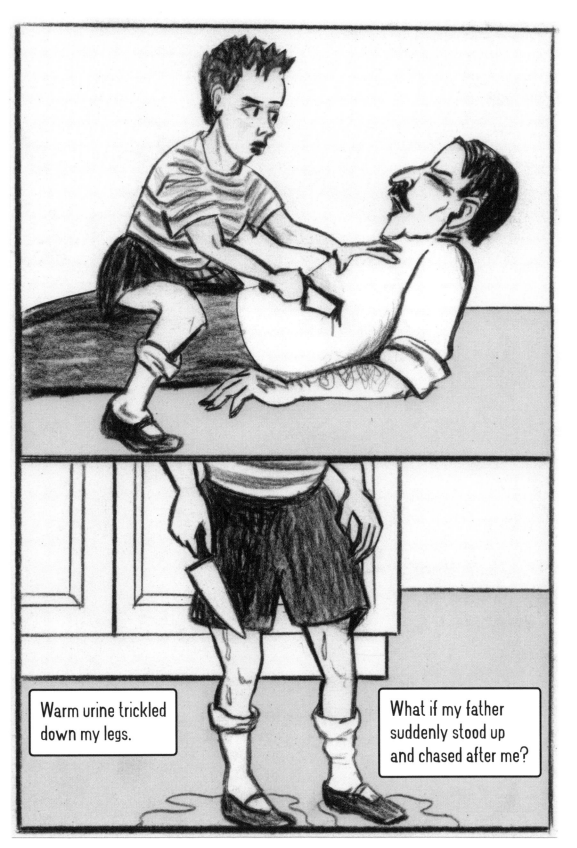

Warm urine trickled down my legs.

What if my father suddenly stood up and chased after me?

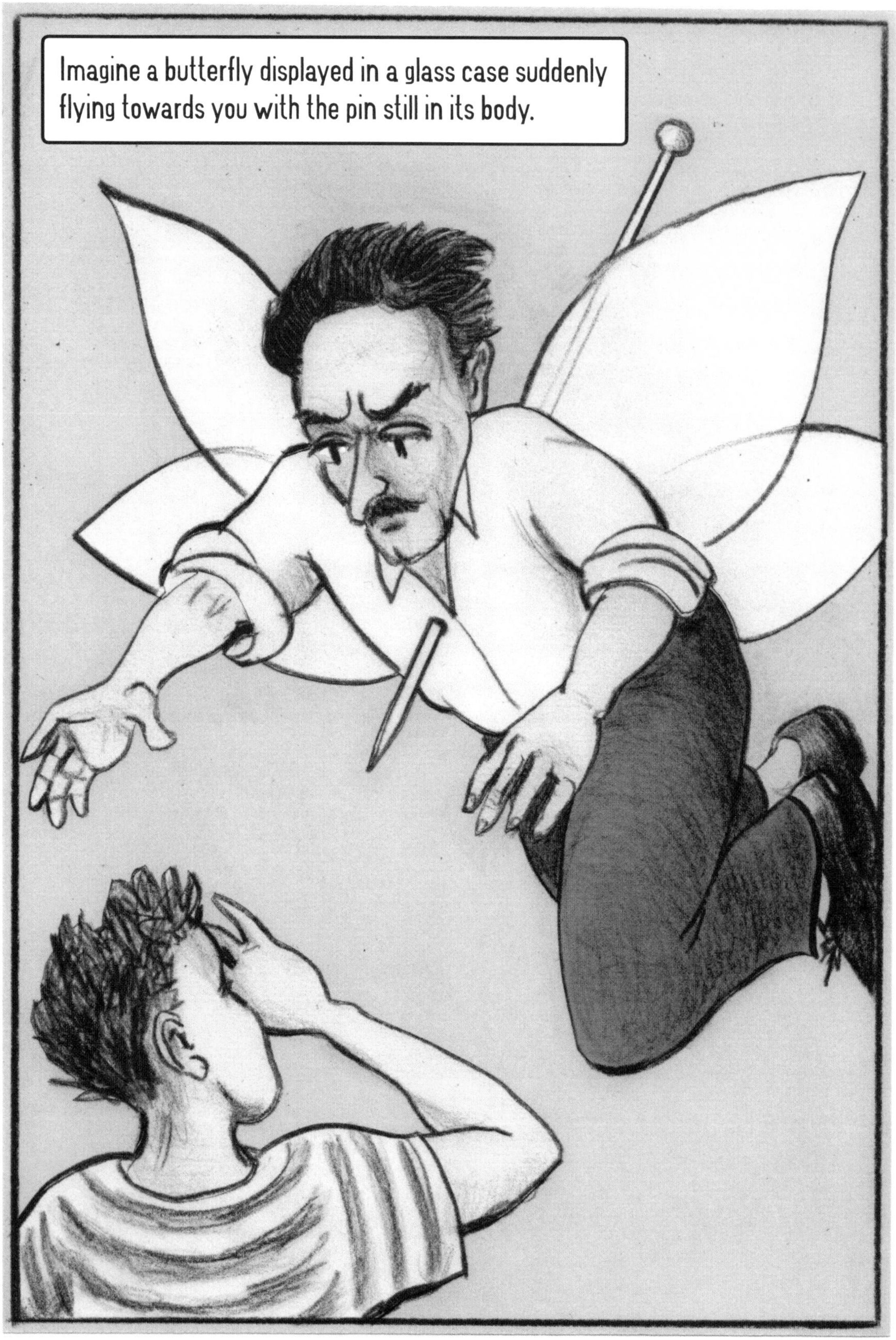
Imagine a butterfly displayed in a glass case suddenly flying towards you with the pin still in its body.

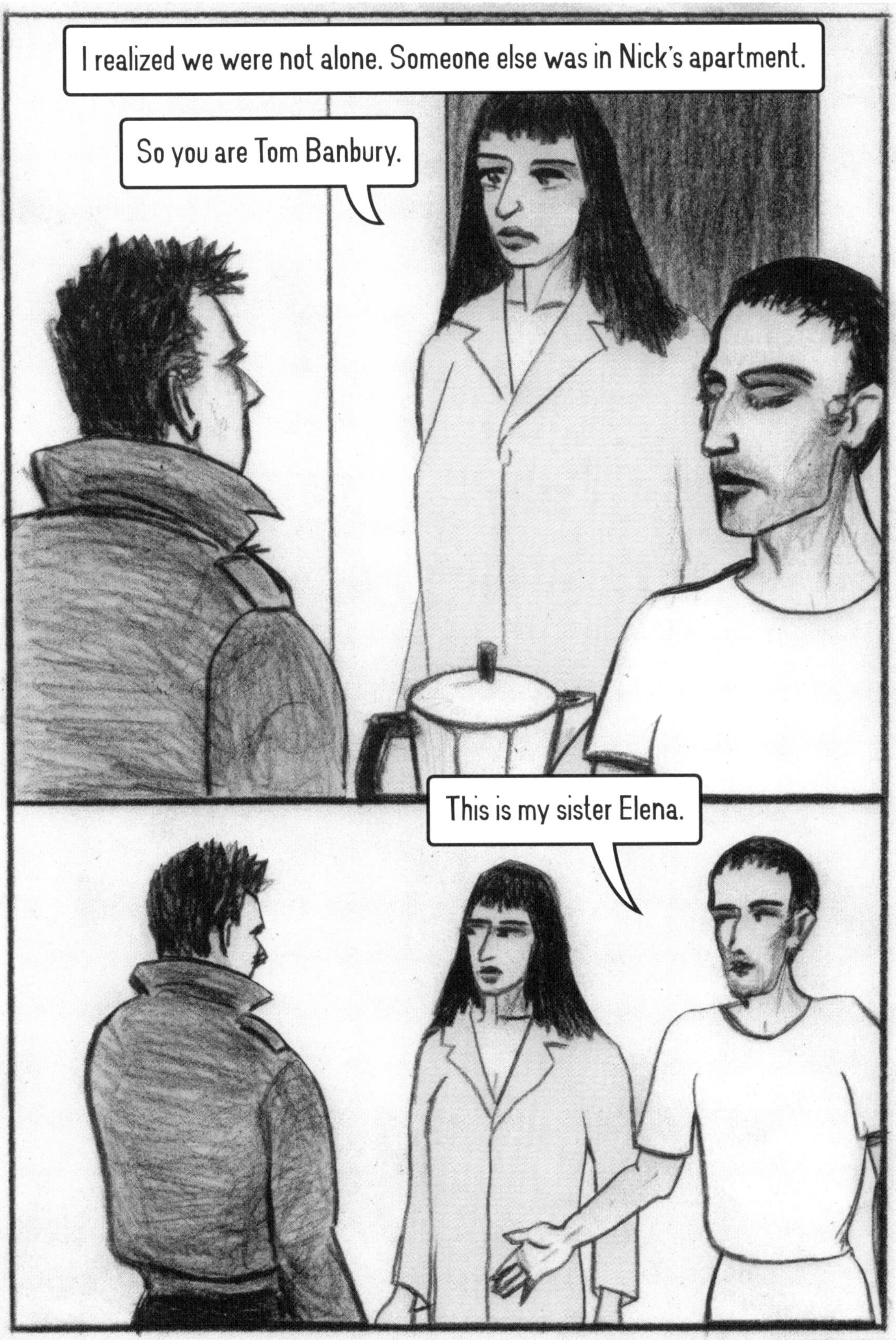
I realized we were not alone. Someone else was in Nick's apartment.
So you are Tom Banbury.
This is my sister Elena.

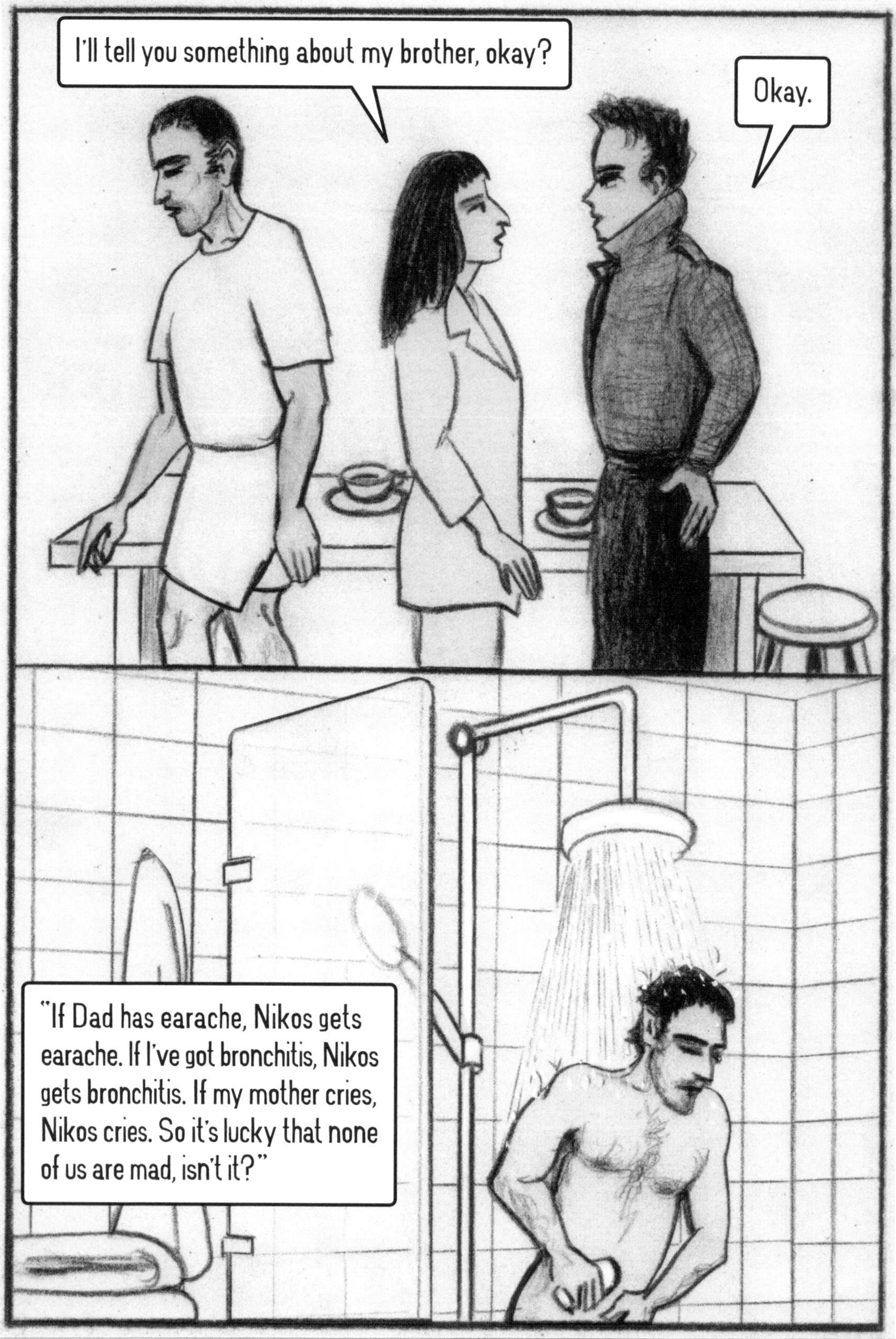
I'll tell you something about my brother, okay?
Okay.
"If Dad has earache, Nikos gets earache. If I've got bronchitis, Nikos gets bronchitis. If my mother cries, Nikos cries. So it's lucky that none of us are mad, isn't it?"

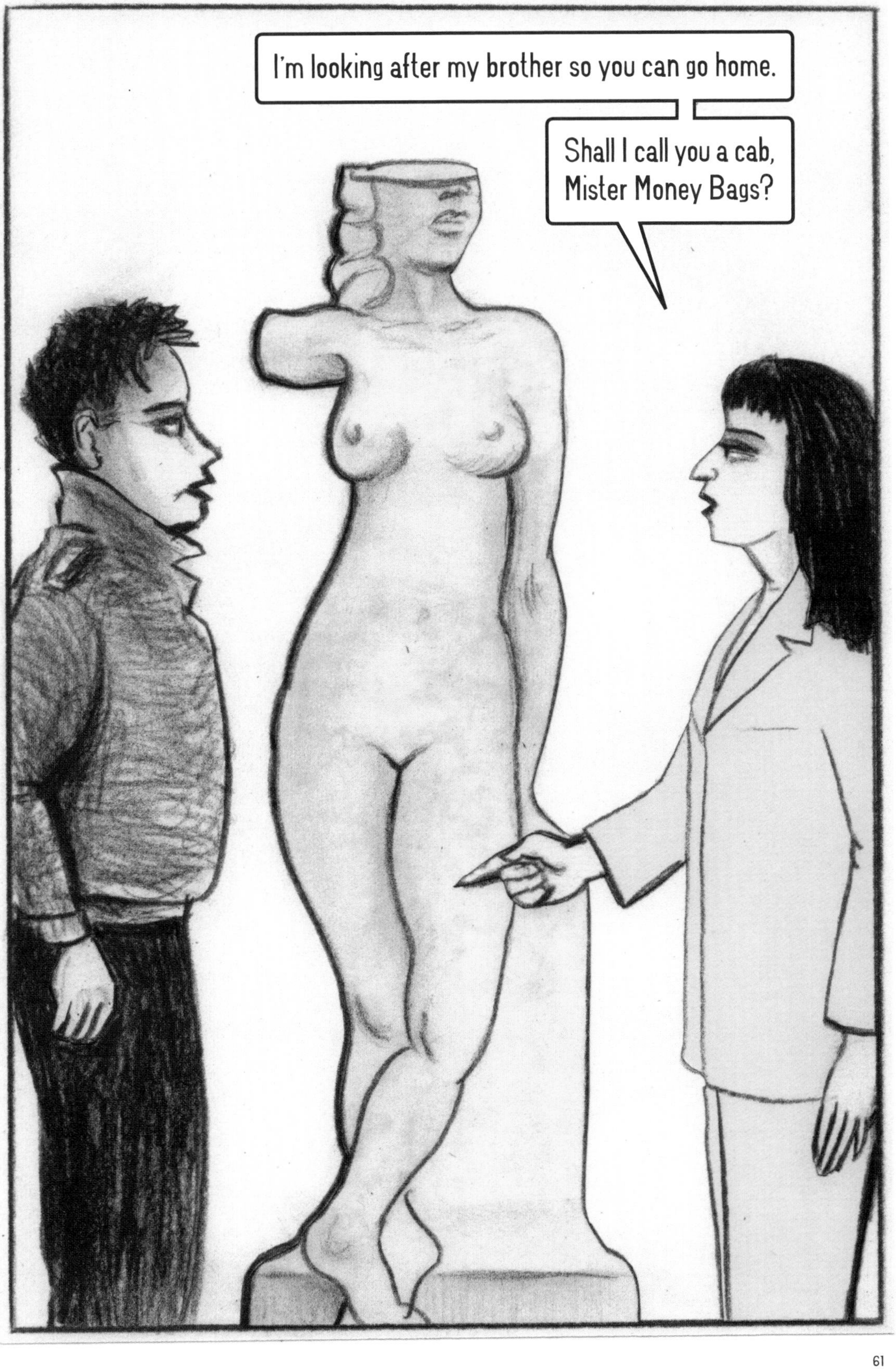
I'm looking after my brother so you can go home.
Shall I call you a cab, Mister Money Bags?

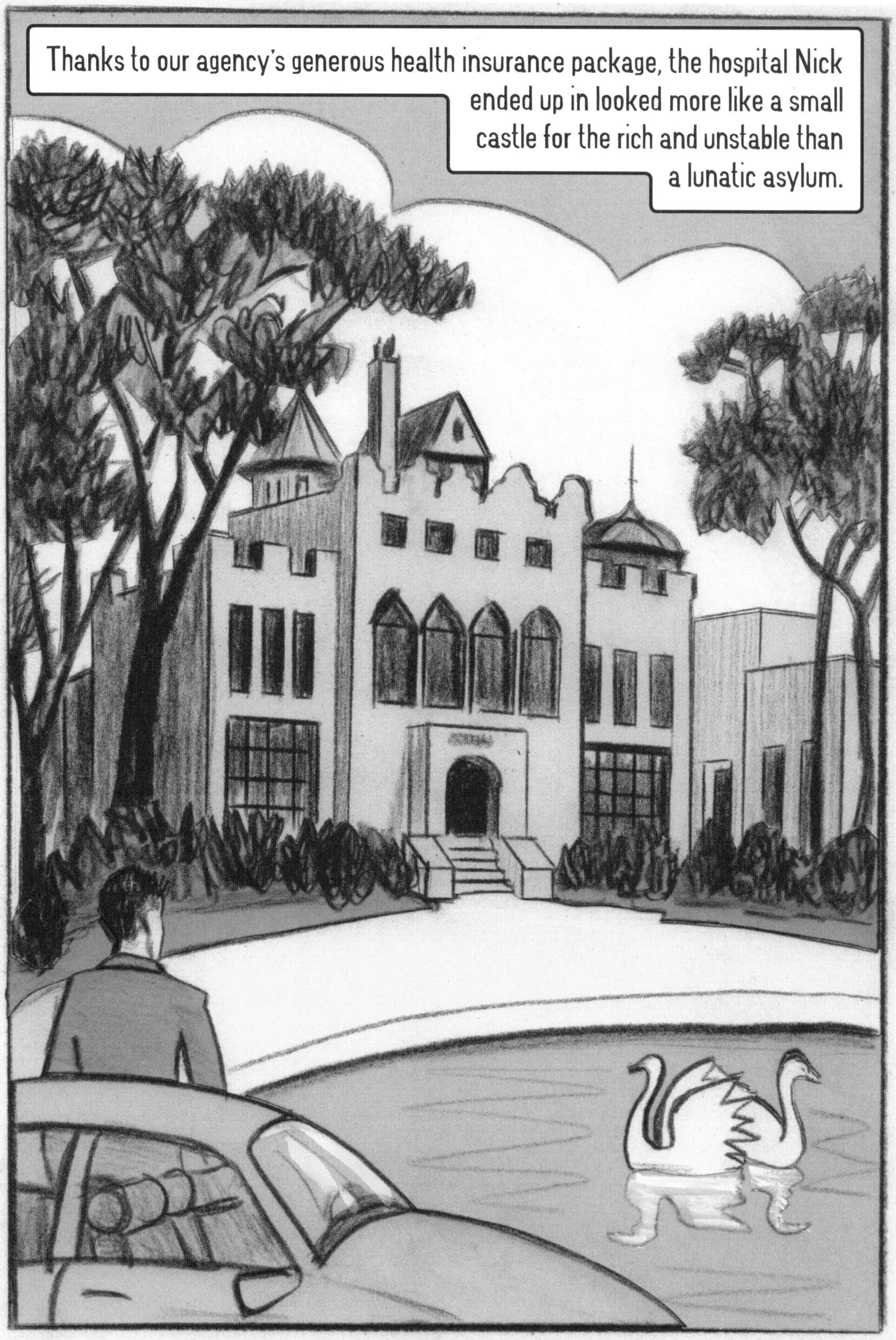
Thanks to our agency's generous health insurance package, the hospital Nick ended up in looked more like a small castle for the rich and unstable than a lunatic asylum.

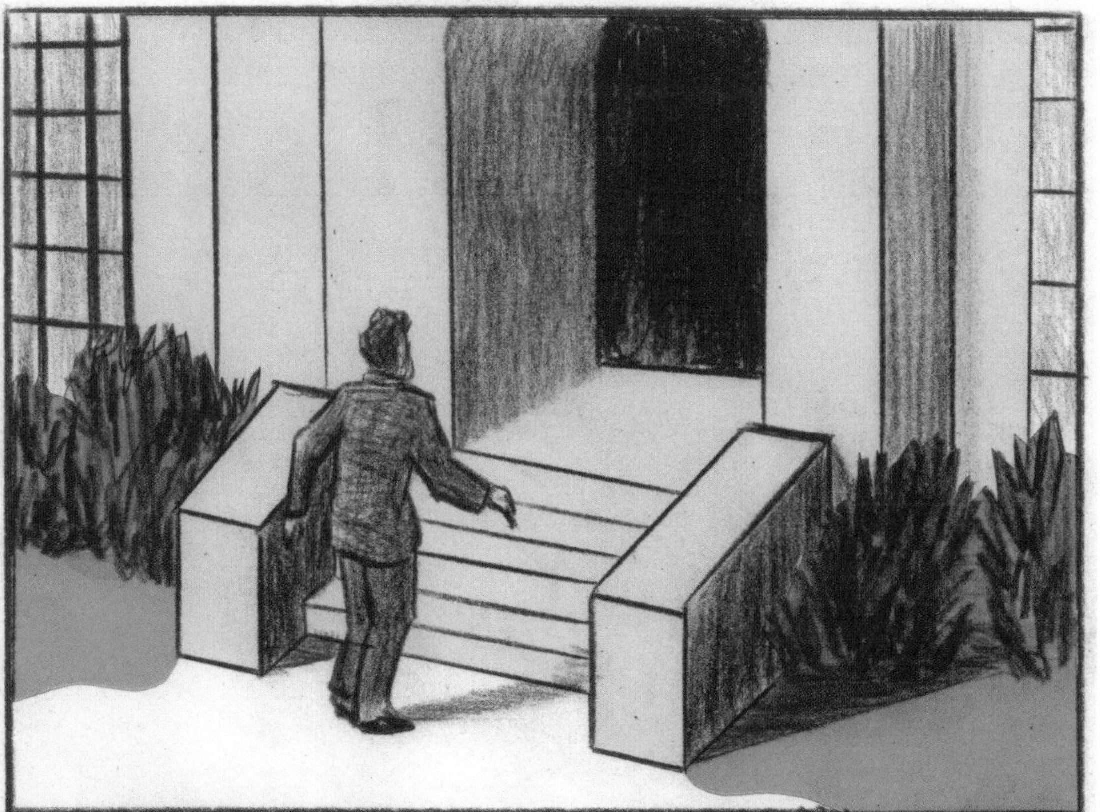

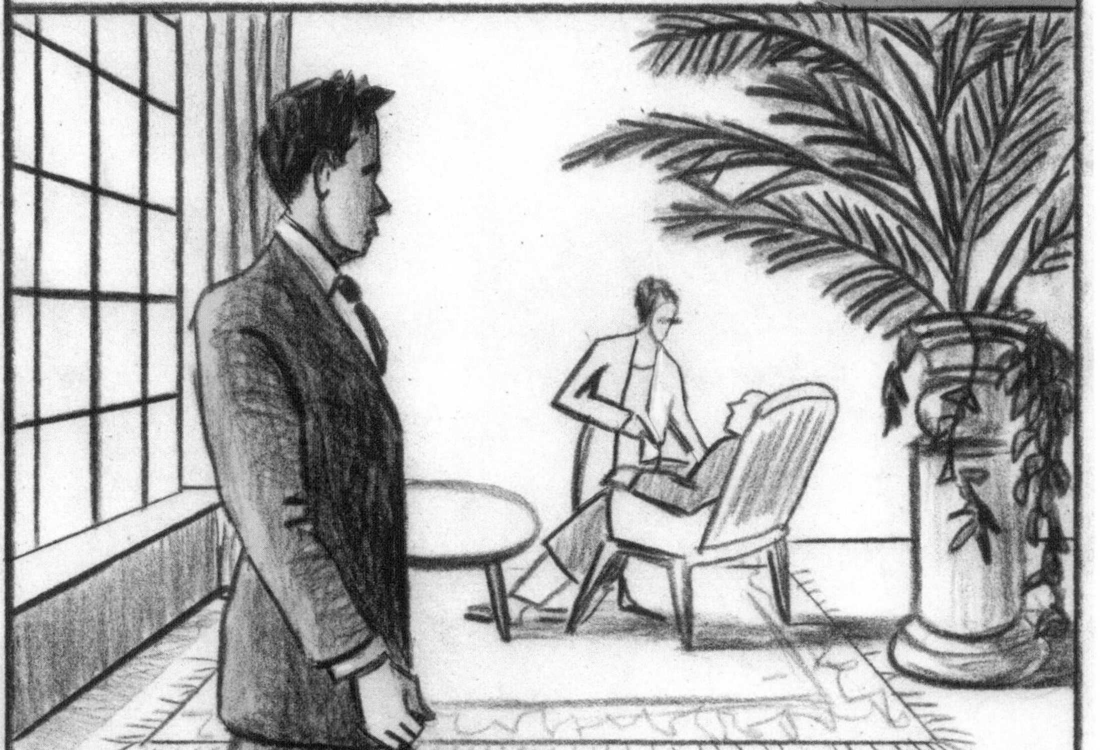

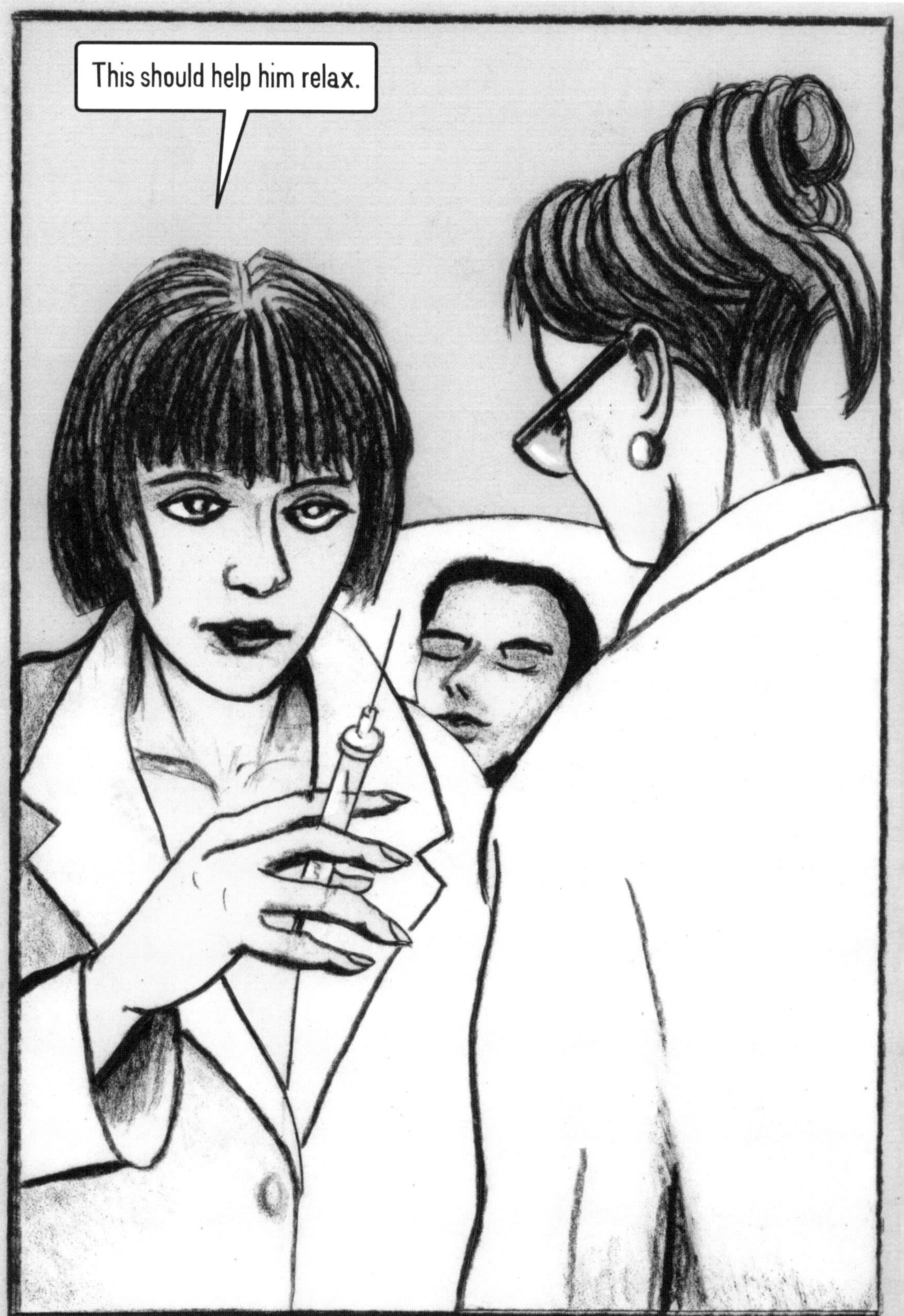
This should help him relax.

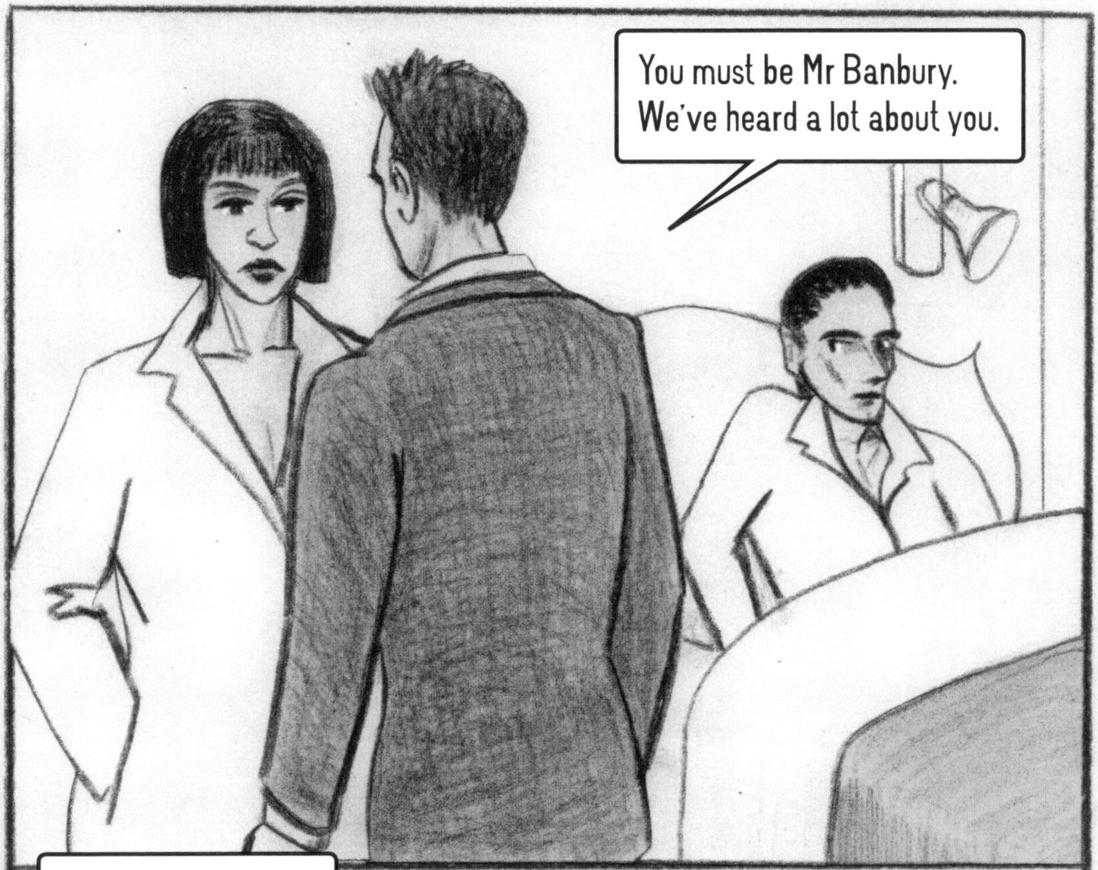
You must be Mr Banbury. We've heard a lot about you.

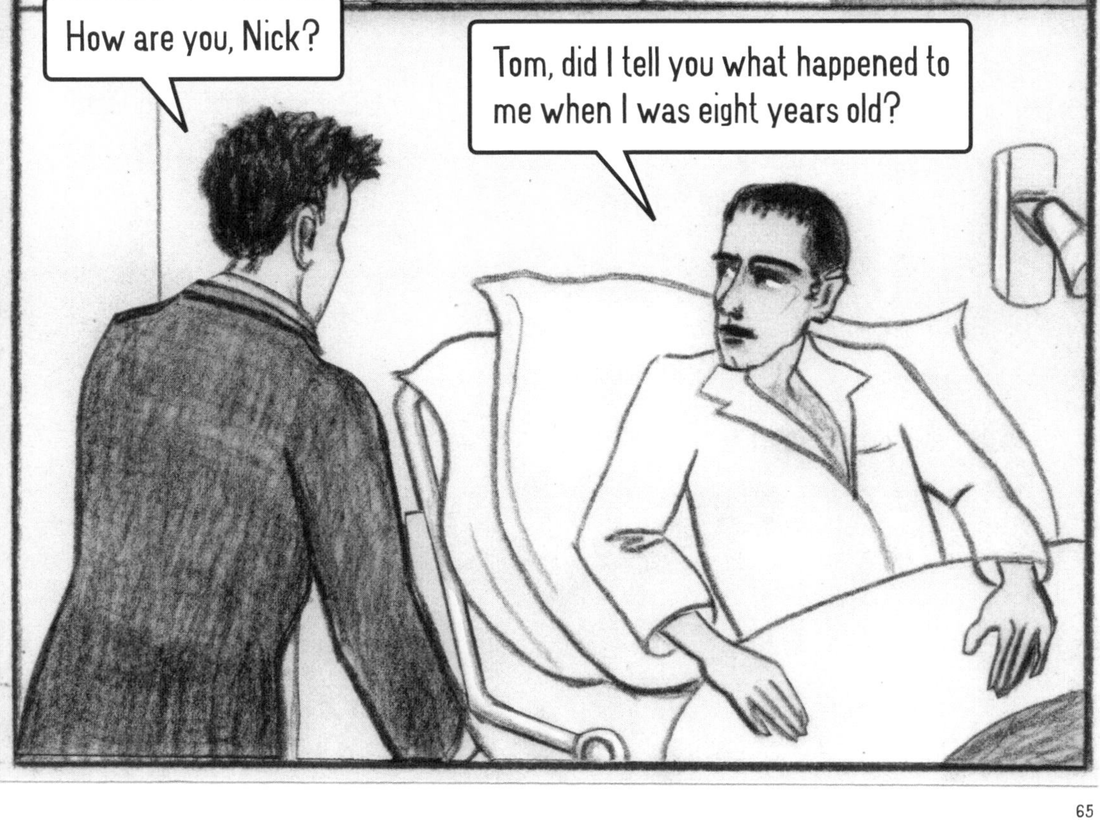
How are you, Nick?
Tom, did I tell you what happened to me when I was eight years old?

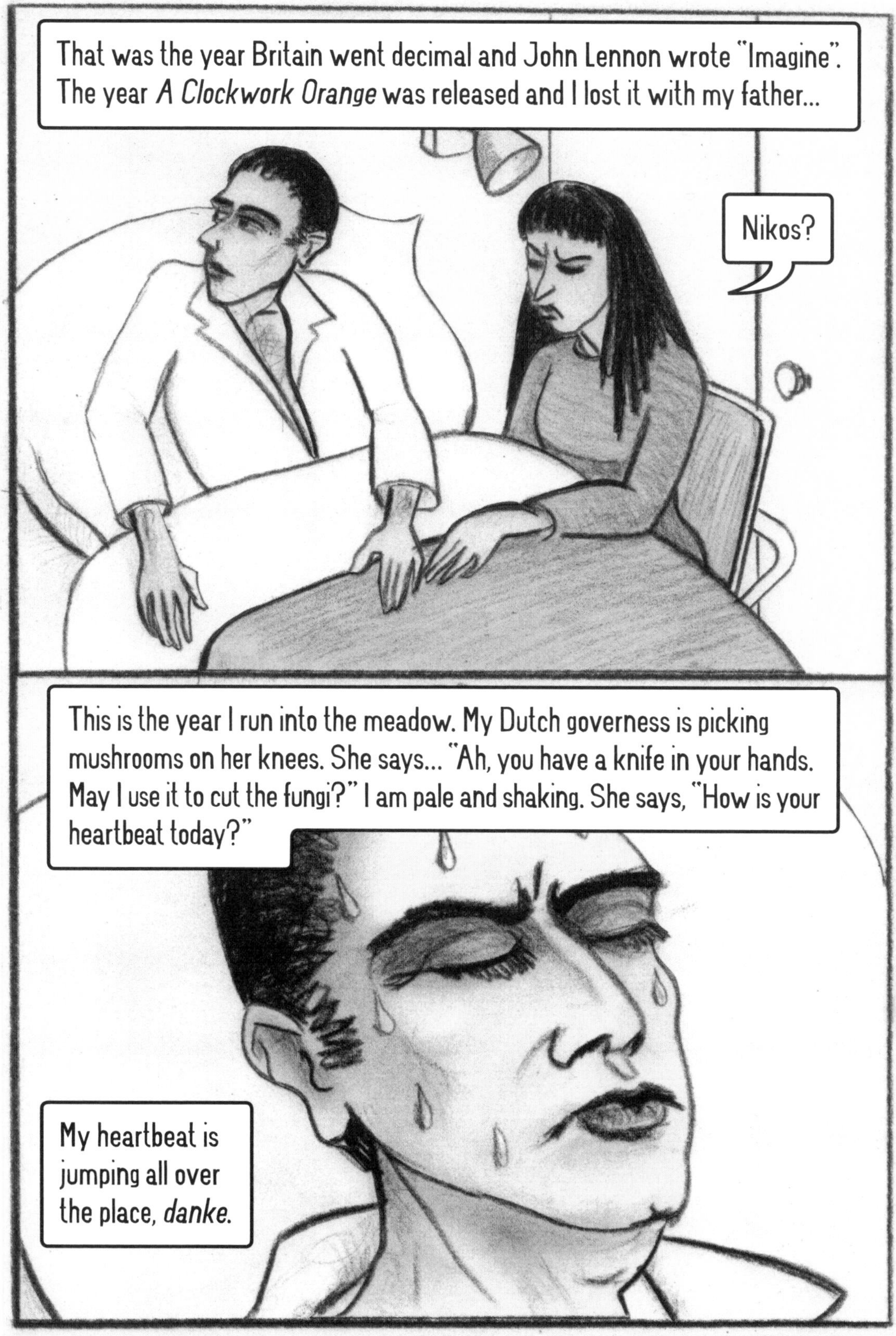
That was the year Britain went decimal and John Lennon wrote "Imagine". The year *A Clockwork Orange* was released and I lost it with my father...
Nikos?
This is the year I run into the meadow. My Dutch governess is picking mushrooms on her knees. She says... "Ah, you have a knife in your hands. May I use it to cut the fungi?" I am pale and shaking. She says, "How is your heartbeat today?"
My heartbeat is jumping all over the place, *danke*.

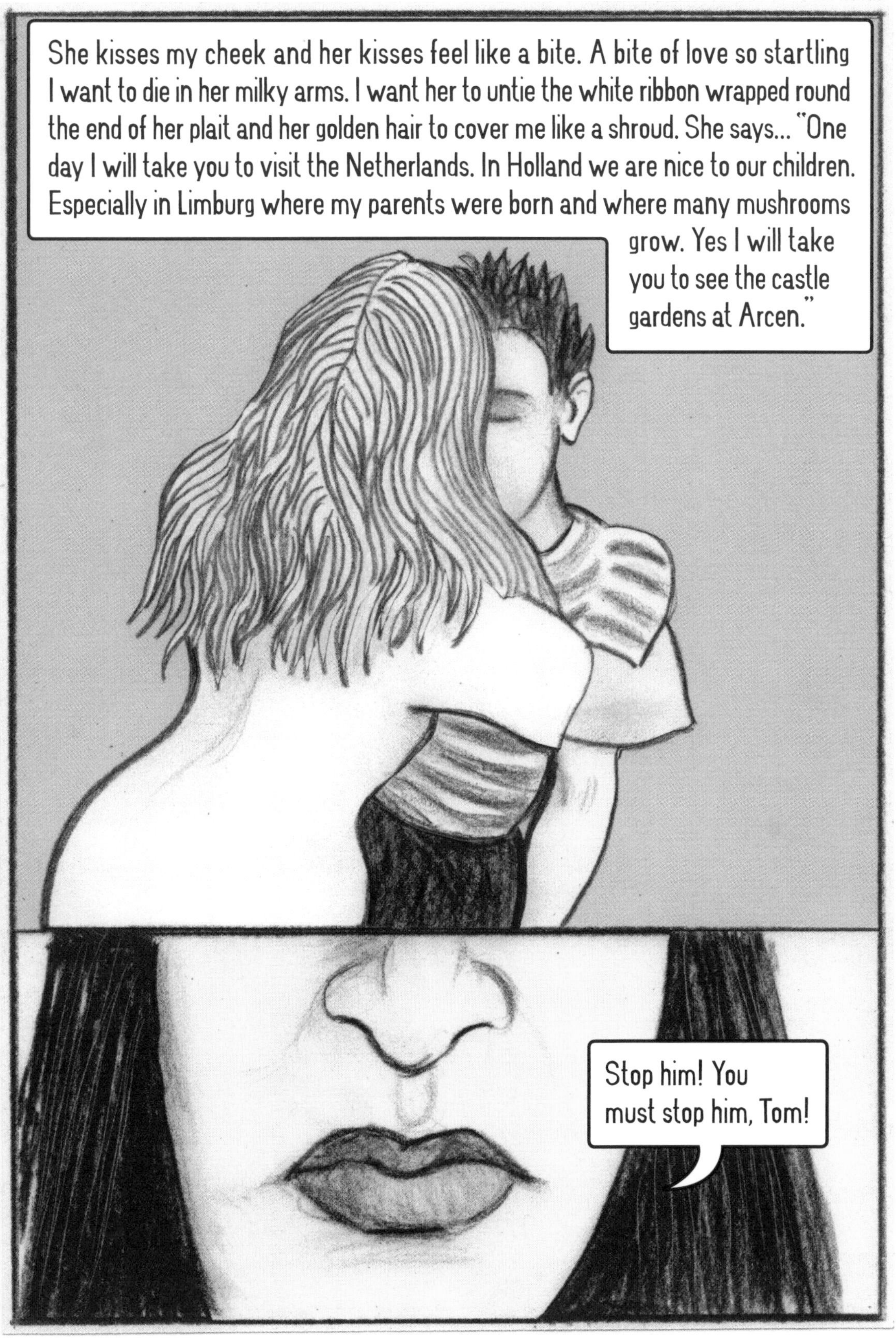
She kisses my cheek and her kisses feel like a bite. A bite of love so startling I want to die in her milky arms. I want her to untie the white ribbon wrapped round the end of her plait and her golden hair to cover me like a shroud. She says... "One day I will take you to visit the Netherlands. In Holland we are nice to our children. Especially in Limburg where my parents were born and where many mushrooms grow. Yes I will take you to see the castle gardens at Arcen."
Stop him! You must stop him, Tom!

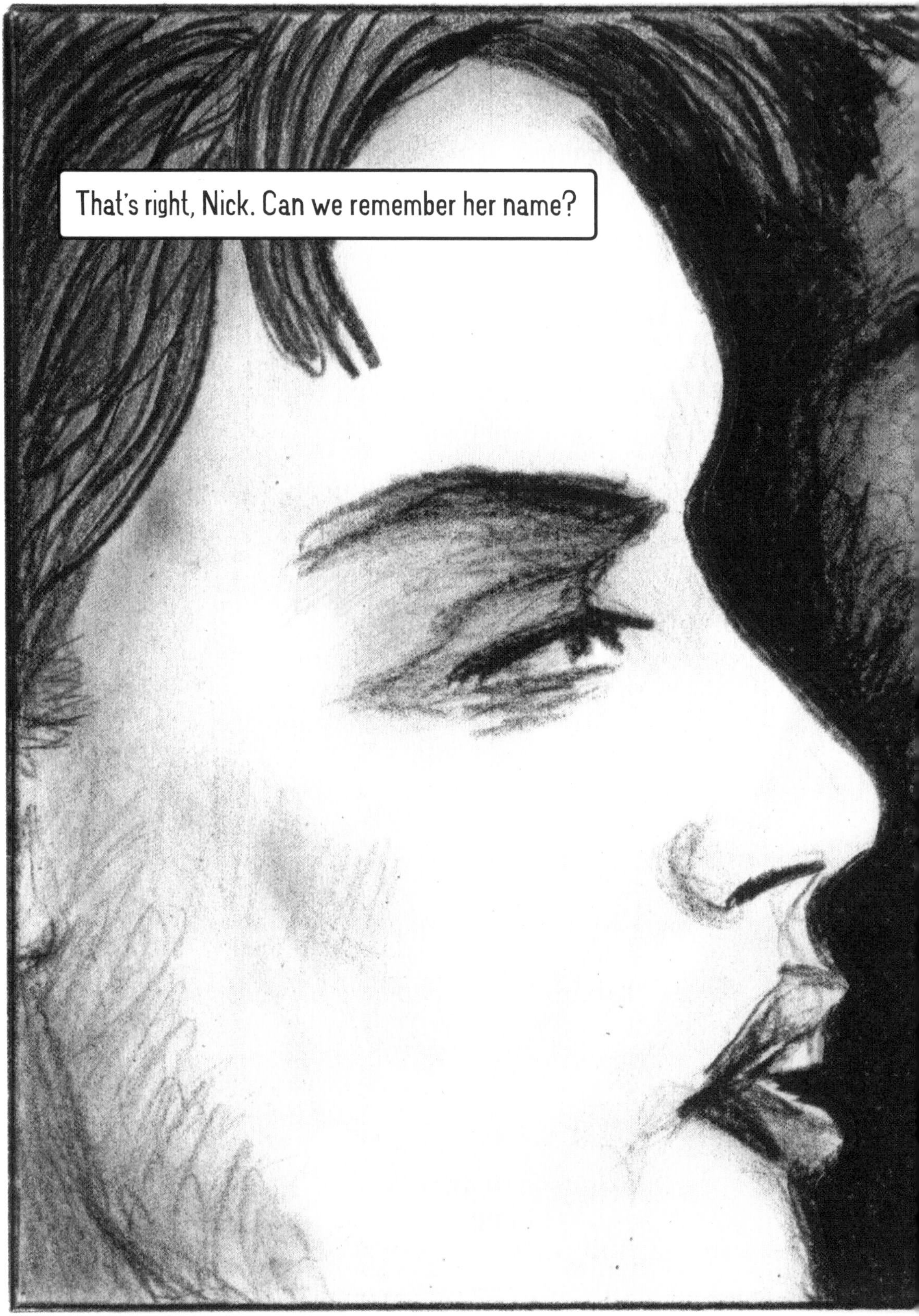
That's right, Nick. Can we remember her name?

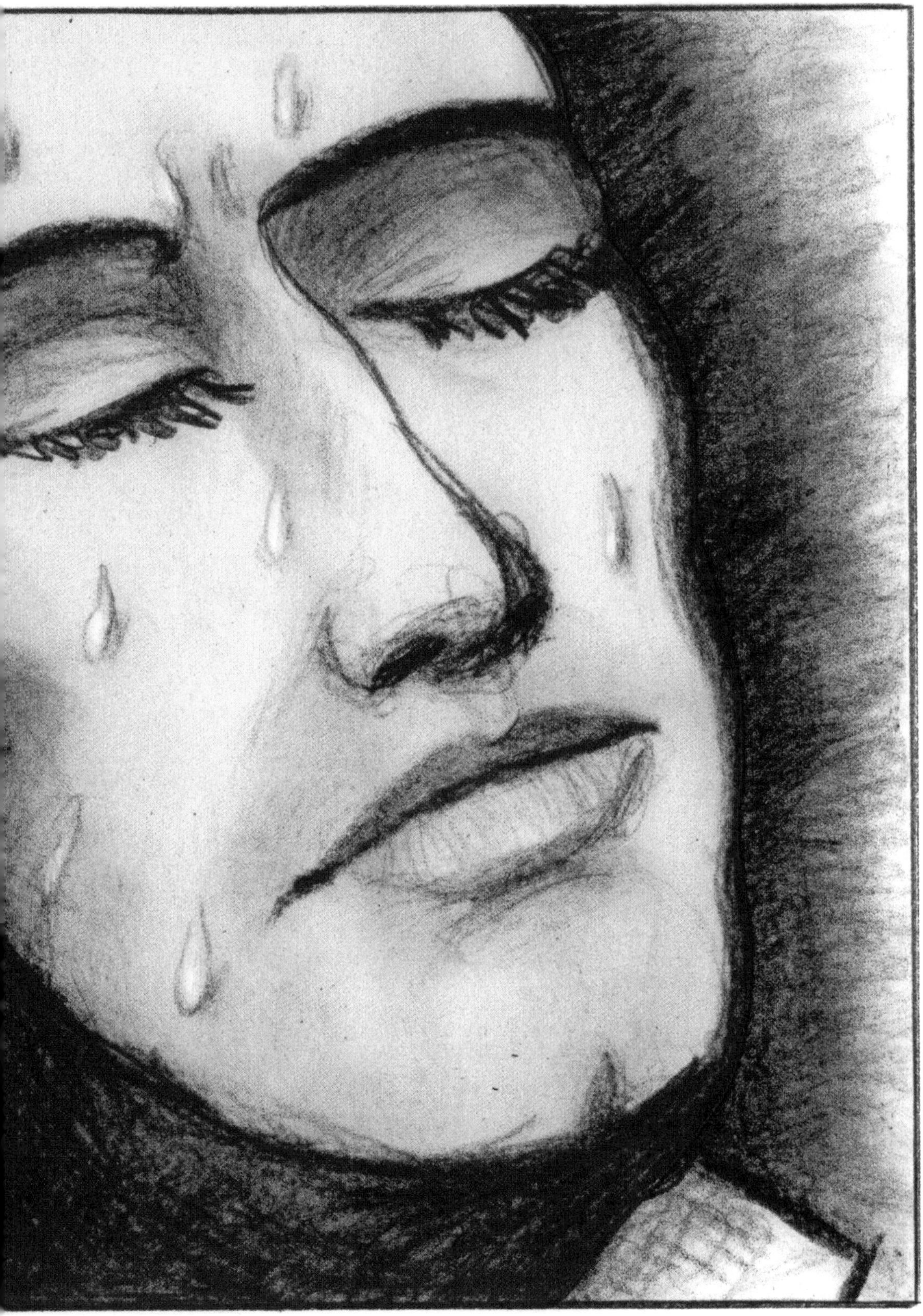

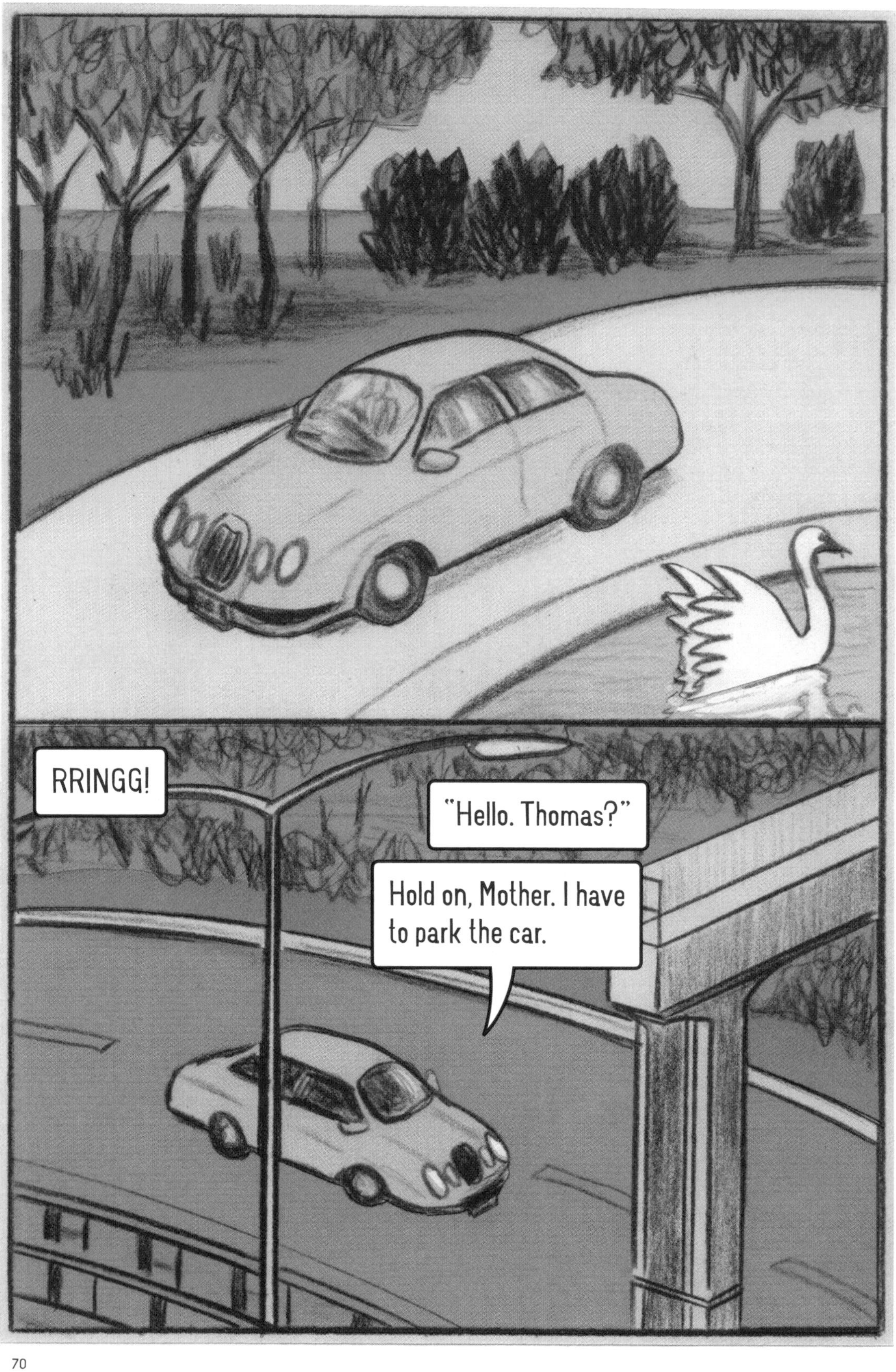
RRINGG!
"Hello. Thomas?"
Hold on, Mother. I have to park the car.

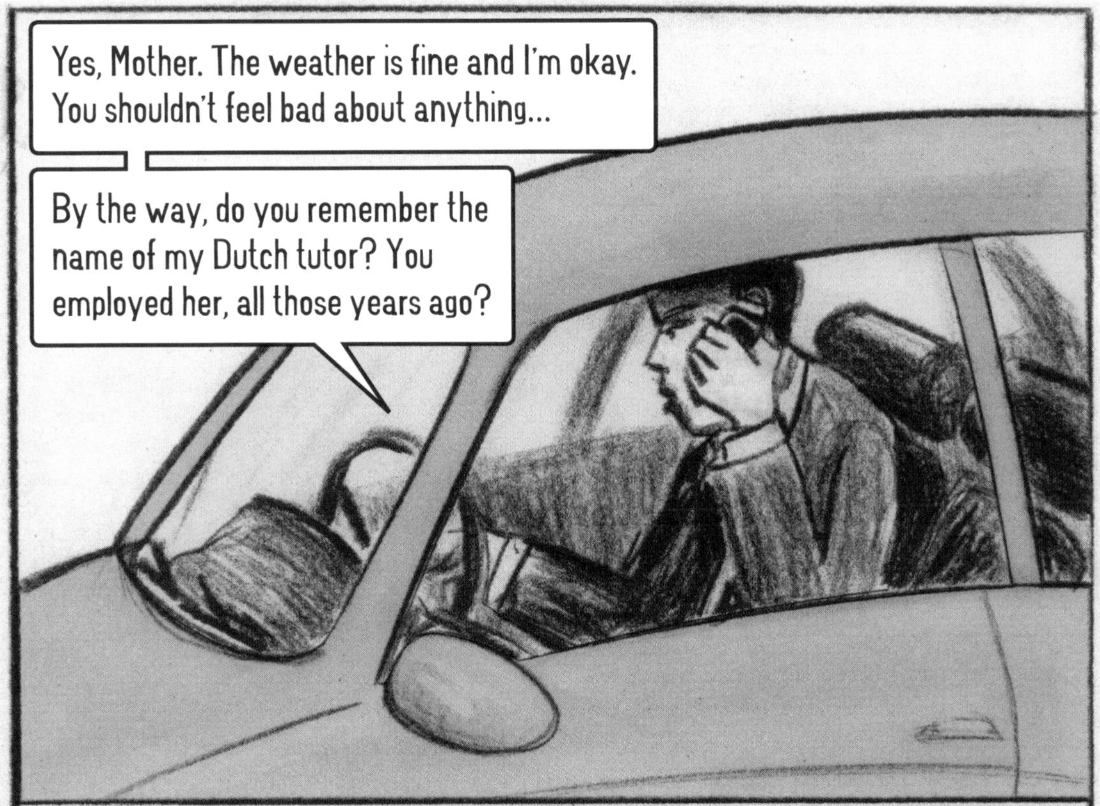
Yes, Mother. The weather is fine and I'm okay. You shouldn't feel bad about anything...
By the way, do you remember the name of my Dutch tutor? You employed her, all those years ago?

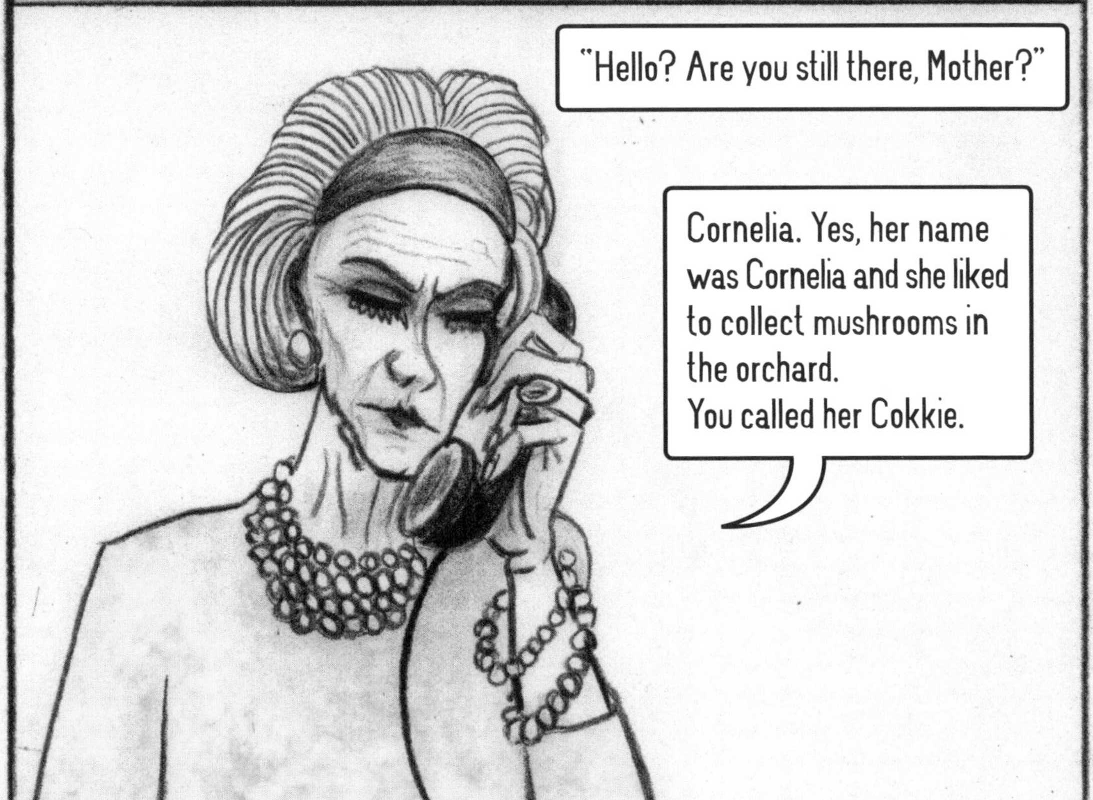
"Hello? Are you still there, Mother?"
Cornelia. Yes, her name was Cornelia and she liked to collect mushrooms in the orchard. You called her Cokkie.

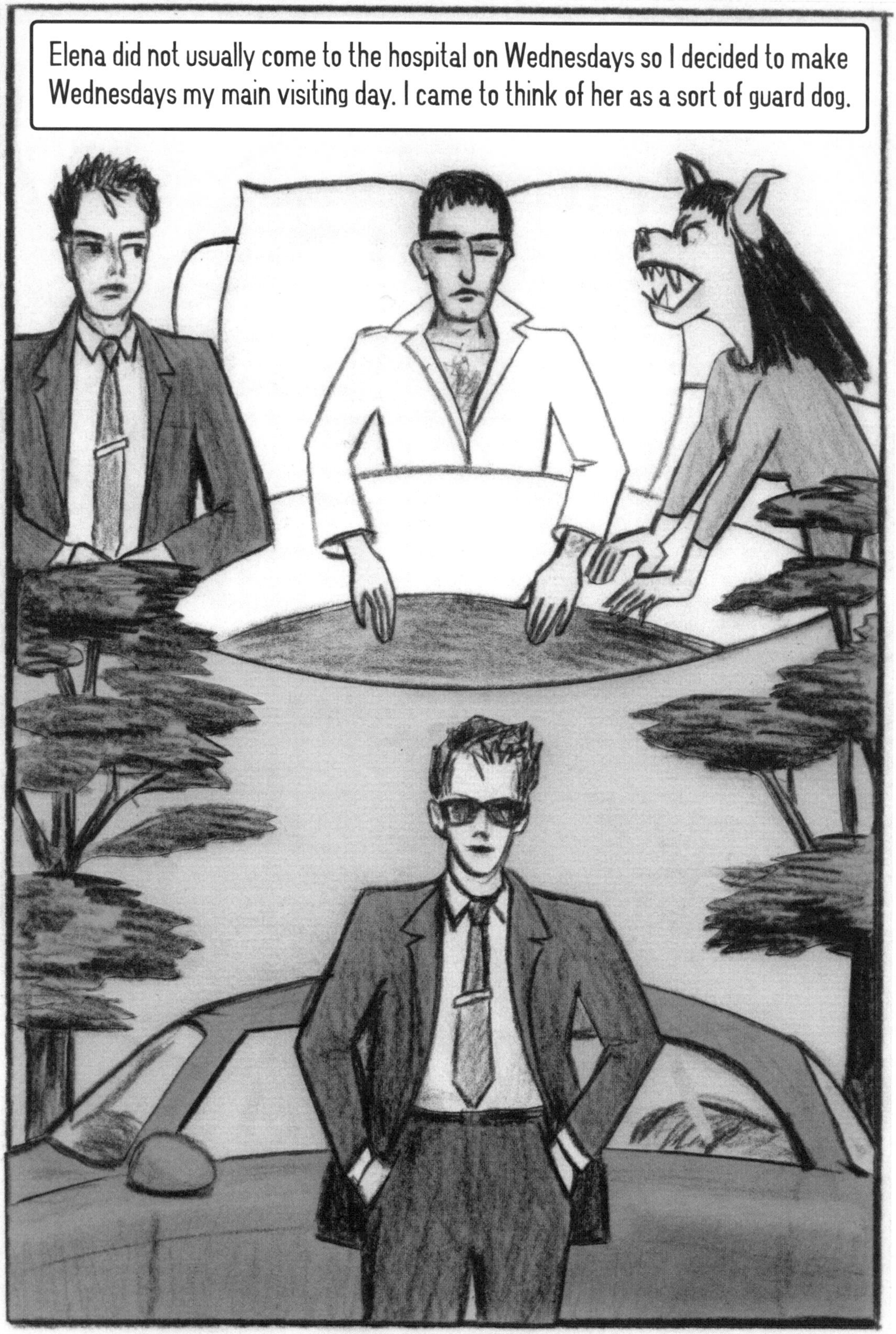
Elena did not usually come to the hospital on Wednesdays so I decided to make Wednesdays my main visiting day. I came to think of her as a sort of guard dog.

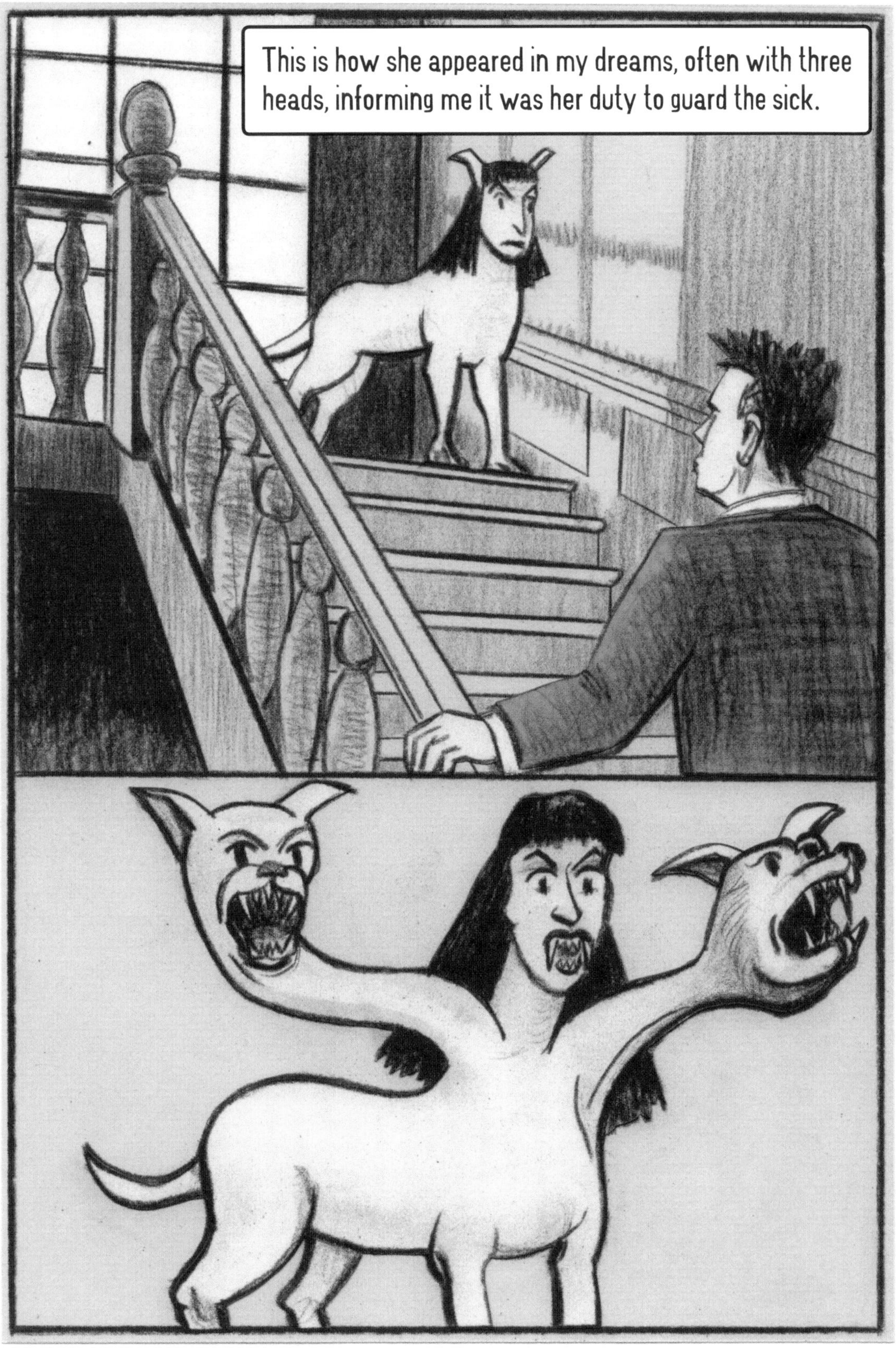
This is how she appeared in my dreams, often with three heads, informing me it was her duty to guard the sick.

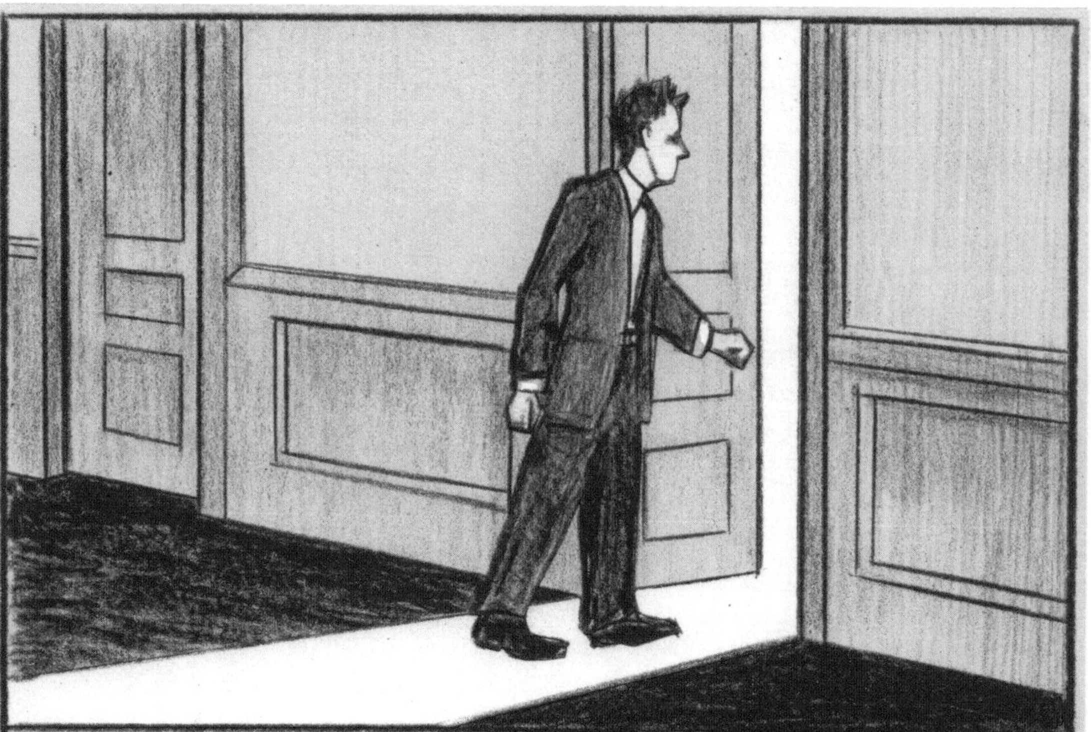

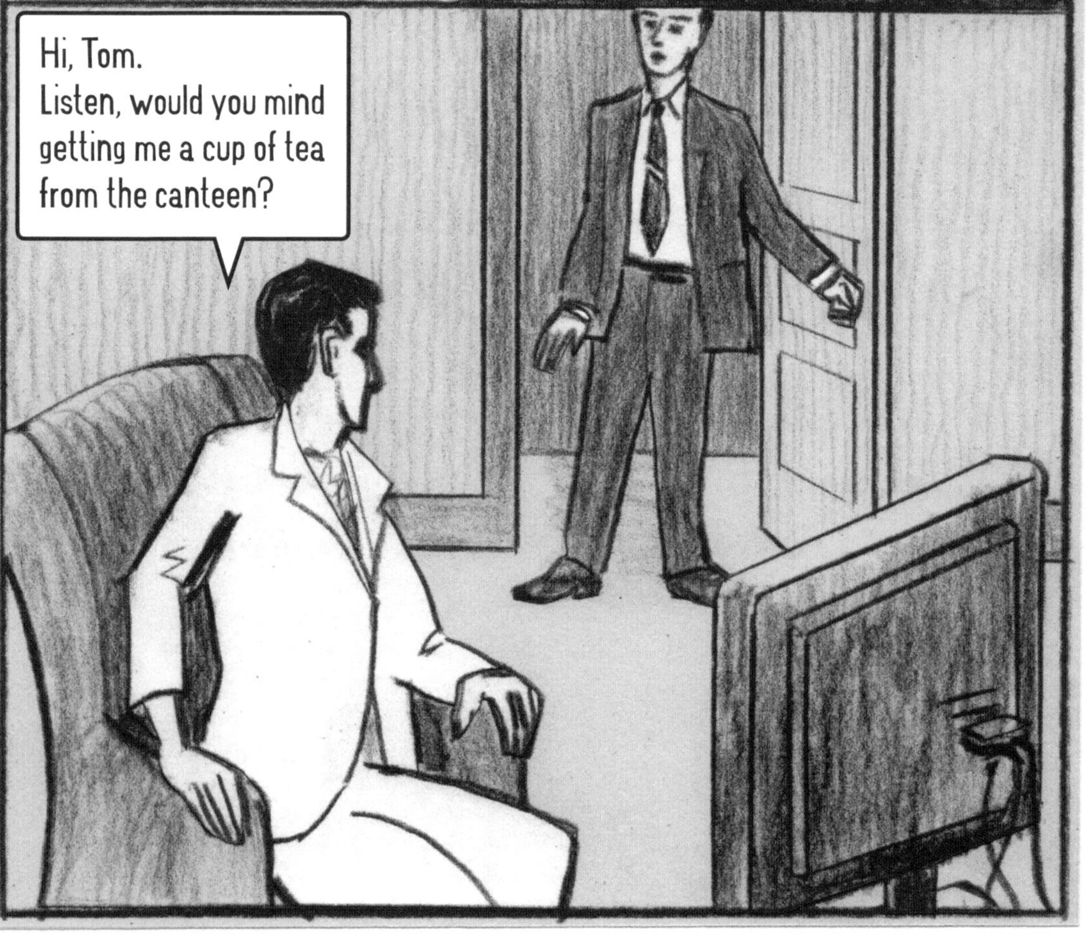
Hi, Tom.
Listen, would you mind getting me a cup of tea from the canteen?

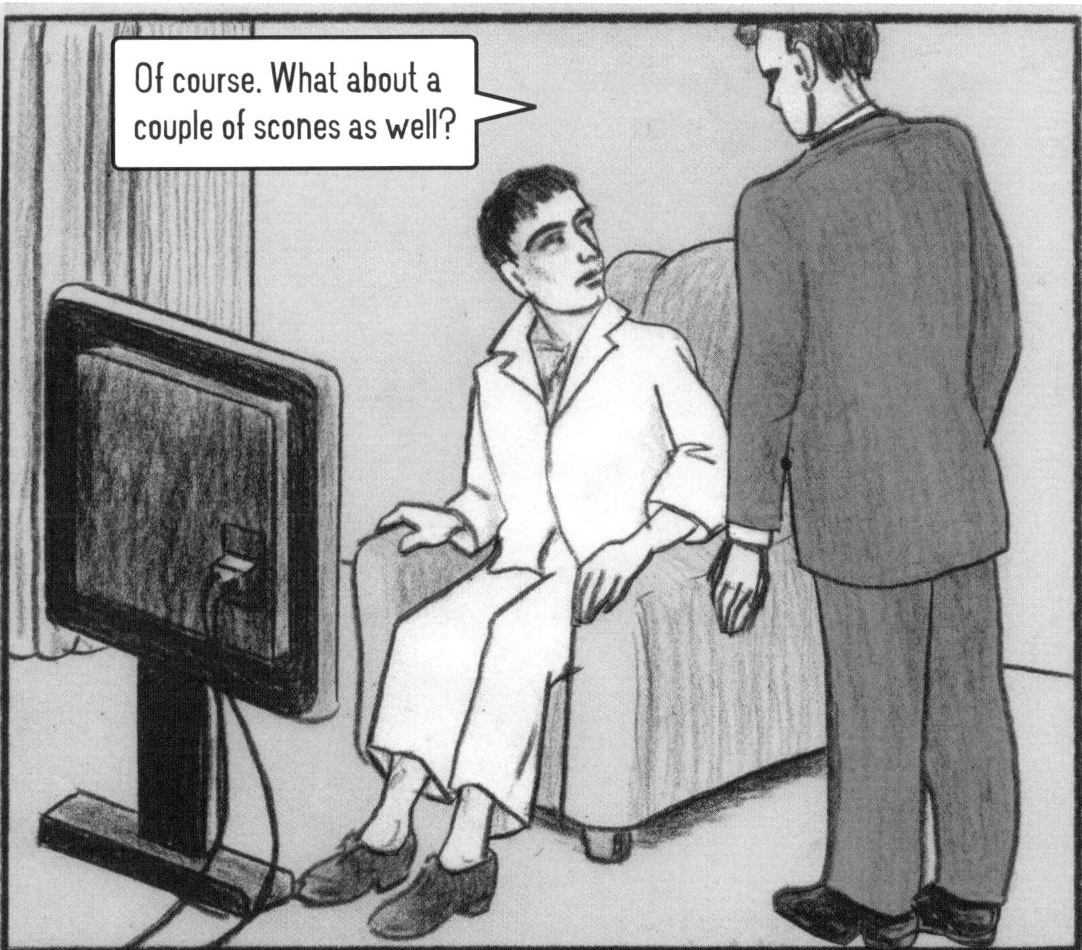
Of course. What about a couple of scones as well?

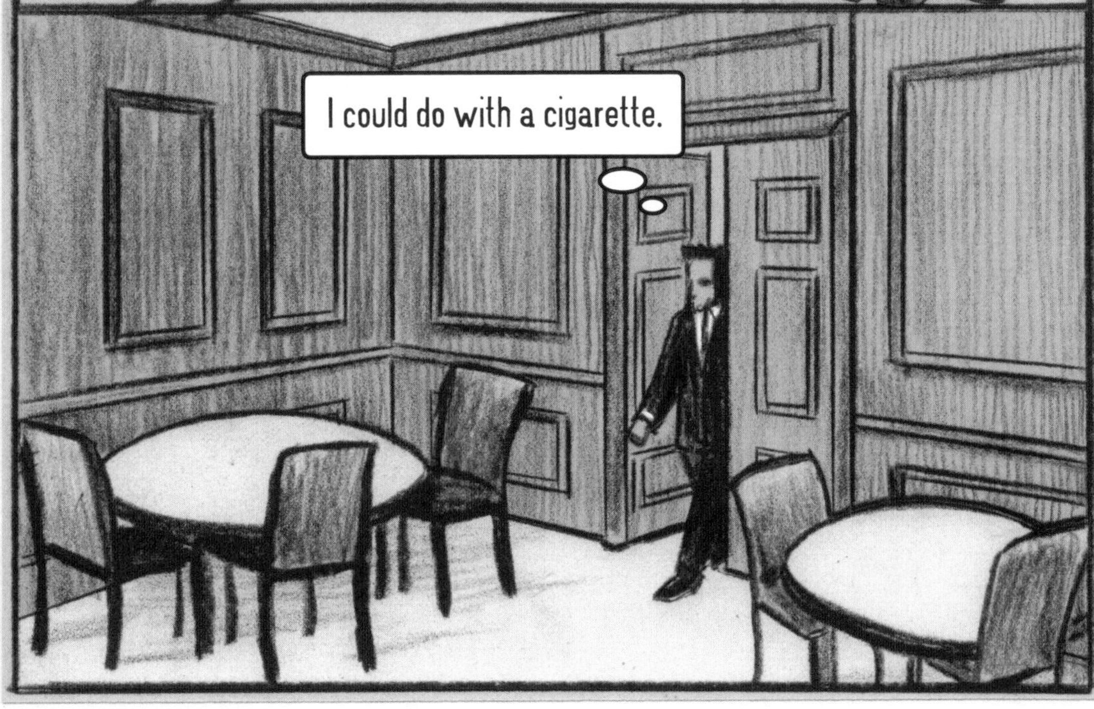
I could do with a cigarette.

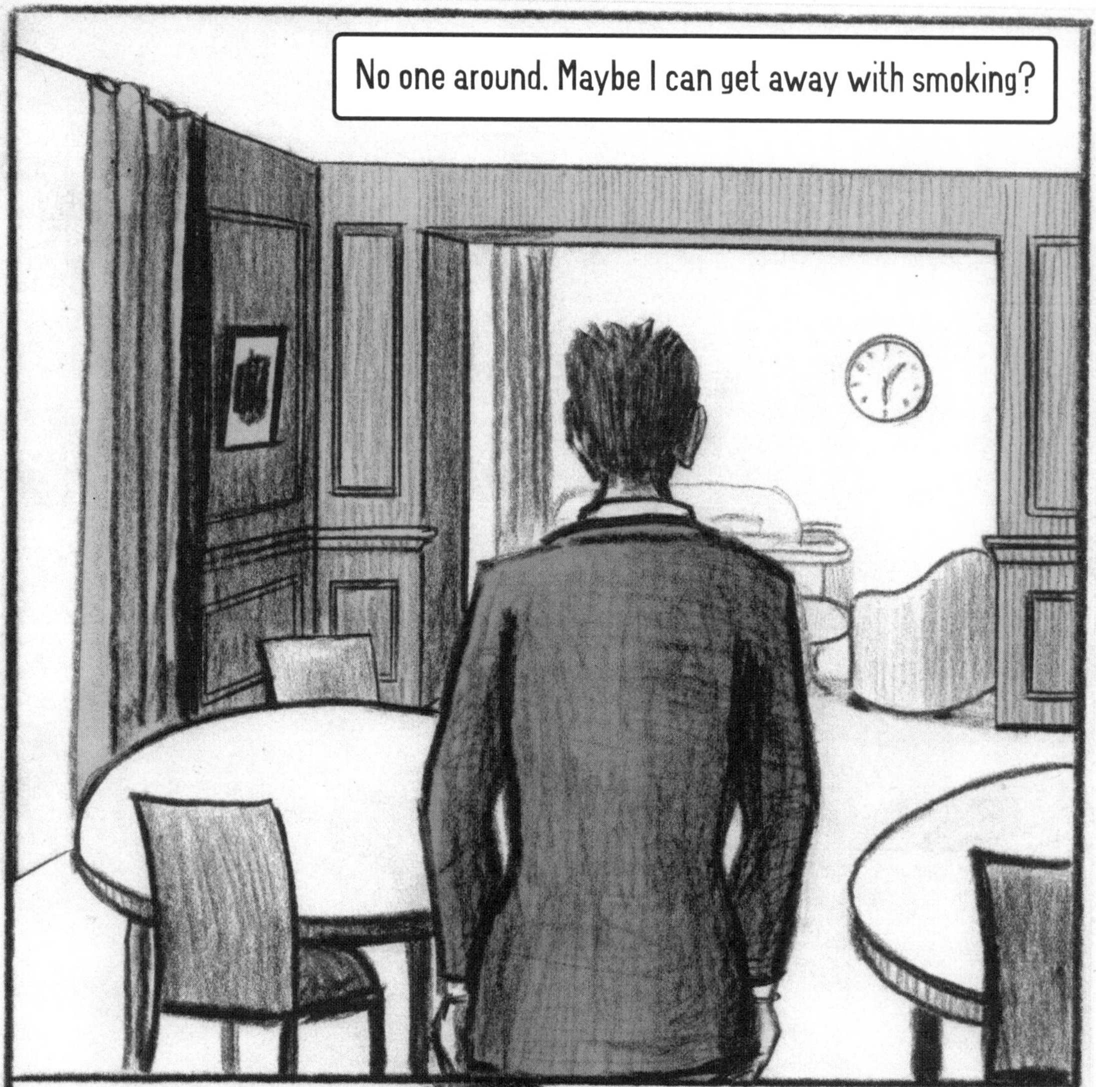
No one around. Maybe I can get away with smoking?

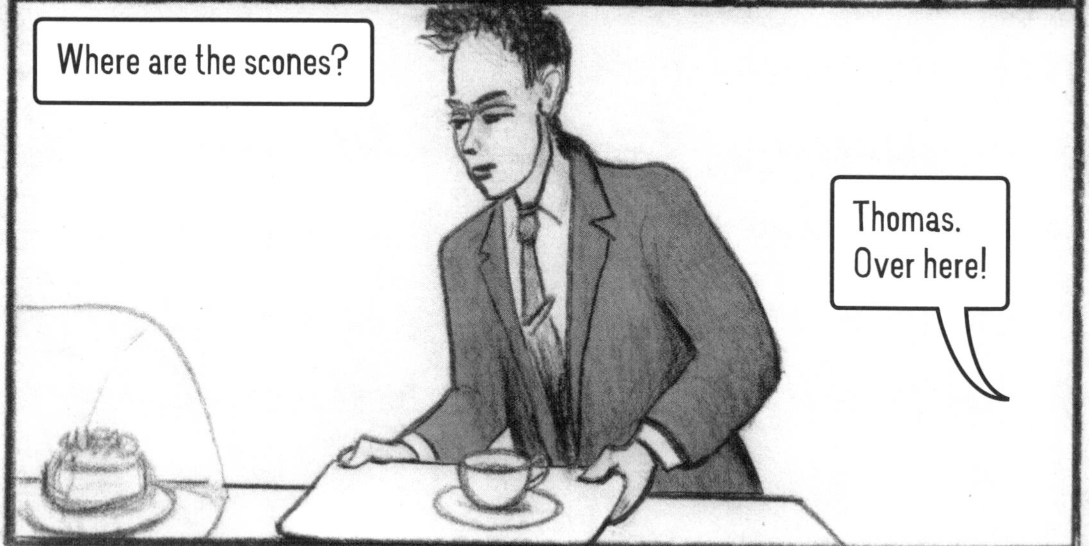
Where are the scones?
Thomas. Over here!

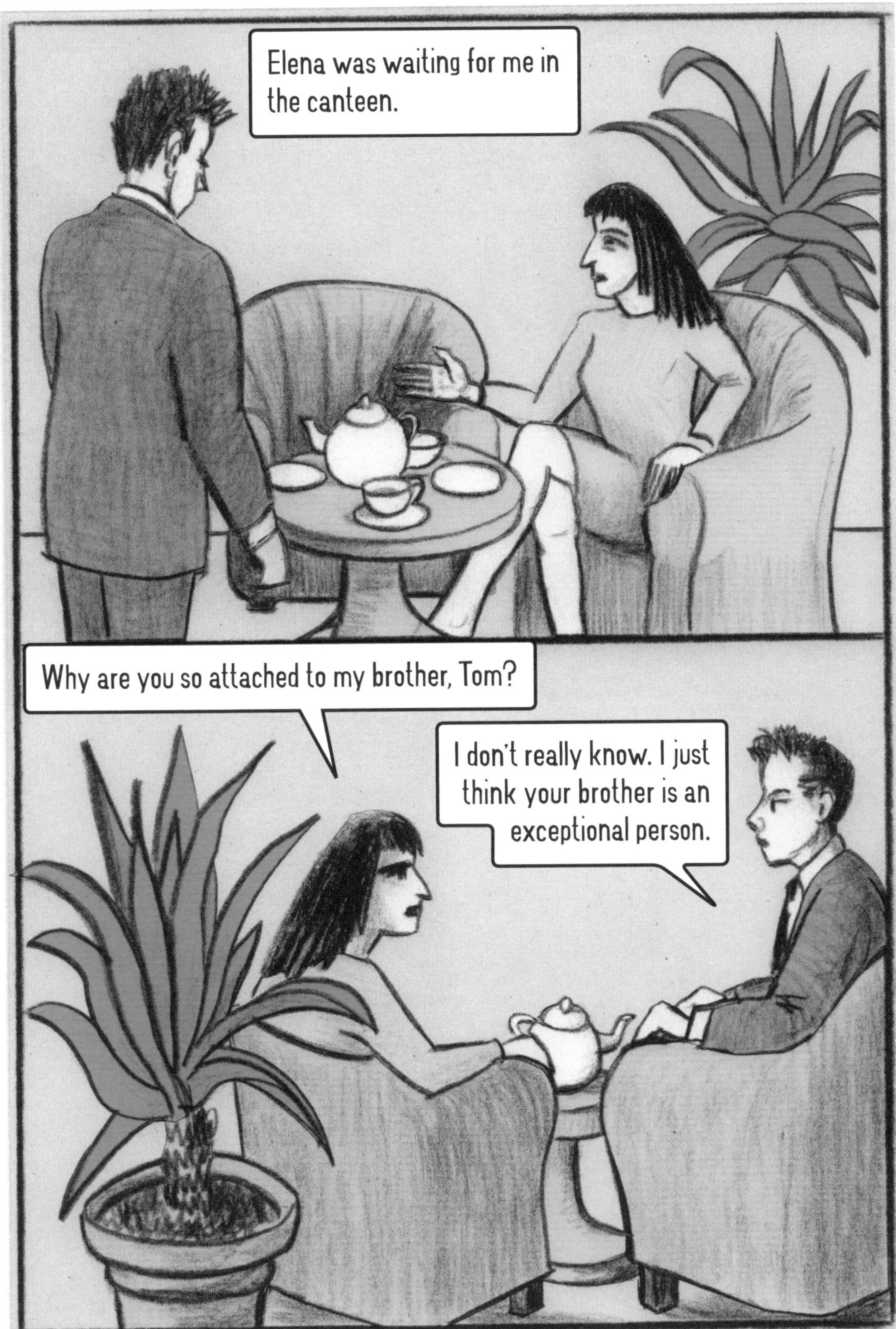
Elena was waiting for me in the canteen.
Why are you so attached to my brother, Tom?
I don't really know. I just think your brother is an exceptional person.

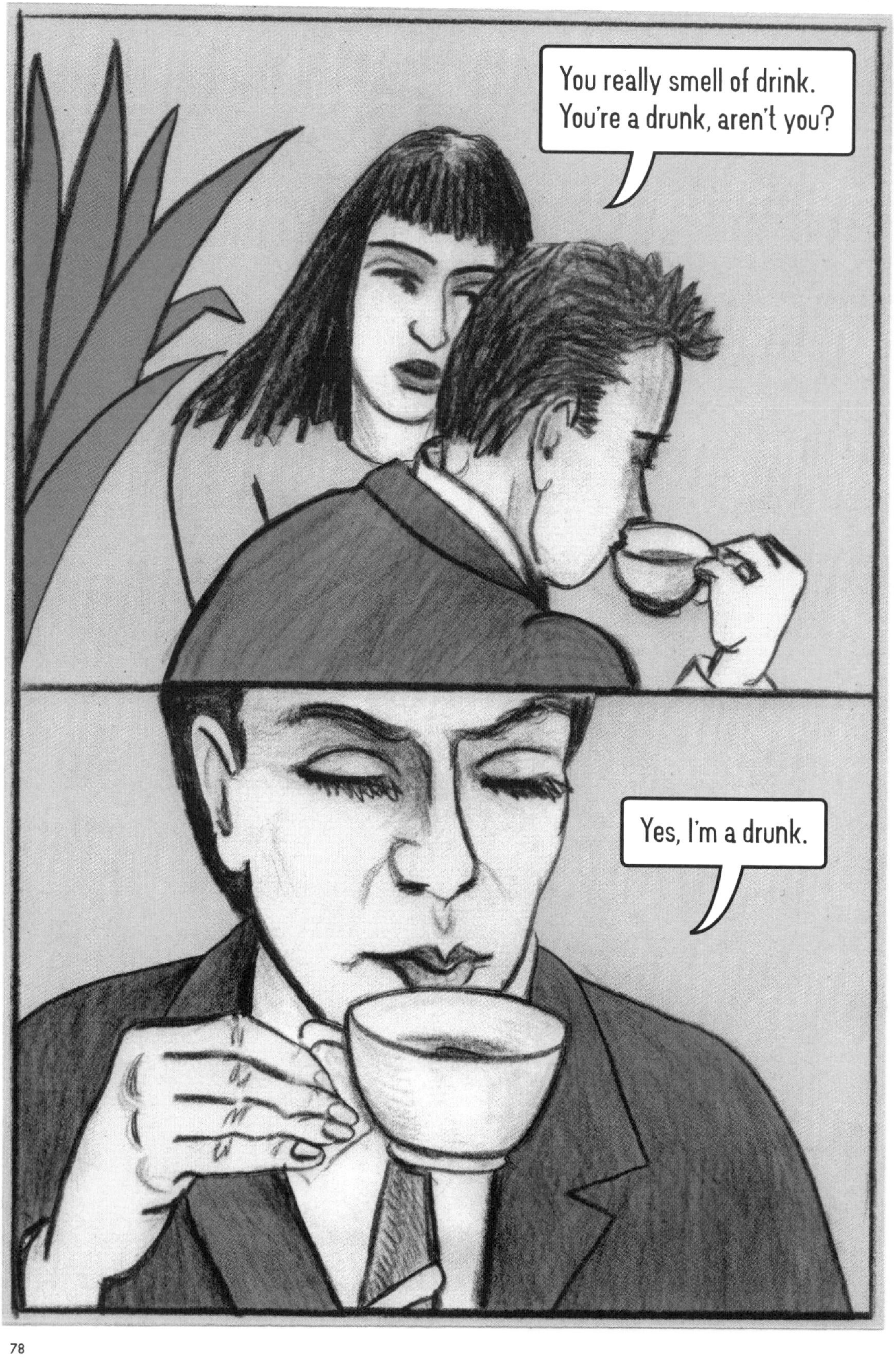
You really smell of drink. You're a drunk, aren't you?
Yes, I'm a drunk.

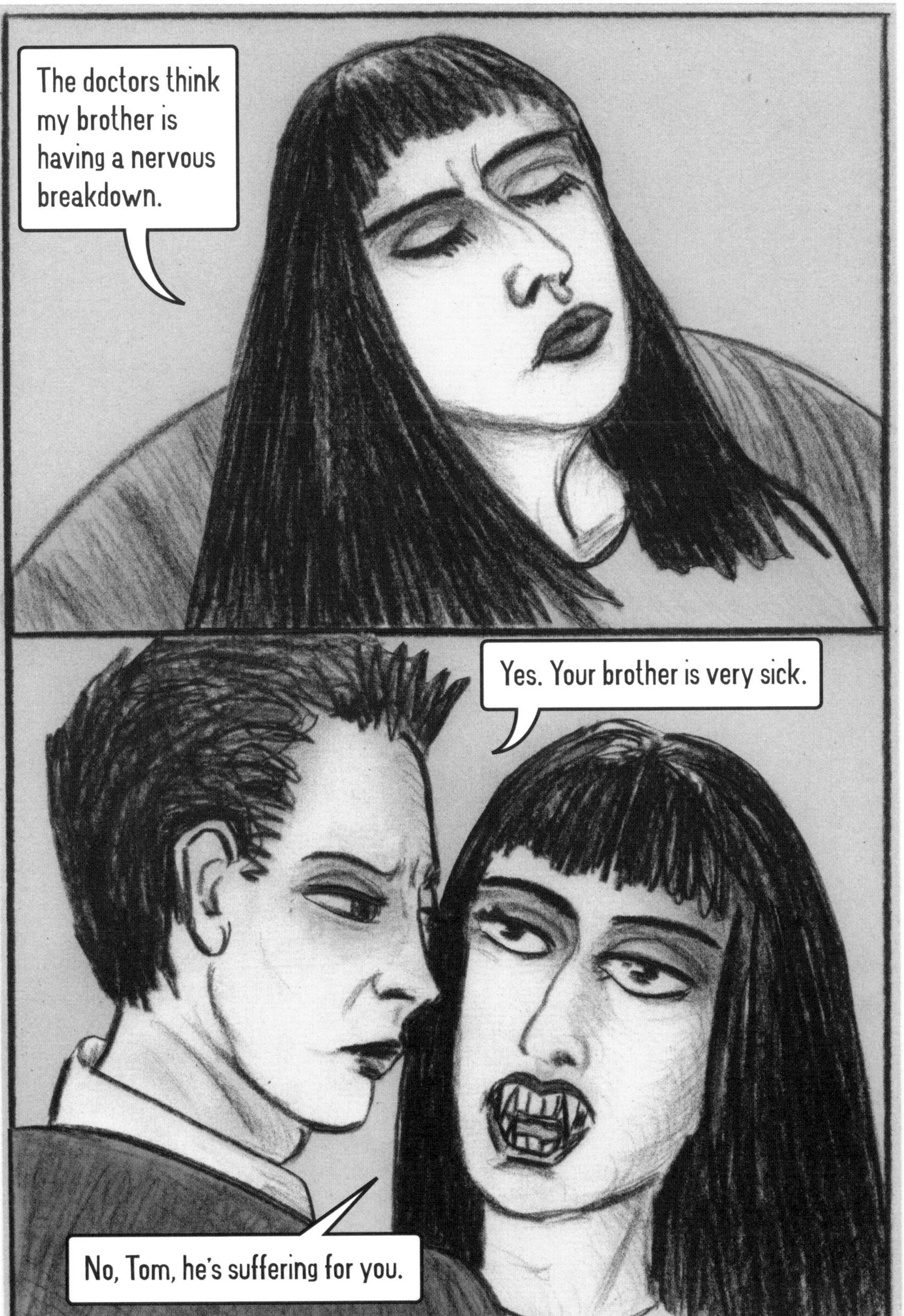
The doctors think my brother is having a nervous breakdown.
Yes. Your brother is very sick.
No, Tom, he's suffering for you.

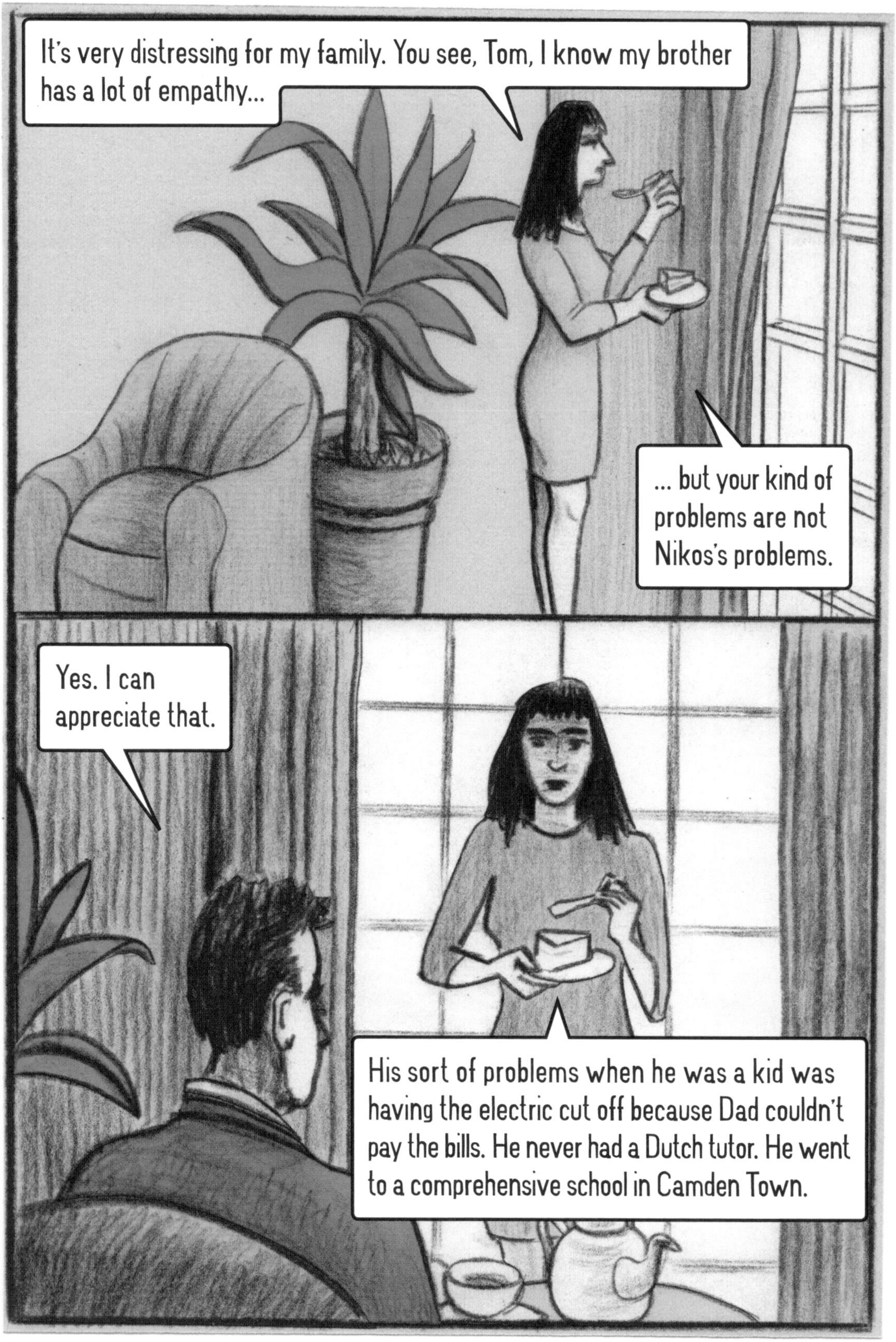
It's very distressing for my family. You see, Tom, I know my brother has a lot of empathy...
... but your kind of problems are not Nikos's problems.
Yes. I can appreciate that.
His sort of problems when he was a kid was having the electric cut off because Dad couldn't pay the bills. He never had a Dutch tutor. He went to a comprehensive school in Camden Town.

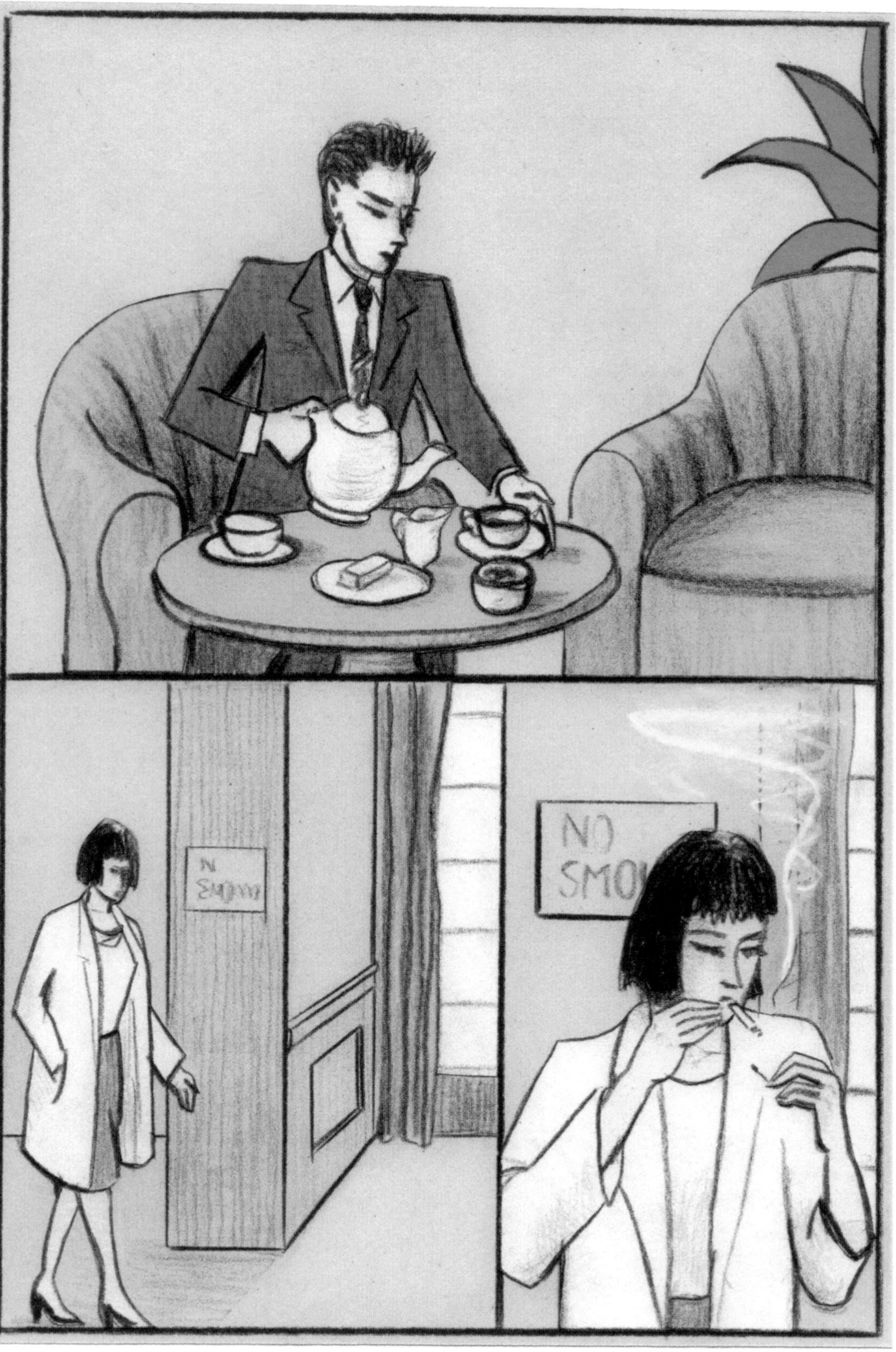
NO
SMO

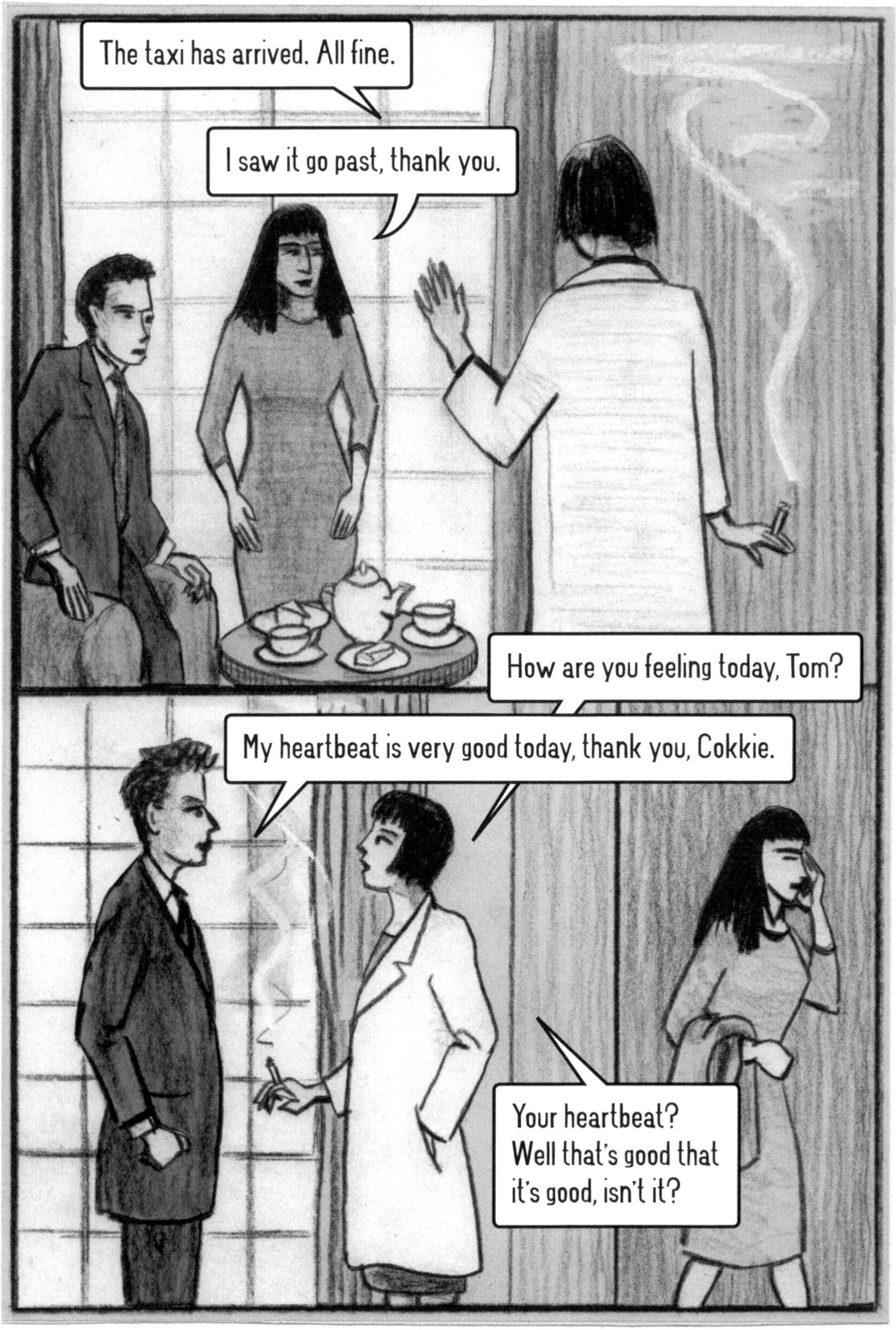
The taxi has arrived. All fine.
I saw it go past, thank you.
How are you feeling today, Tom?
My heartbeat is very good today, thank you, Cokkie.
Your heartbeat? Well that's good that it's good, isn't it?

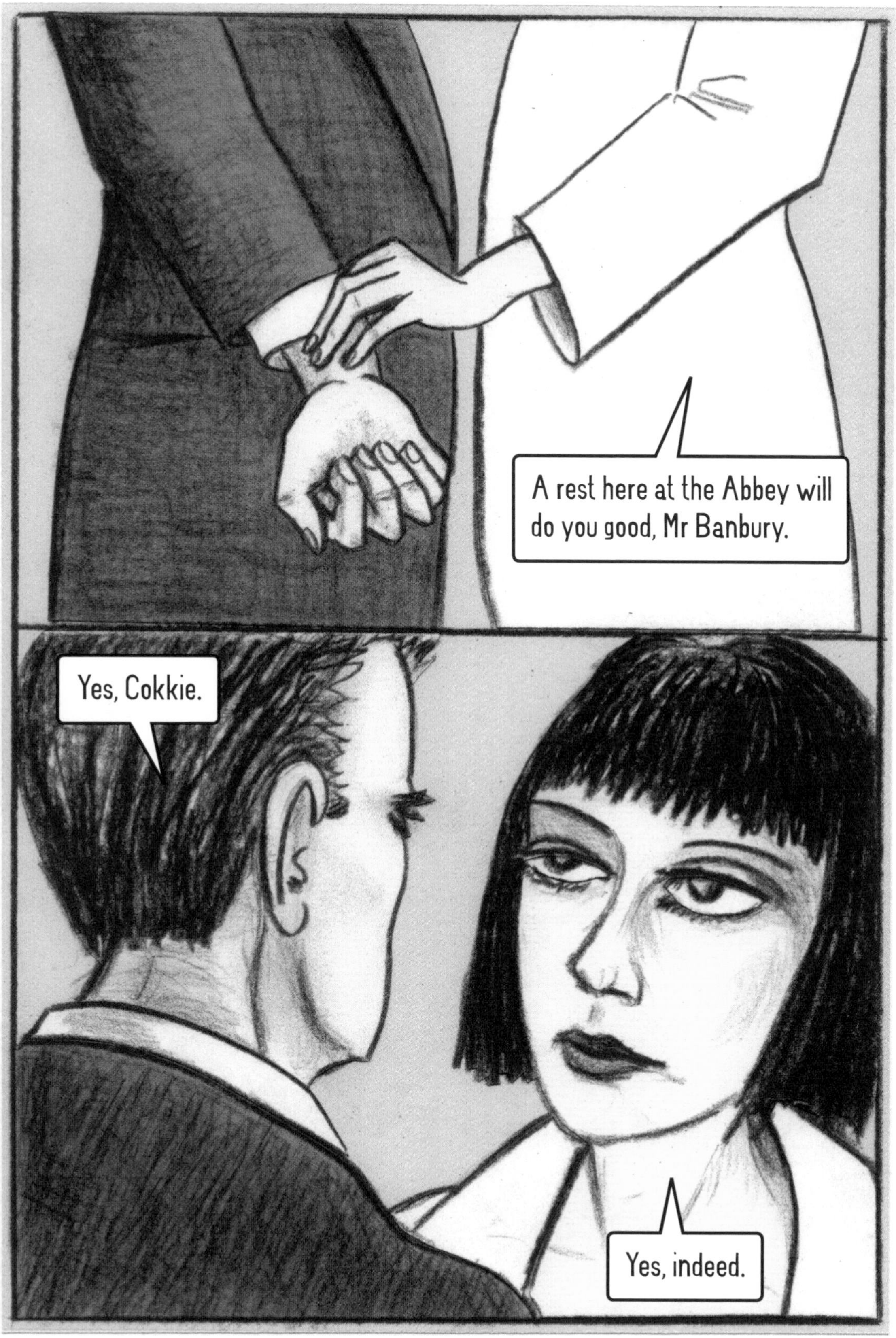
A rest here at the Abbey will do you good, Mr Banbury.
Yes, Cokkie.
Yes, indeed.

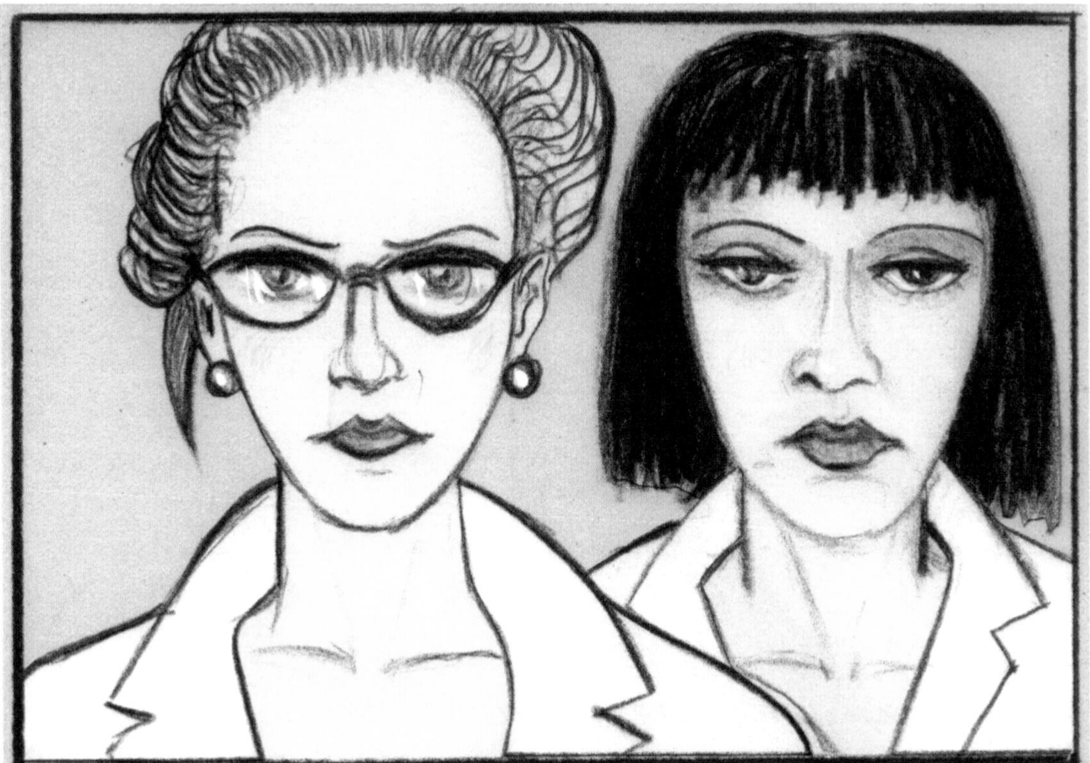

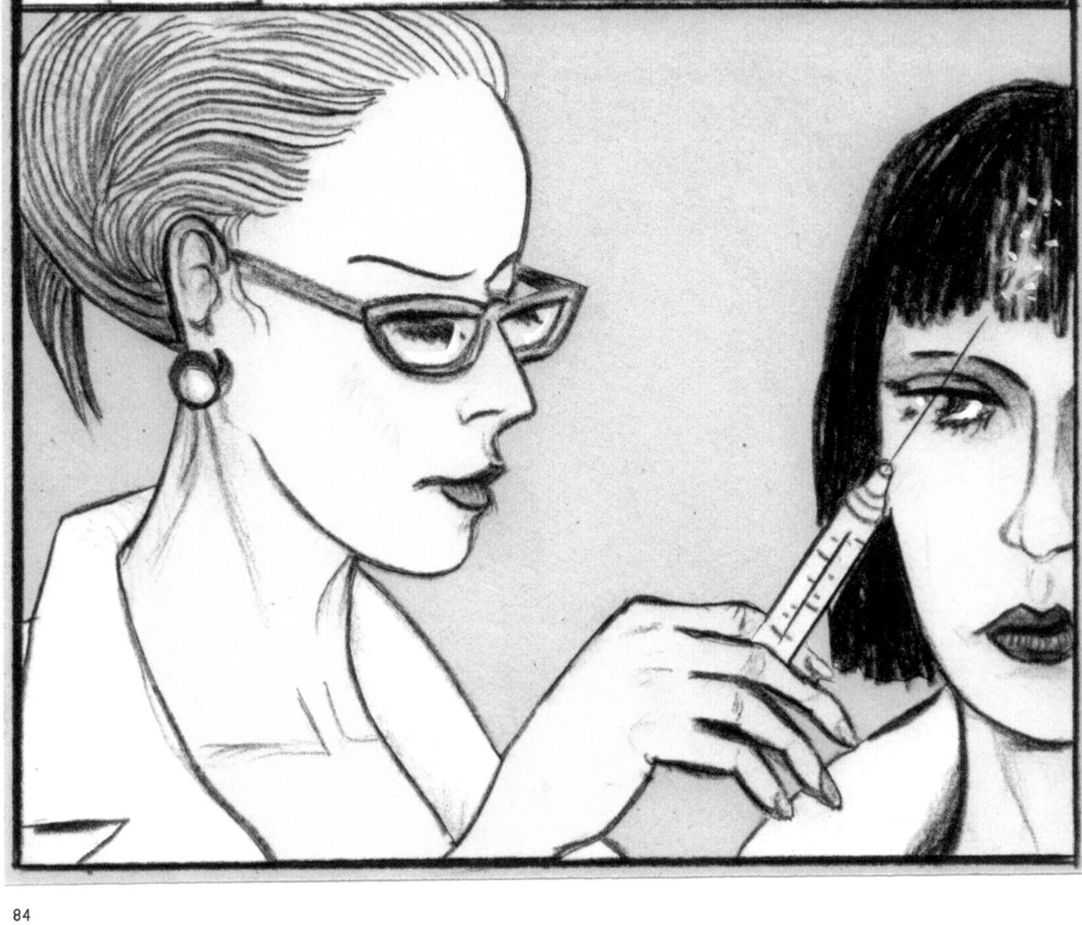

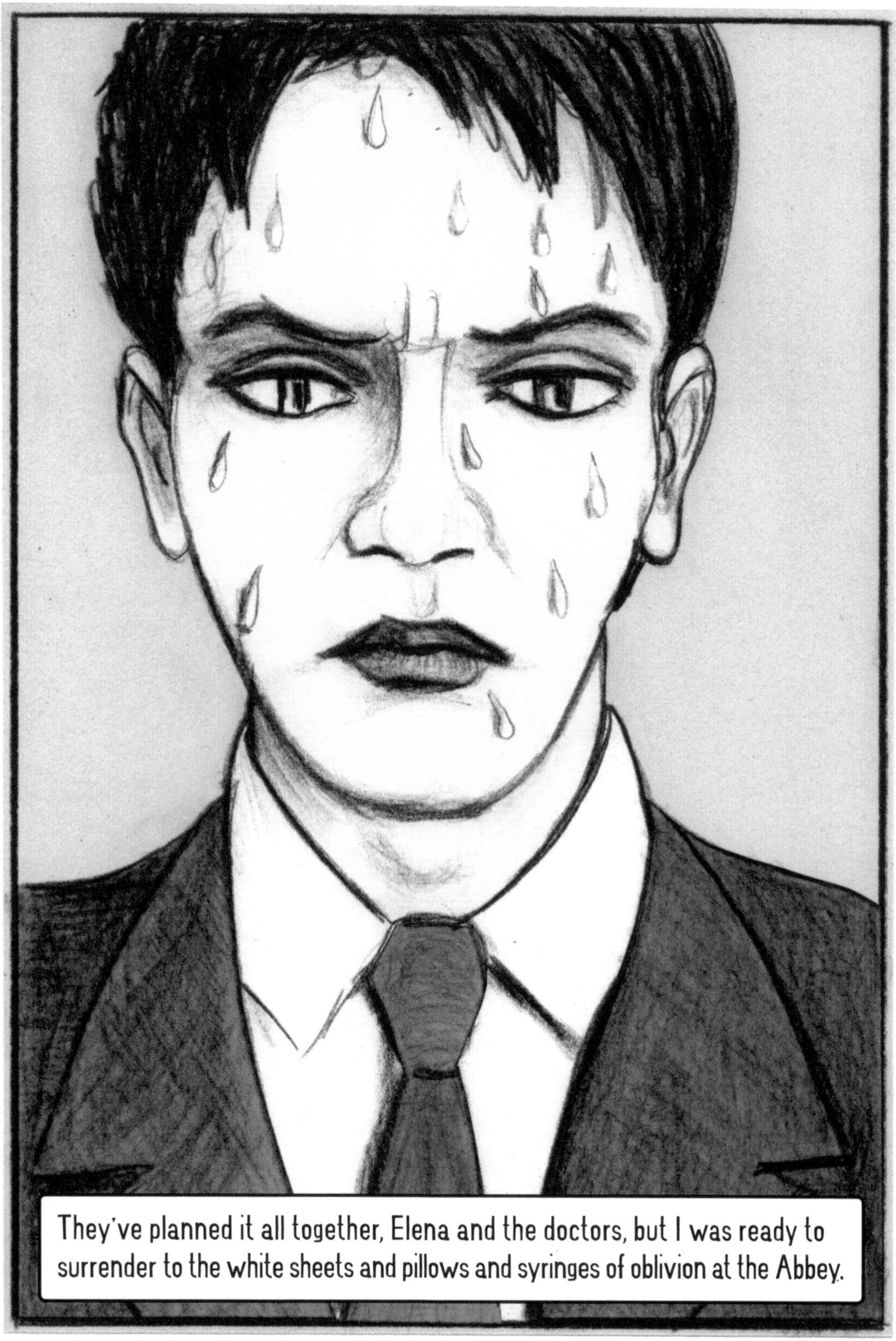
They've planned it all together, Elena and the doctors, but I was ready to surrender to the white sheets and pillows and syringes of oblivion at the Abbey.

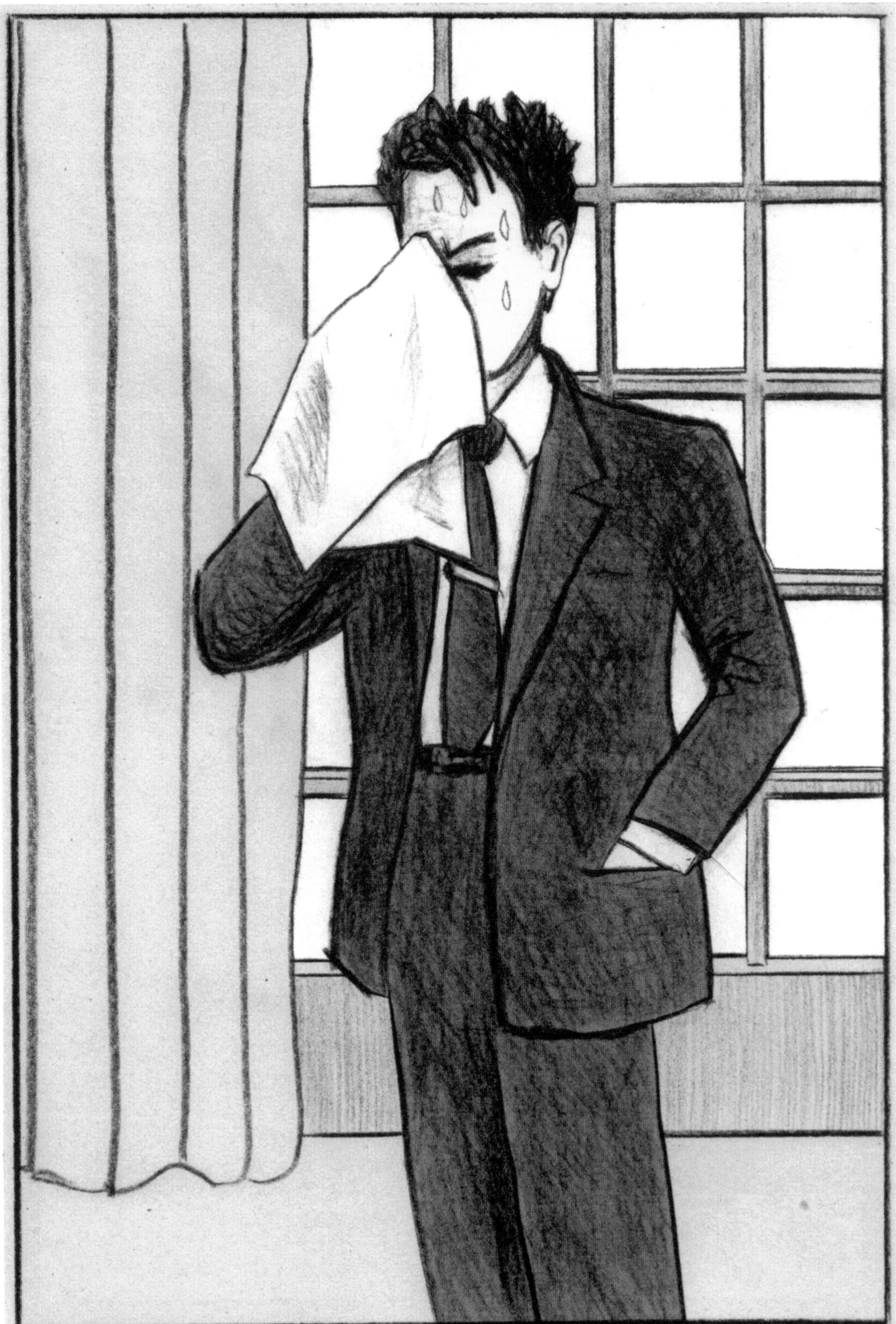

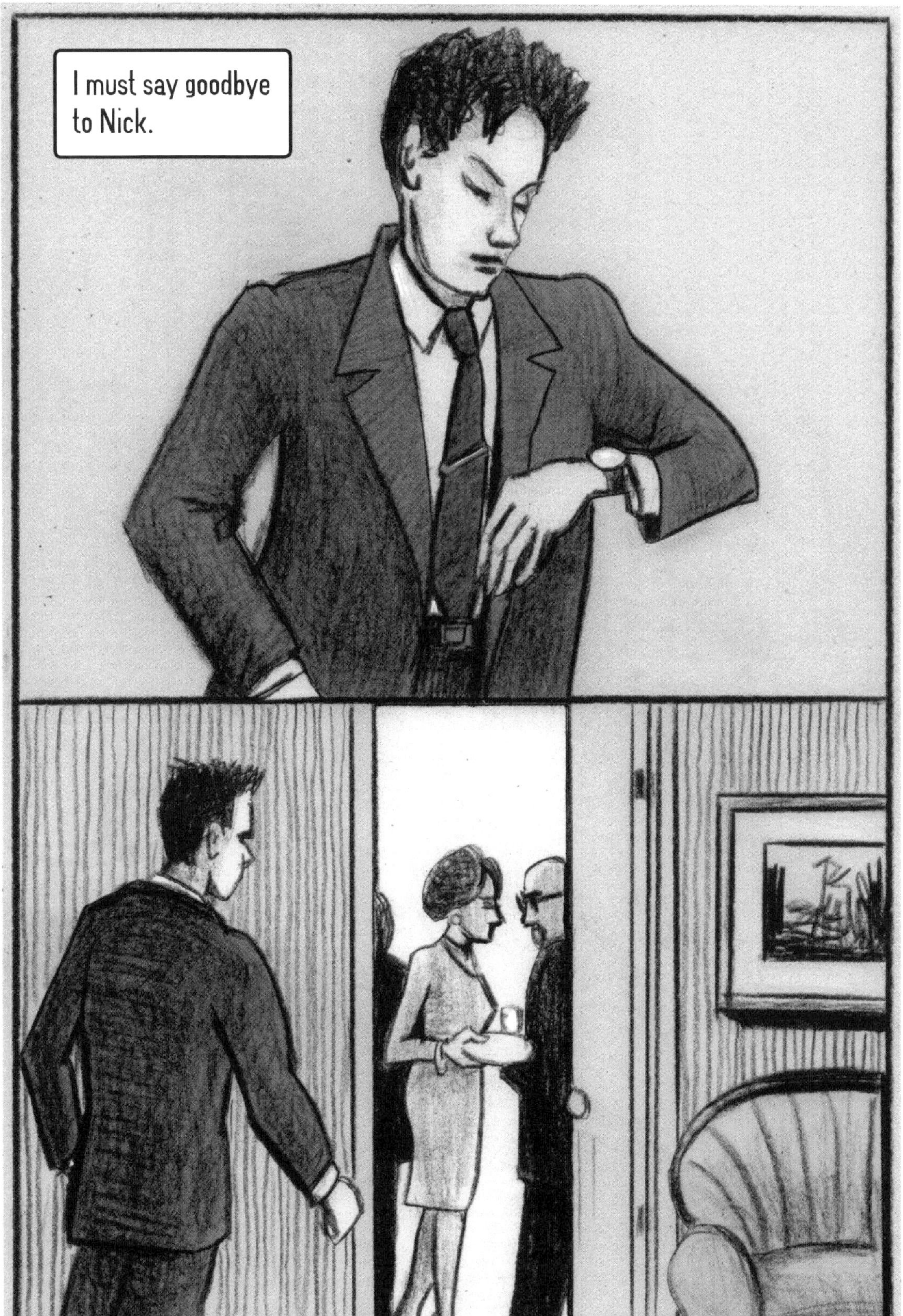
I must say goodbye to Nick.

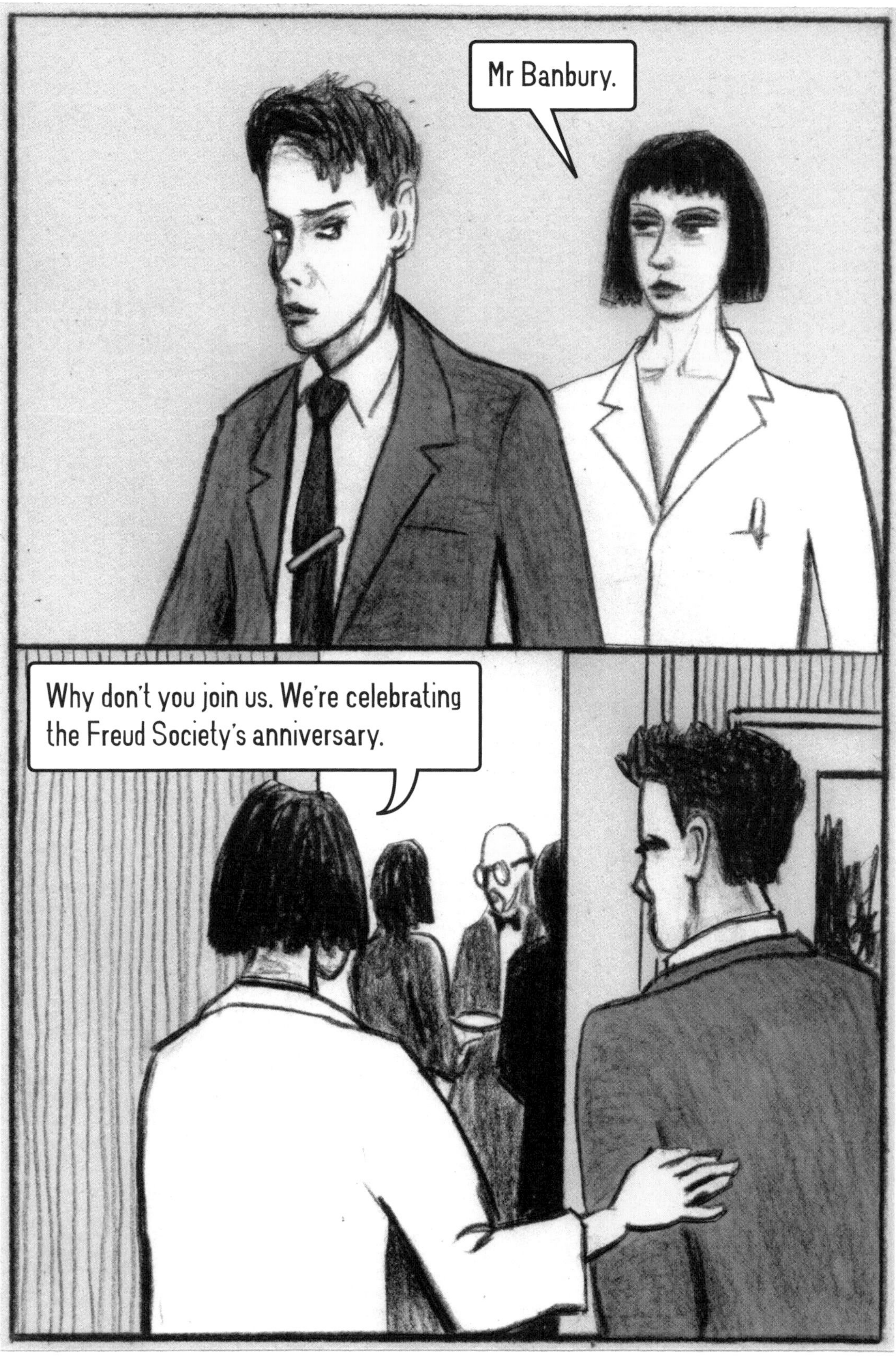
Mr Banbury.
Why don't you join us. We're celebrating the Freud Society's anniversary.

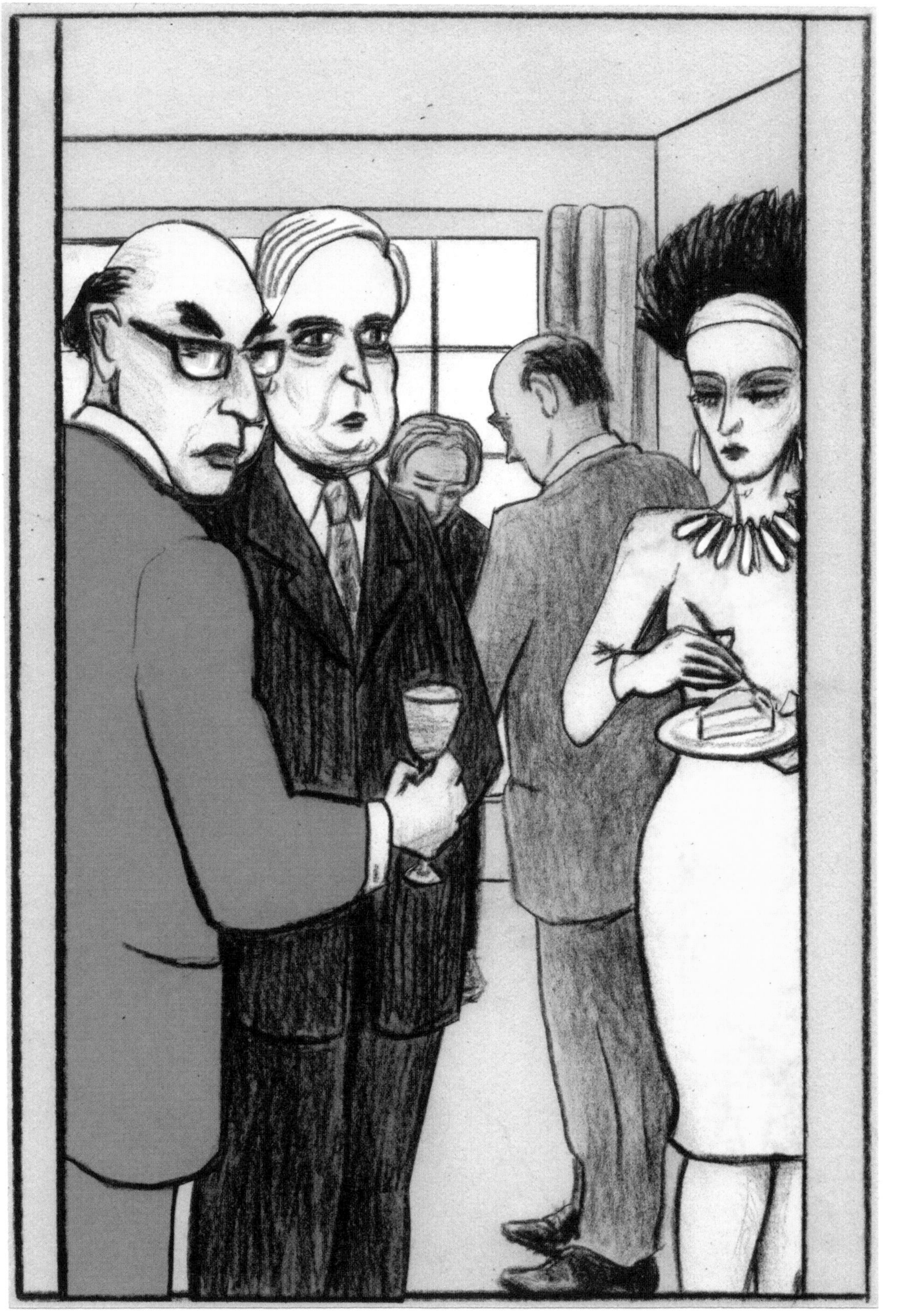

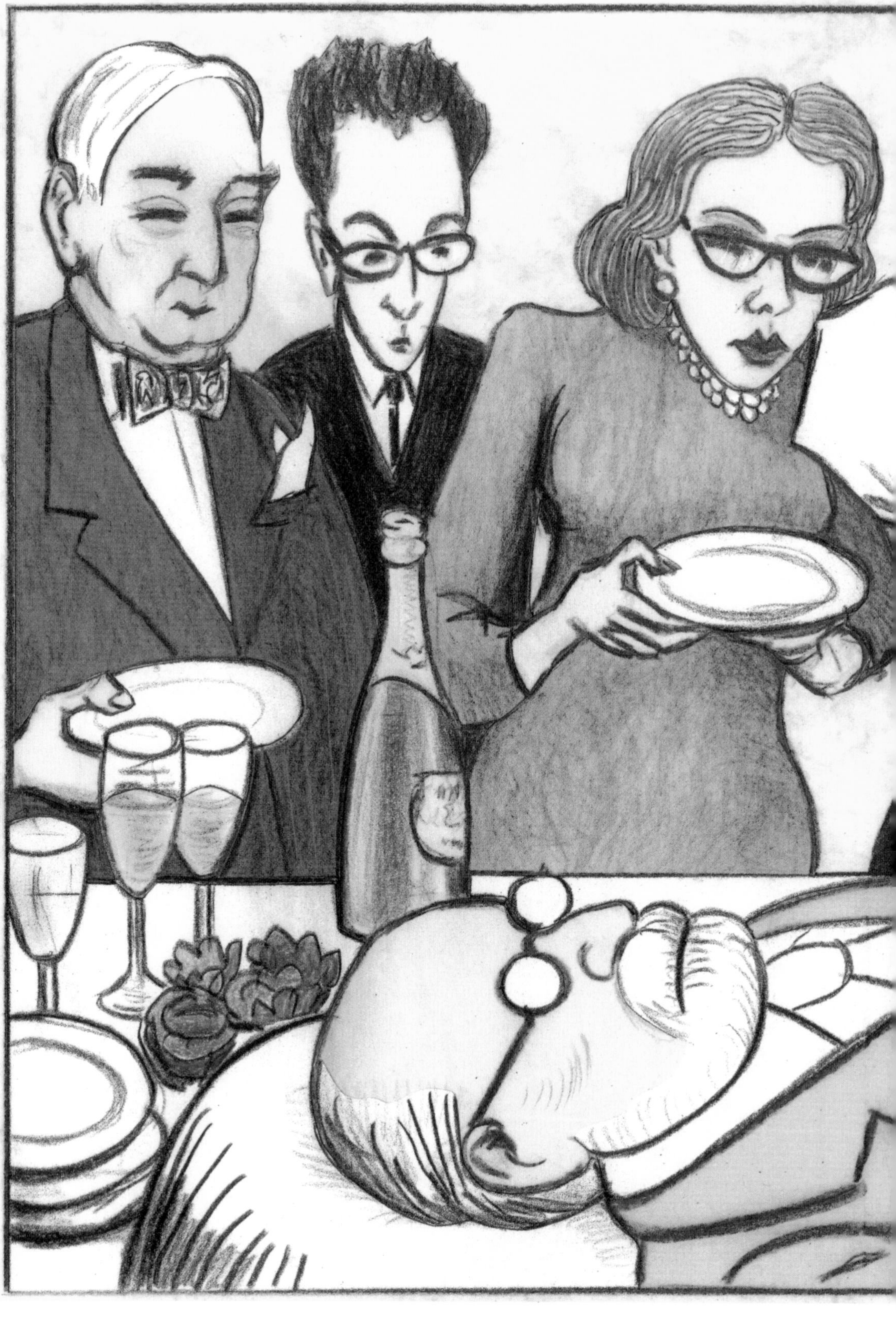

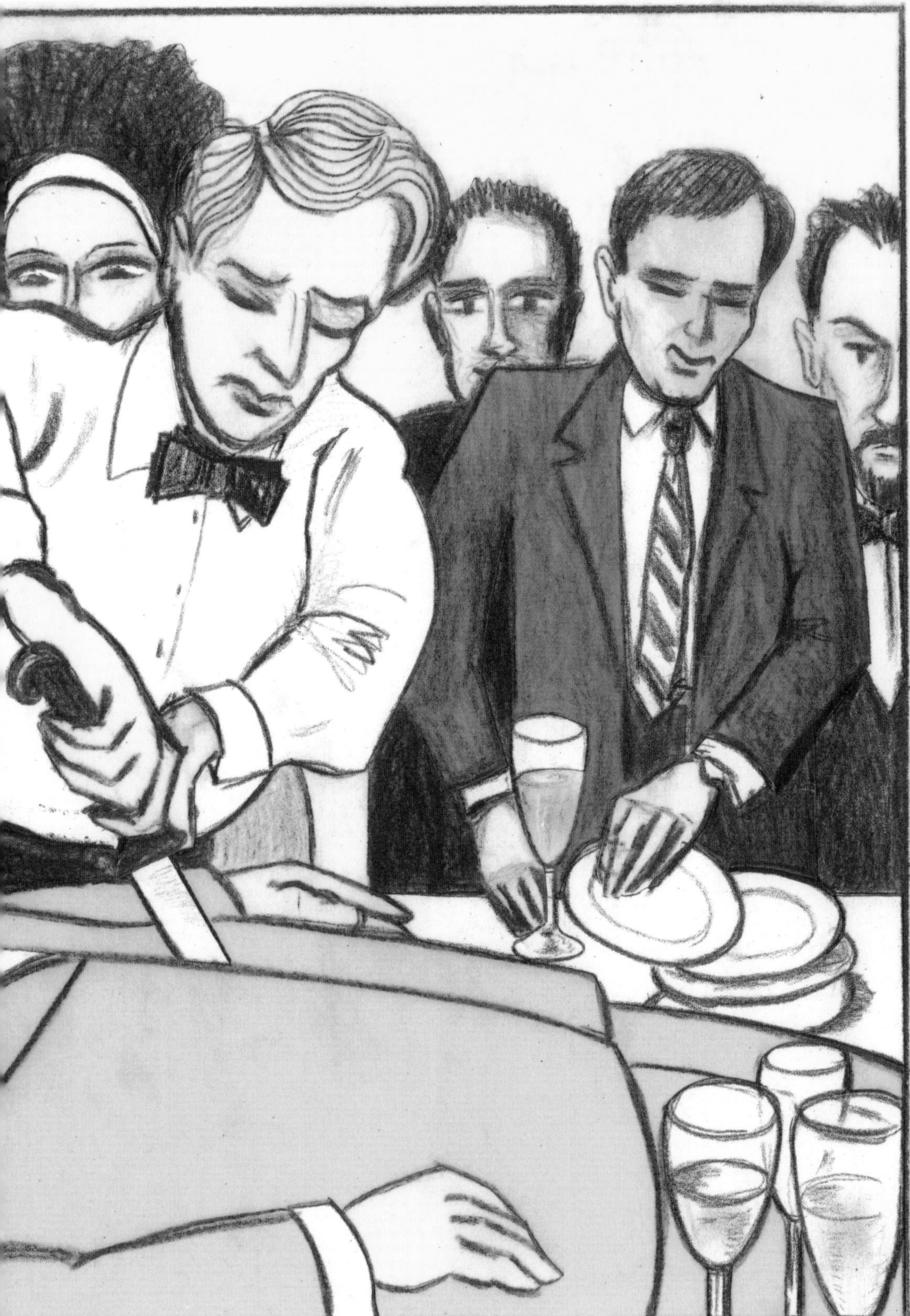

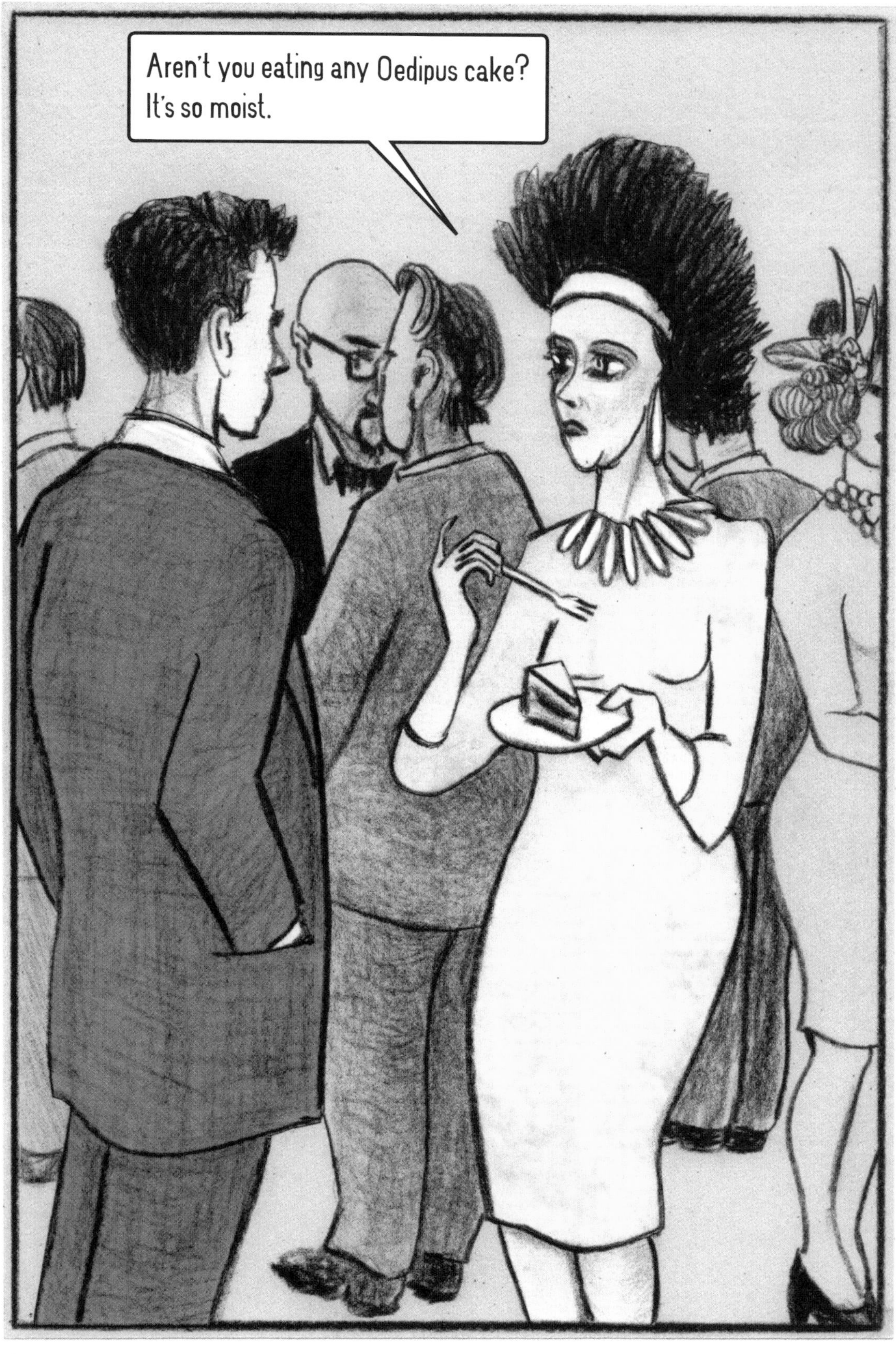
Aren't you eating any Oedipus cake? It's so moist.

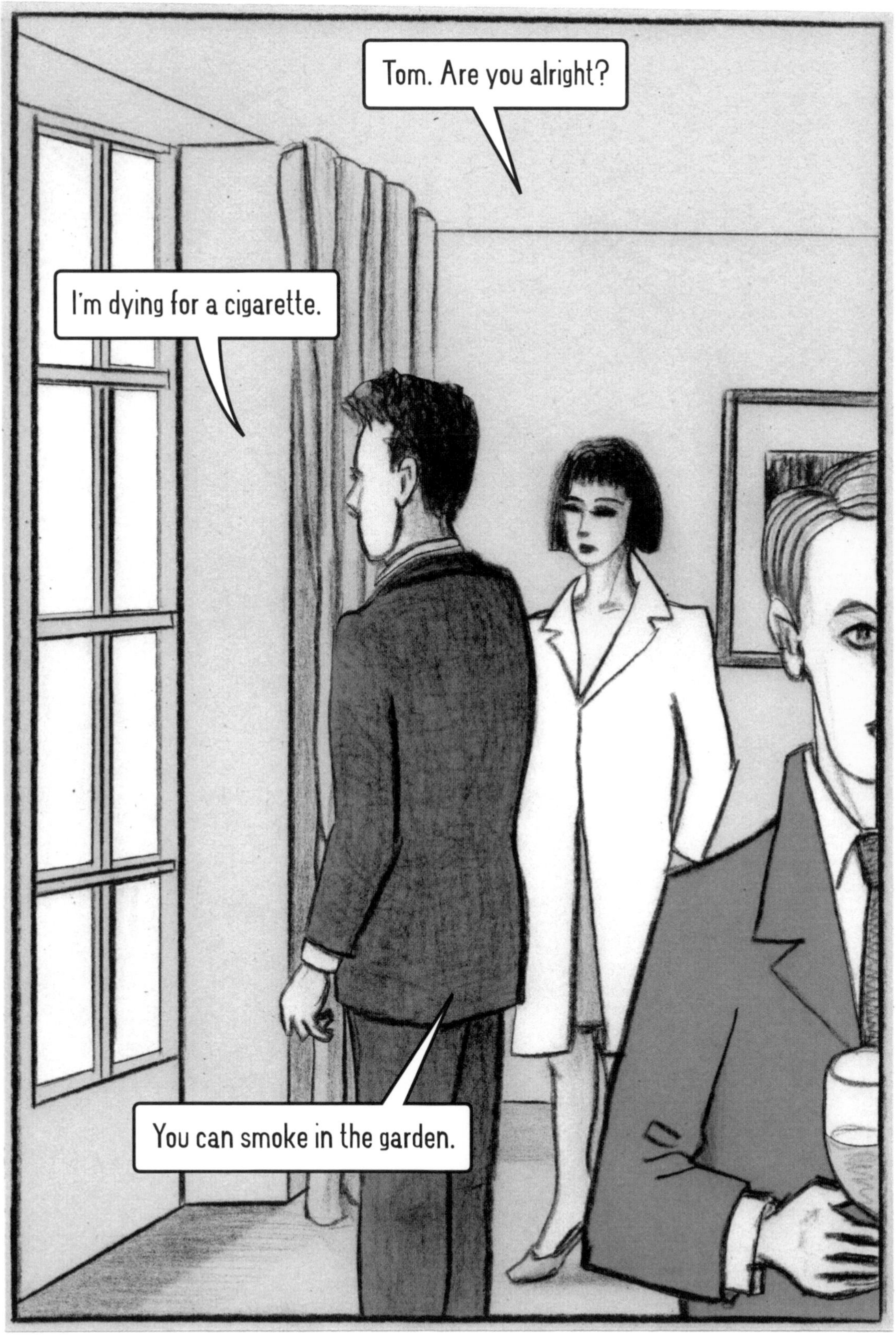
Tom. Are you alright?
I'm dying for a cigarette.
You can smoke in the garden.

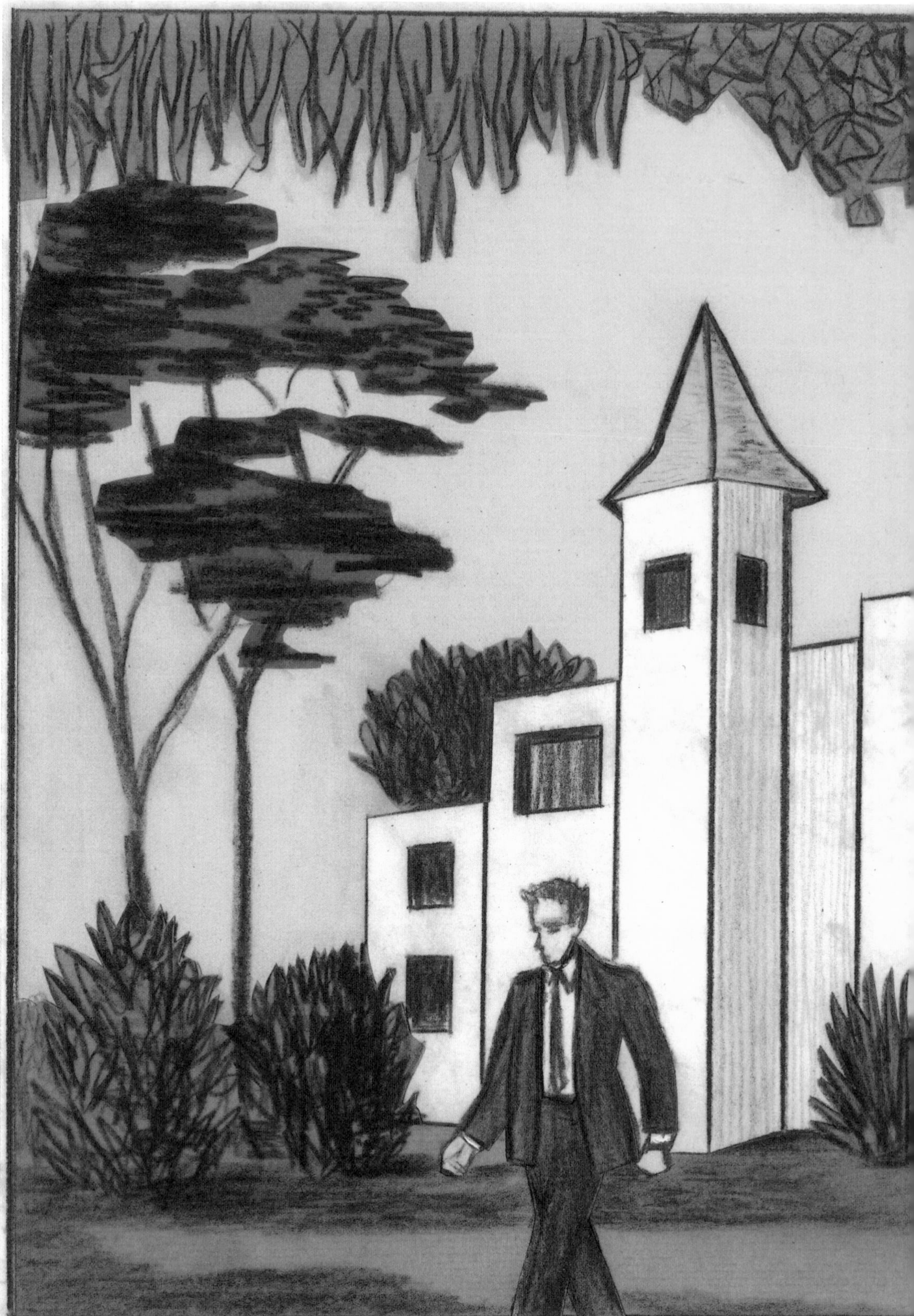

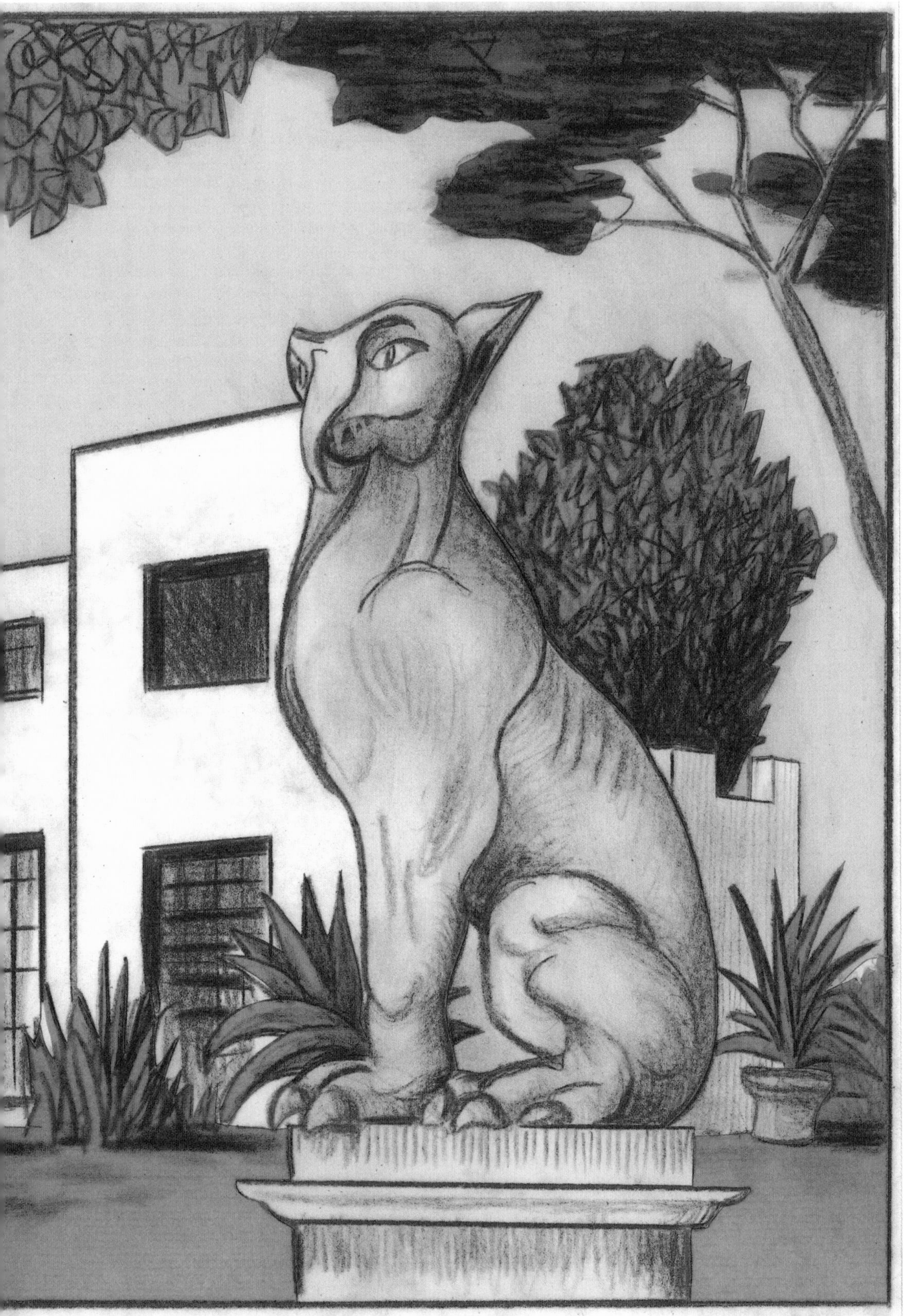

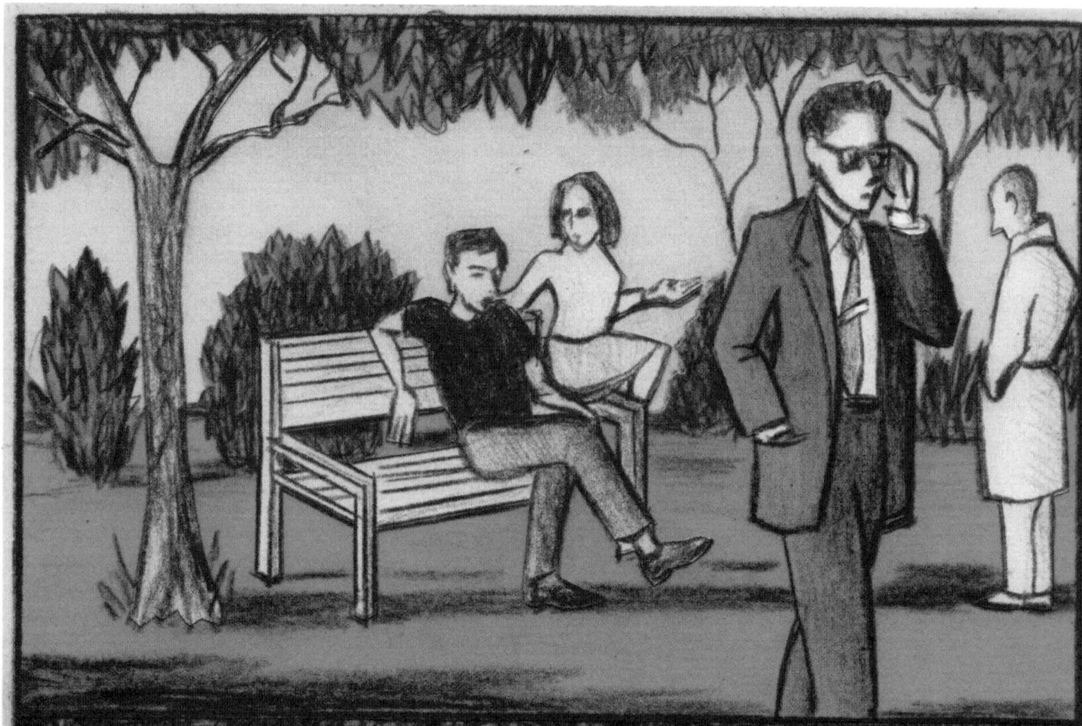

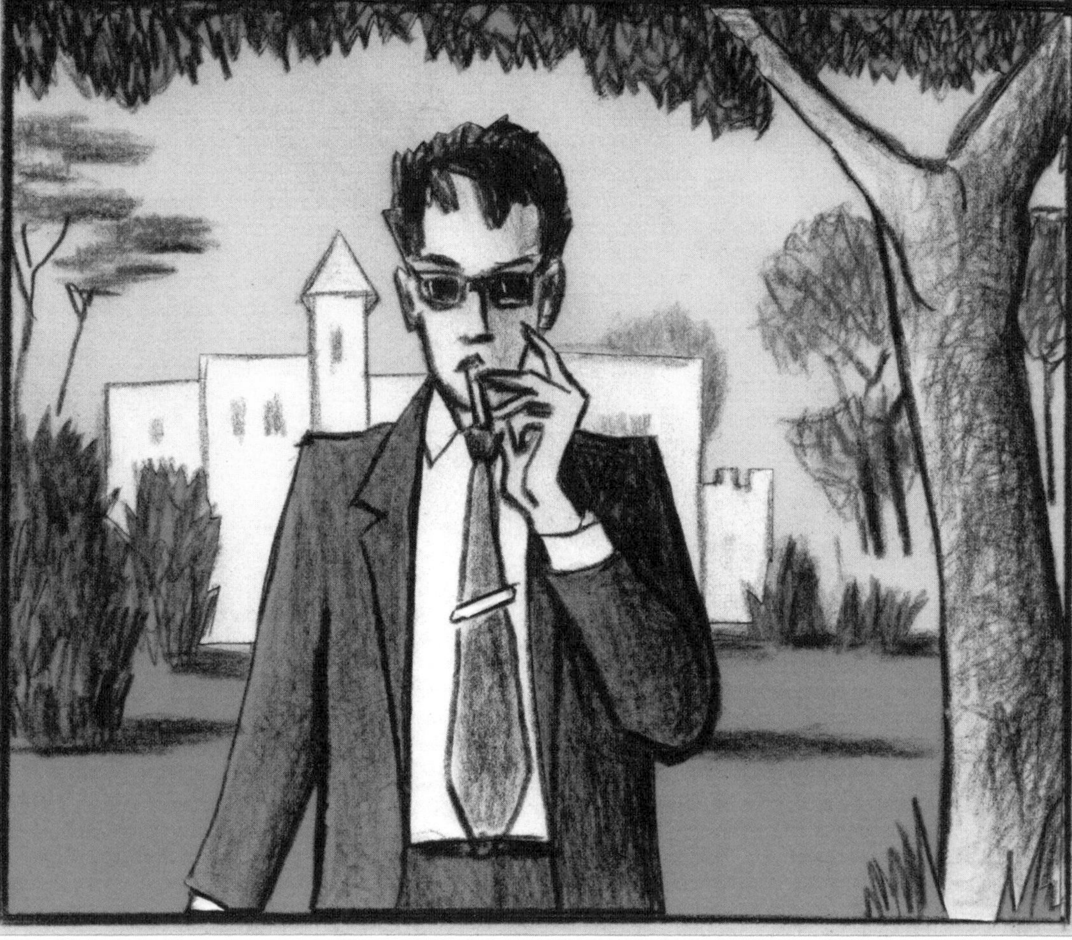

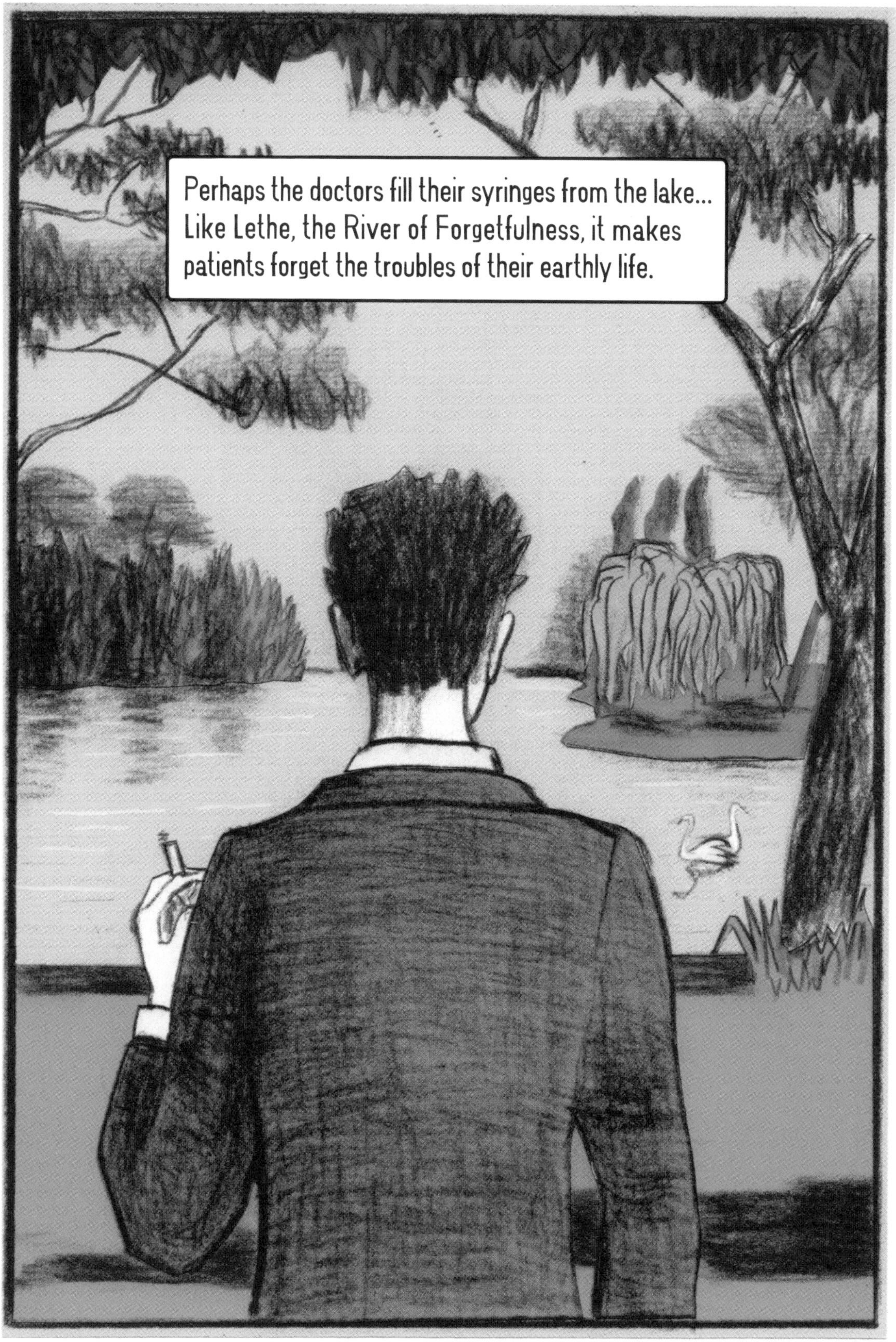
Perhaps the doctors fill their syringes from the lake... Like Lethe, the River of Forgetfulness, it makes patients forget the troubles of their earthly life.

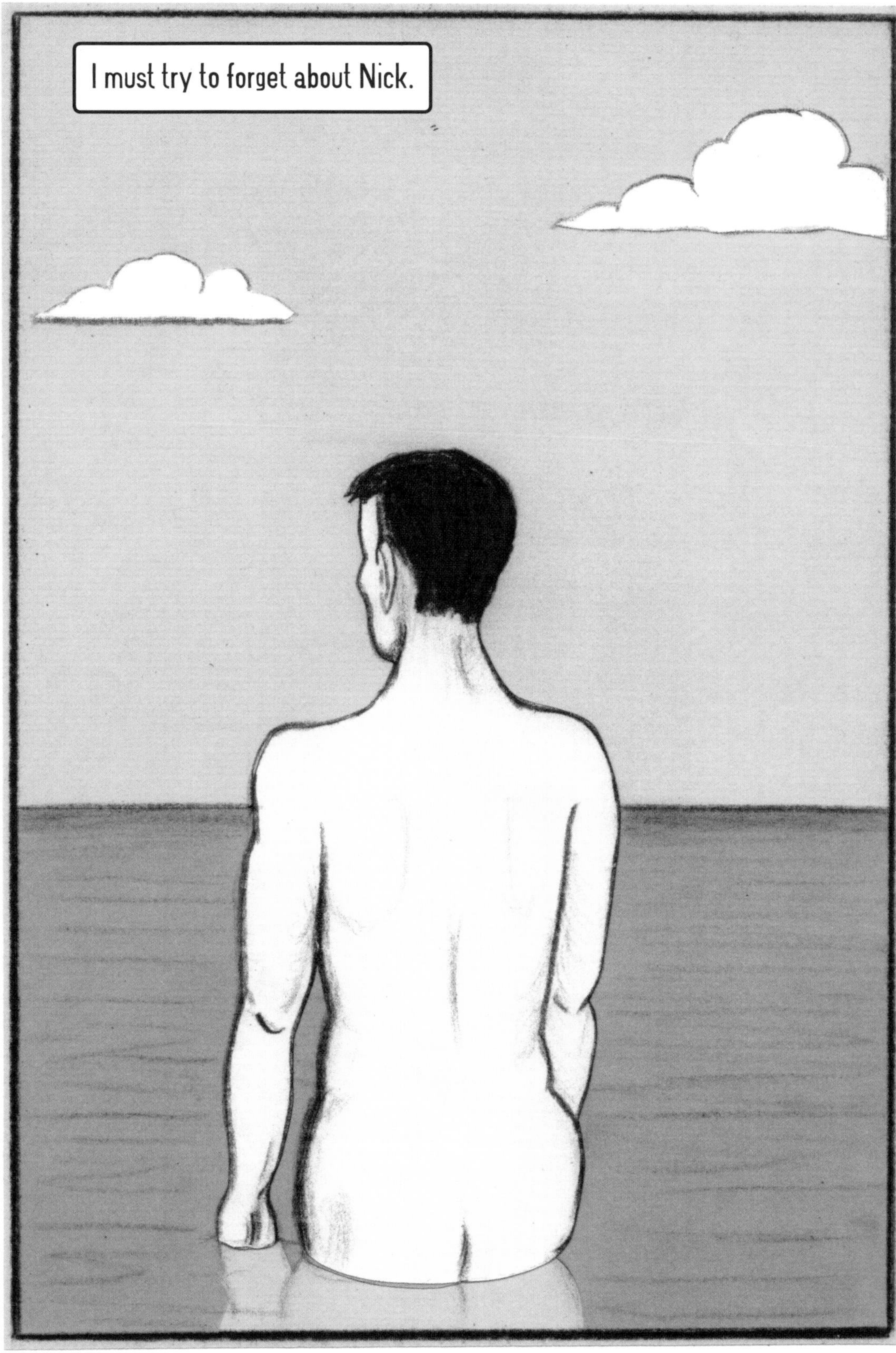
I must try to forget about Nick.

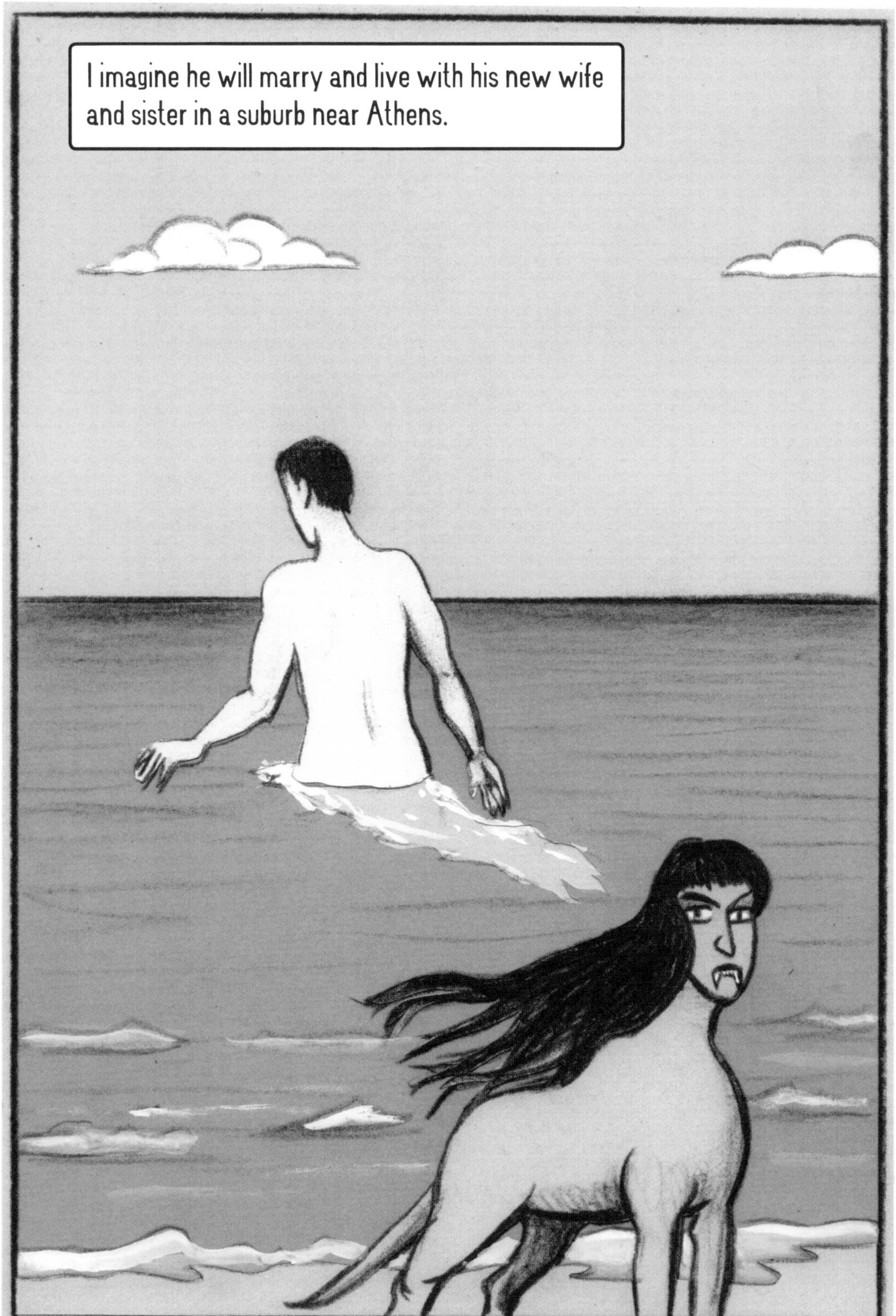
I imagine he will marry and live with his new wife and sister in a suburb near Athens.

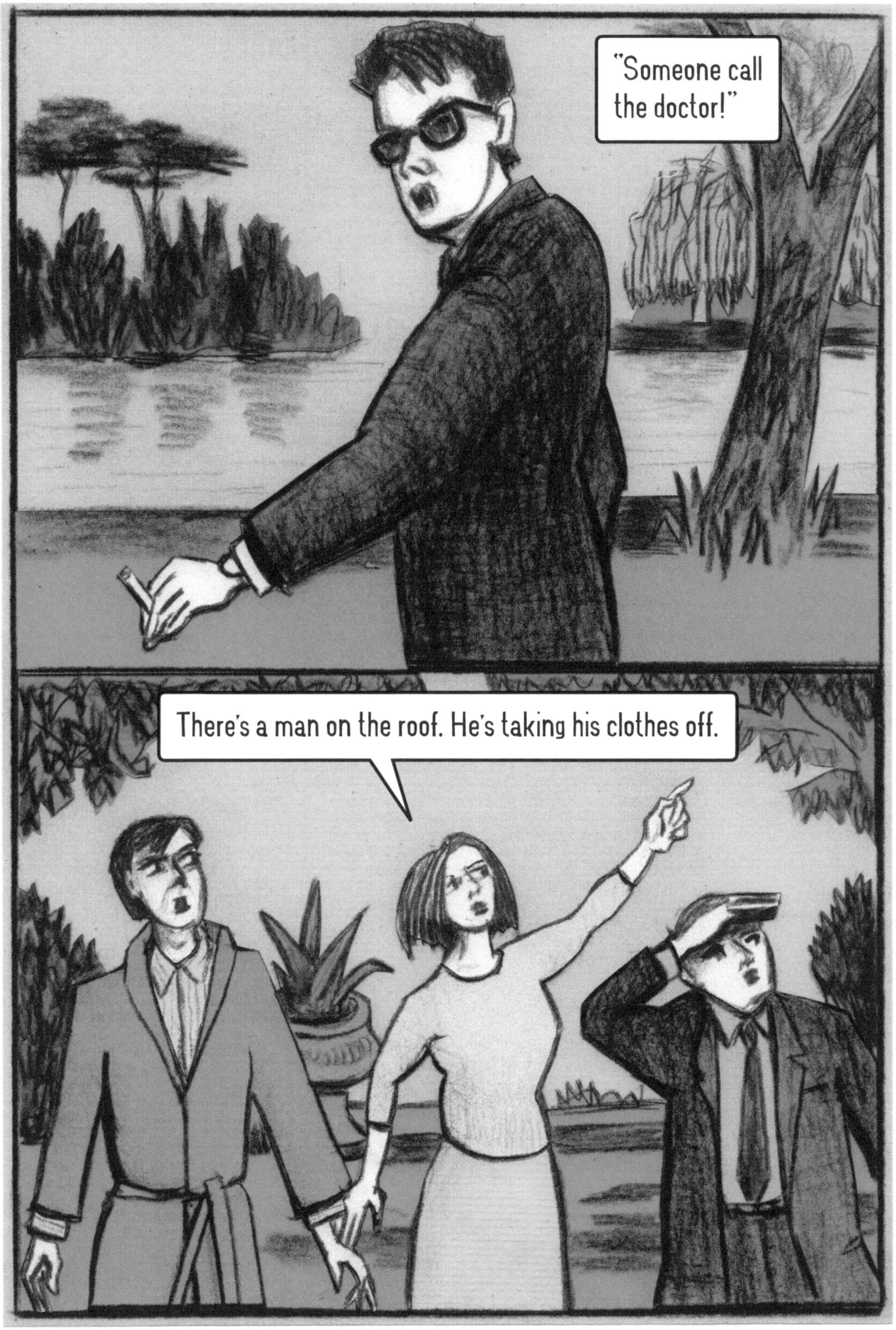
"Someone call the doctor!"
There's a man on the roof. He's taking his clothes off.

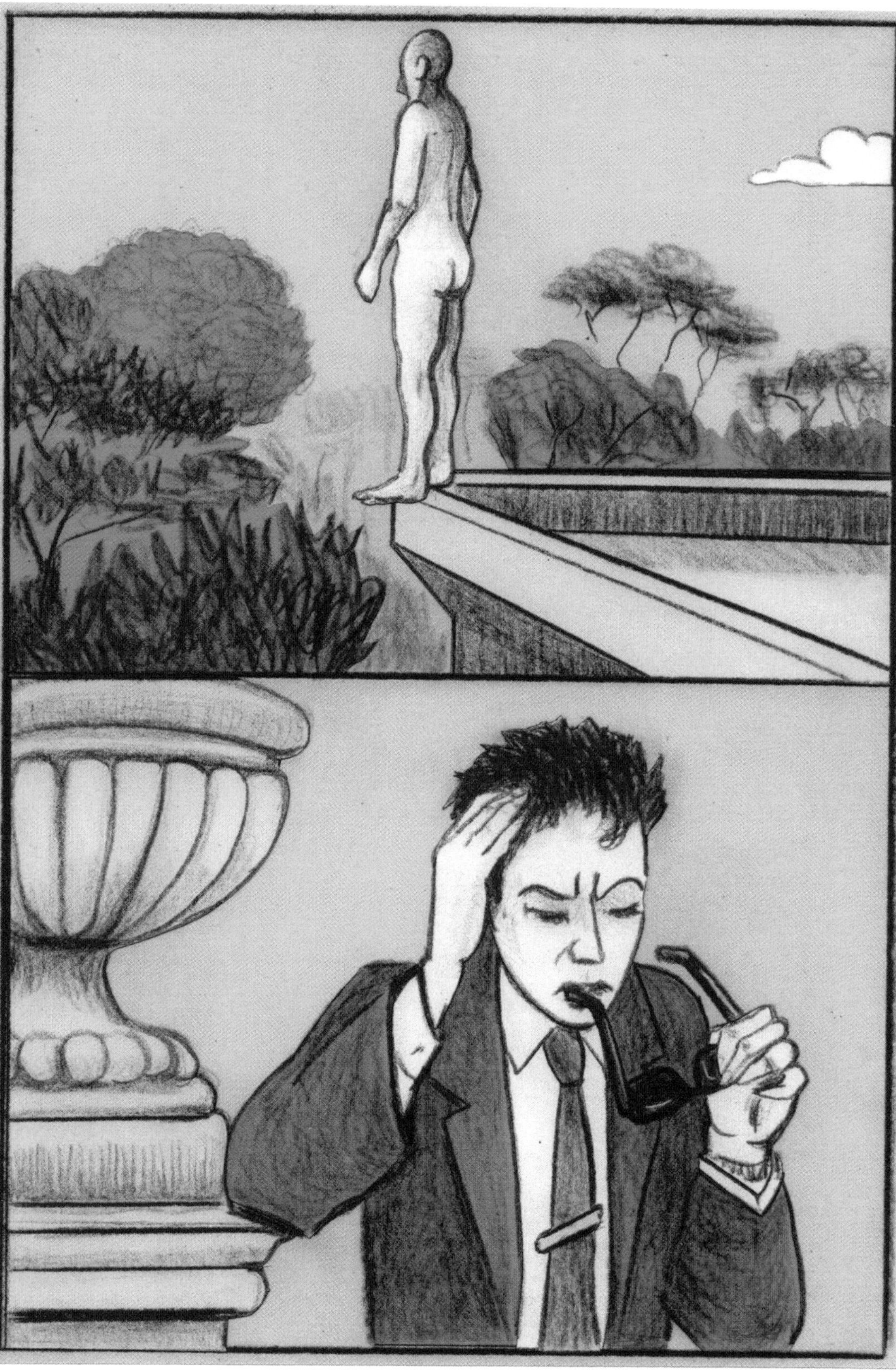

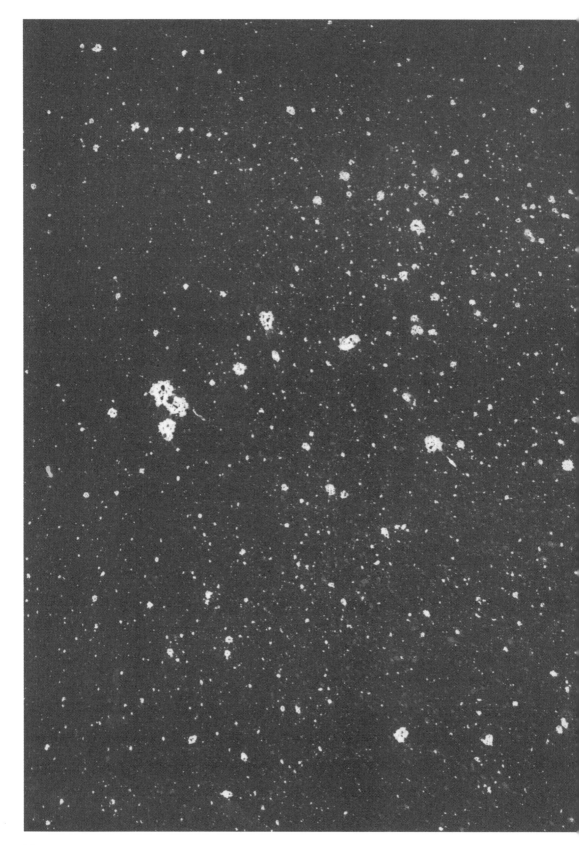

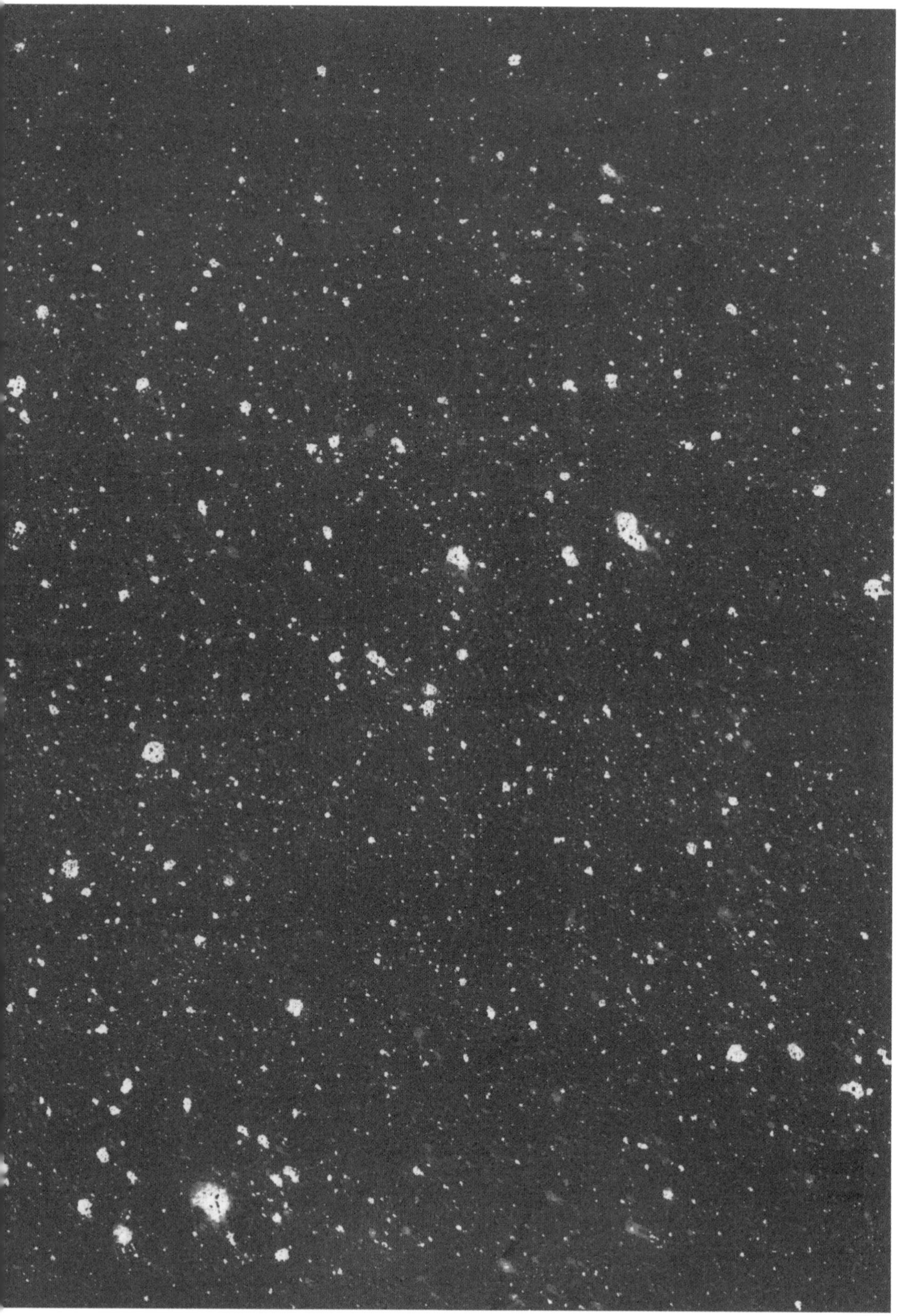

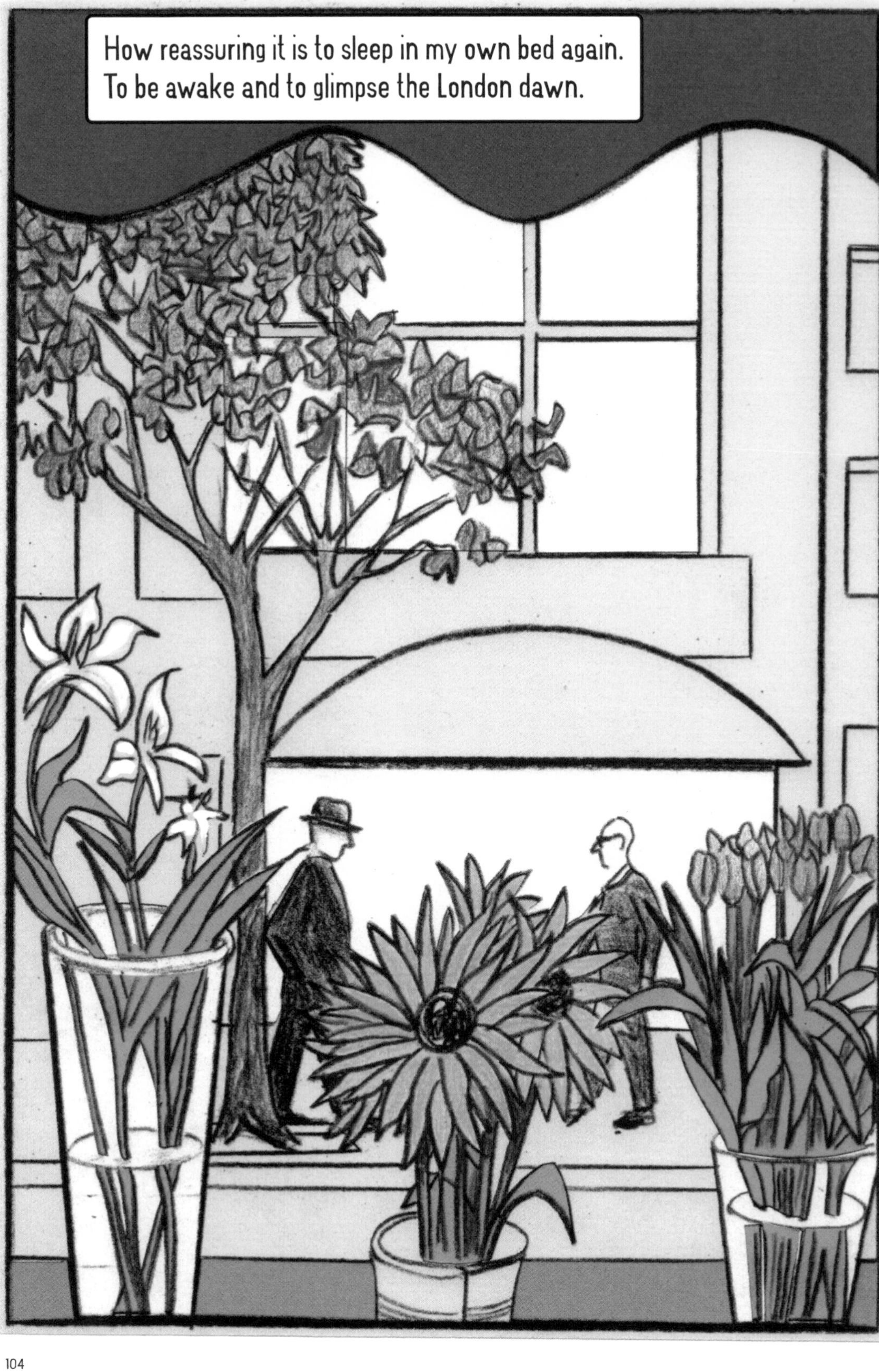
How reassuring it is to sleep in my own bed again. To be awake and to glimpse the London dawn.

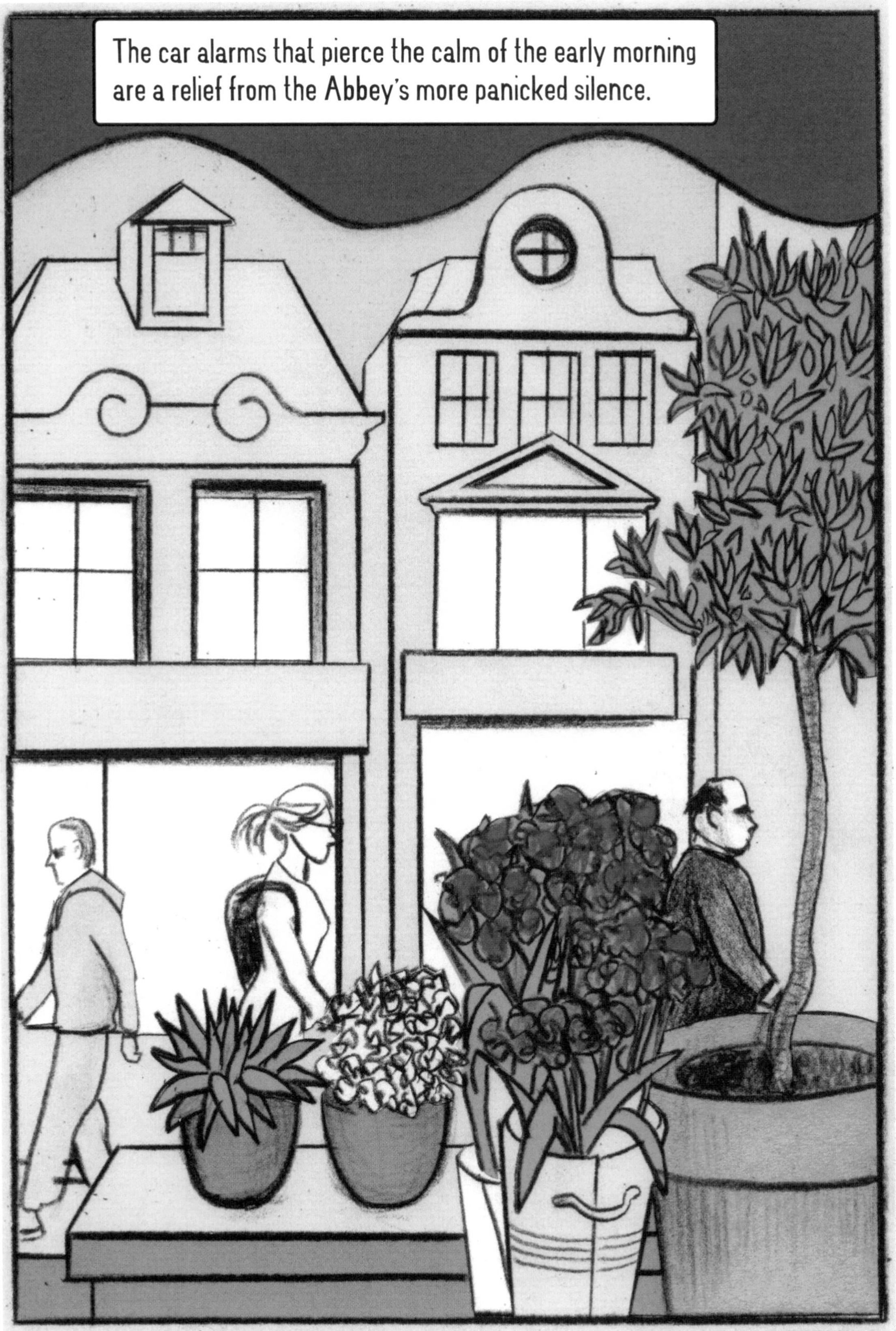
The car alarms that pierce the calm of the early morning are a relief from the Abbey's more panicked silence.

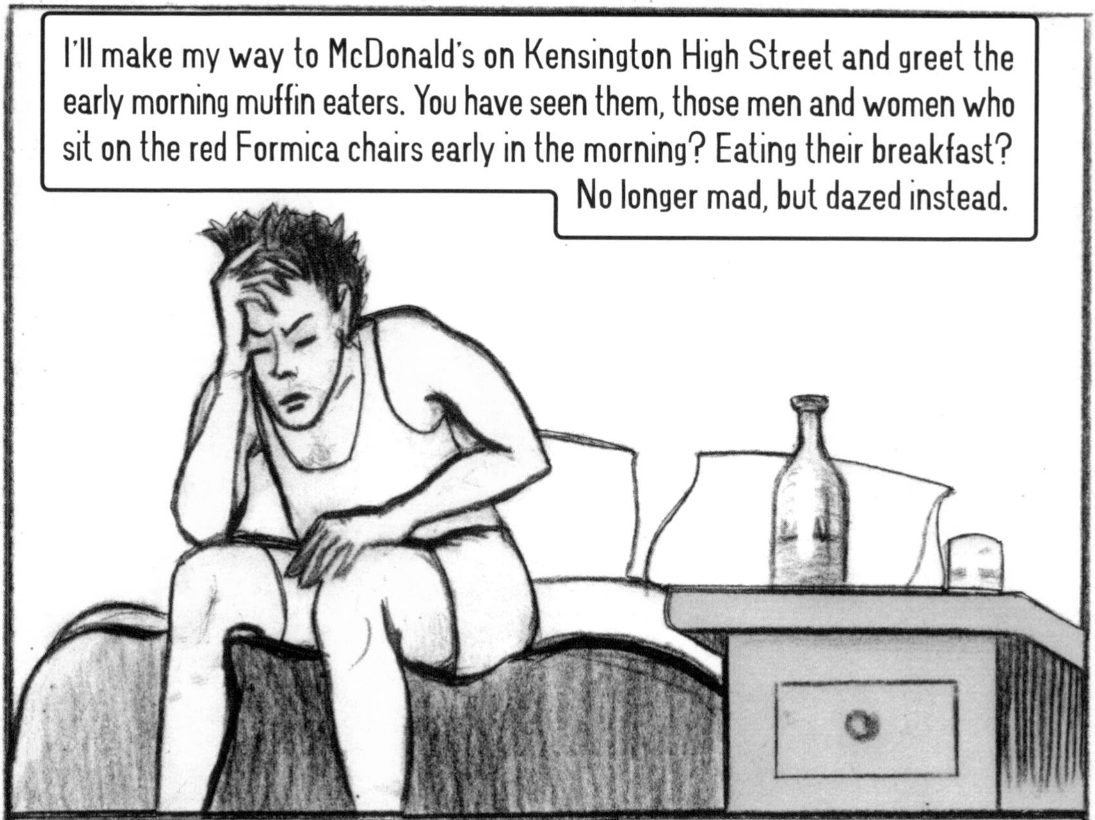
I'll make my way to McDonald's on Kensington High Street and greet the early morning muffin eaters. You have seen them, those men and women who sit on the red Formica chairs early in the morning? Eating their breakfast?
No longer mad, but dazed instead.

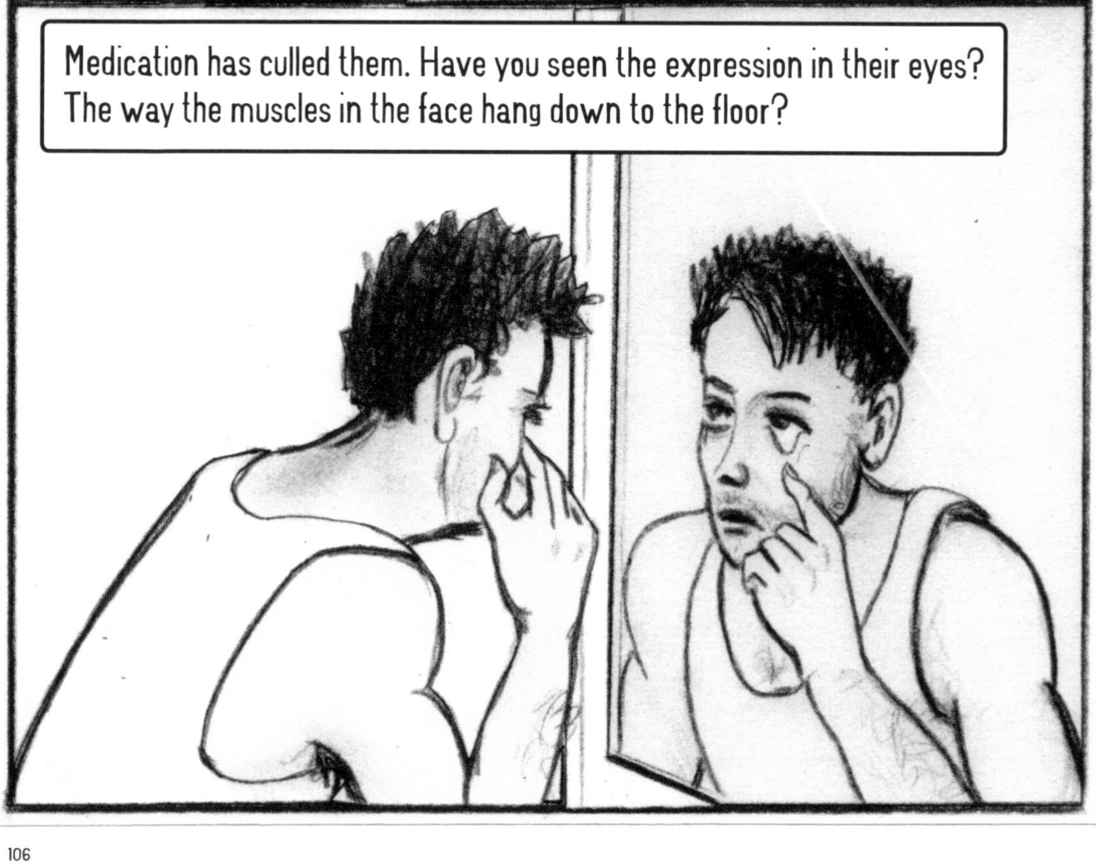
Medication has culled them. Have you seen the expression in their eyes? The way the muscles in the face hang down to the floor?

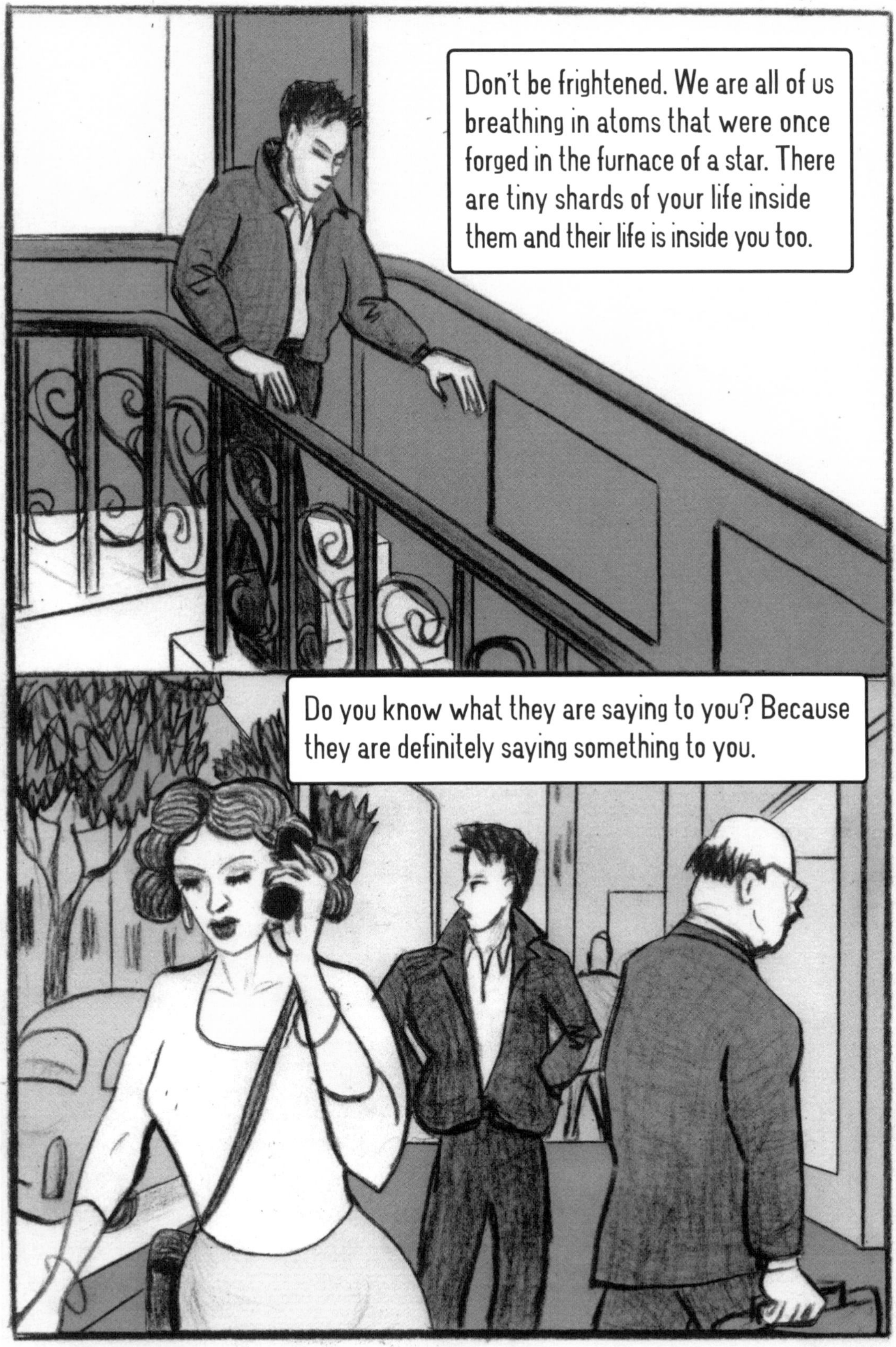
Don't be frightened. We are all of us breathing in atoms that were once forged in the furnace of a star. There are tiny shards of your life inside them and their life is inside you too.
Do you know what they are saying to you? Because they are definitely saying something to you.

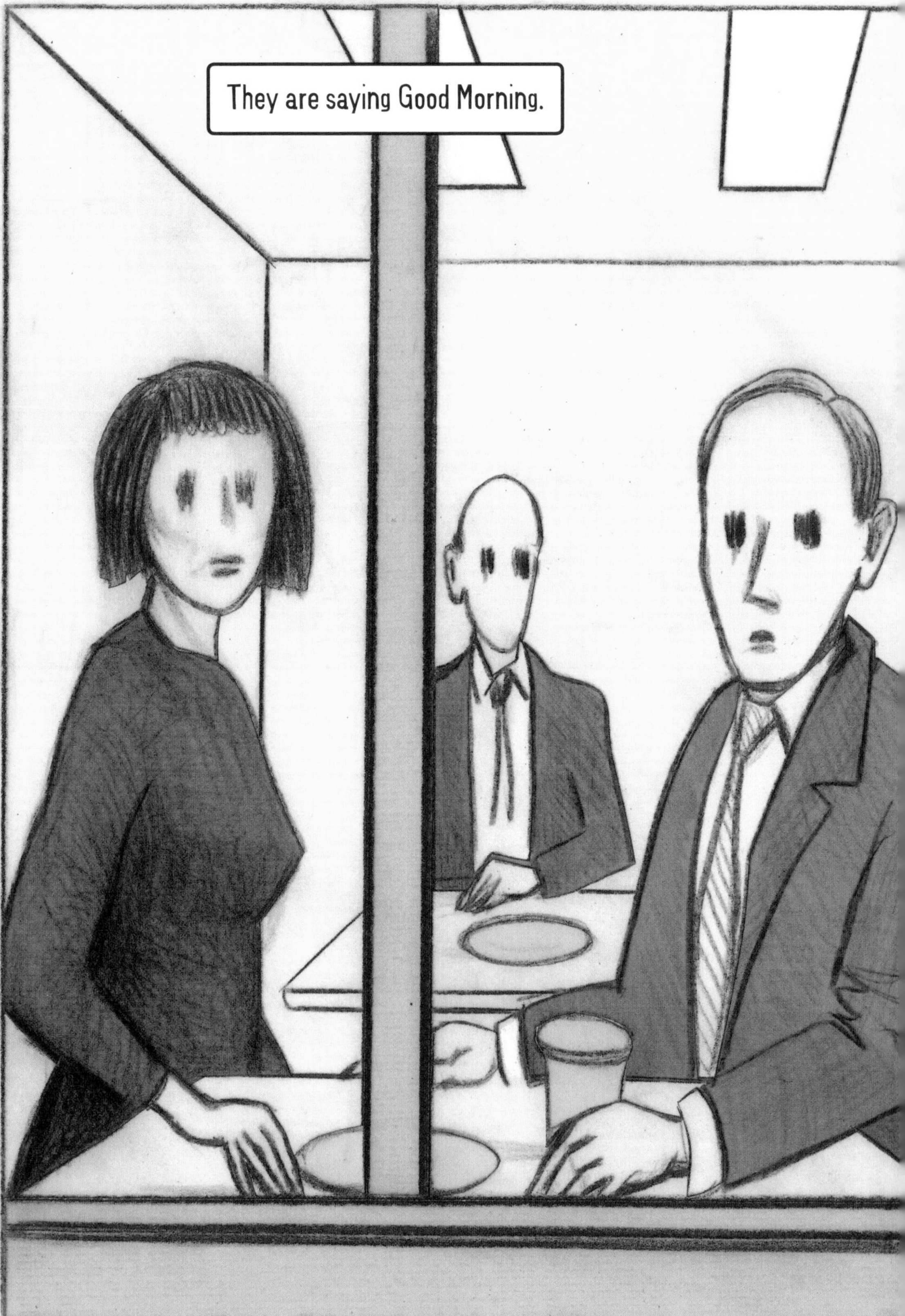
They are saying Good Morning.

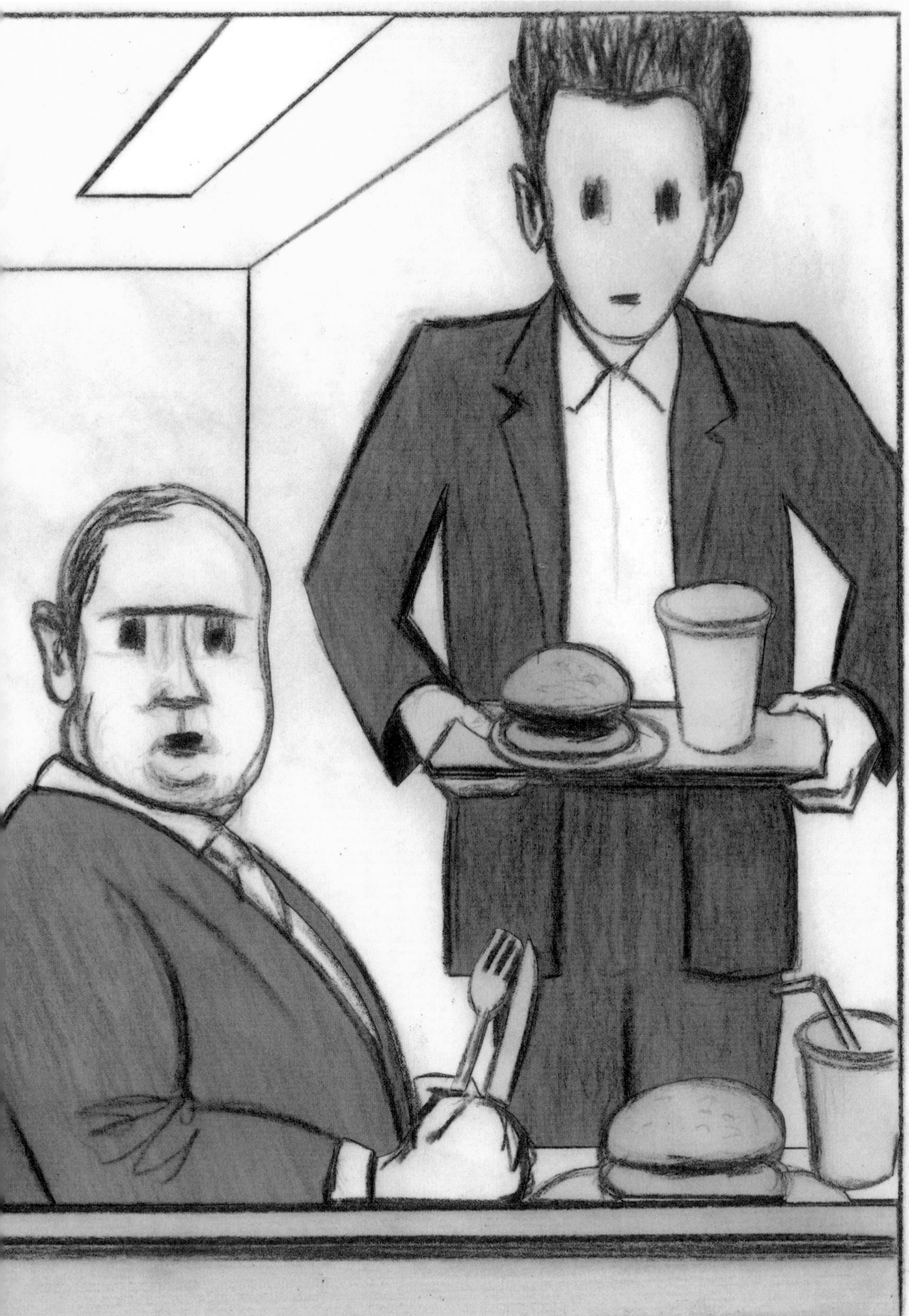